"This is a dark fantasy romance from Katee Robert, and honestly, this is exactly what I hoped she'd always write."

—Culturess

"Katee Robert knows how to capture romance readers' hearts."

—*Entertainment Weekly*

"Full of unique world-building and compelling characters."

—Paste

"Thanks to its wildly fun romance and adventure, *Hunt on Dark Waters* will soon be a staple for any romantasy lover's bookshelf."

—BookTrib

"This promises more good things to come in future installments."

—*Publishers Weekly*

"Robert continues to shine with their inclusive characters and flawlessly executed romance tropes. . . . A clever-witch-meets-stern-pirate, open-door, one-bed delight."

—*Library Journal*

"Robert fans will enjoy this fresh, new setting on the high seas, as well as the enticing spice."

—*Booklist*

"Katee Robert's *Hunt on Dark Waters* is a fast-paced and delightful fever dream of fantasy creatures, mysterious magic, and sizzling sexual innuendo."

—*BookPage* (starred review)

BERKLEY TITLES BY KATEE ROBERT

Hunt on Dark Waters
Blood on the Tide
Rebel in the Deep

Rebel in the Deep

KATEE ROBERT

BERKLEY ROMANCE
New York

BERKLEY ROMANCE
Published by Berkley
An imprint of Penguin Random House LLC
1745 Broadway, New York, NY 10019
penguinrandomhouse.com

Book design by Daniel Brount

Library of Congress Cataloging-in-Publication Data

Names: Robert, Katee, author.
Title: Rebel in the deep / Katee Robert.
Description: First edition. | New York: Berkley Romance, 2025. | Series: Crimson sails; 3
Identifiers: LCCN 2024039008 (print) | LCCN 2024039009 (ebook) |
ISBN 9780593639122 (trade paperback) | ISBN 9780593639139 (ebook)
Subjects: LCGFT: Romance fiction. | Fantasy fiction. | Novels.
Classification: LCC PS3618.O31537 R43 2025 (print) |
LCC PS3618.O31537 (ebook) | DDC 813/.6—dc23/eng/20240823
LC record available at https://lccn.loc.gov/2024039008
LC ebook record available at https://lccn.loc.gov/2024039009

First Edition: May 2025

Printed in the United States of America
1st Printing

The authorized representative in the EU for product safety and compliance
is Penguin Random House Ireland, Morrison Chambers, 32 Nassau Street,
Dublin D02 YH68, Ireland, https://eu-contact.penguin.ie.

Rebel in the Deep

CHAPTER 1

Nox

SOME DAYS, I HAVE TO ACTUALLY DO MY JOB. THOSE TEND to be the bad days. The ones filled with violence and blood and a sorrow so thick, the entire crew can taste it on the air.

Today is shaping up to be a bad day.

"Hold it, Bowen," I snap. "If one of those tentacles makes it through your shield, we're in trouble."

"I *am* holding it," the man at my side grits out. He's easily a head and shoulders taller than me and twice as large, the muscles in his arms standing out in stark relief. He appears to be holding air, but it's just a physical representation of what his magic is doing.

Mainly: protecting my damn ship.

Another tentacle arches out of the sea and slaps down on the invisible barrier of Bowen's shield. Even with his deep well of power, he can't keep this up forever. Not when our primary shield already failed, which isn't something that's happened in the weeks since Evelyn has been aboard.

The woman herself crouches behind us, frantically trying to remake the circle that will re-create the shield. When I dare a glance at her, she's looking shaky and paler than normal, her skin waxen. She meets my gaze, green eyes wide. "Is it the kraken?"

"No. Krakens can be reasoned with. Everyone!" I lift my voice, injecting a boom that will make my crew snap to action. "Attack the tentacles. Bowen, drop the shield when I go over."

"Are you out of your fucking mind, Nox?"

It's not the first time I've been asked this. It won't be the last. I shrug out of my coat and drop it onto the deck next to me. If I've learned one thing, it's that when in doubt, it's best to brazen your way through. I don't have the same scale of power that Bowen does, but I have enough. "I would prefer a peaceful resolution, but this beastie isn't cooperating. I'll get it to the surface. You rip it to shreds."

His dark brows draw together. "How are you—"

"Don't ask questions you don't want the answers to, darling." I yank off my boots—even with magic, they're a pain to get salt water out of—and step onto the railing. "If I die tragically, remember me fondly."

"Nox, damn you!"

I dive over the edge before he can finish berating me. Bowen's got a paladin's sense of honor—which means he's a stick-in-the-mud—and he's always been reluctant to admit that sometimes it takes breaking the rules to come out on top. Since coming out on top of this current conflict means my crew lives and my ship stays intact, there's no room for negotiation.

The water welcomes me like an old friend, my magic rising beneath my skin in response to my intent. It's difficult to see with the beastie churning through the depths, bubbles and tentacles everywhere. That's fine. I've worked in worse conditions.

I pull a small funnel of air down to meet me and enclose my head, allowing me to breathe, and then cut down through the depths, propelled along by my water magic through the small hole Bowen opened in his shield for me. Most people have access to only one element, but I've never been like most people. I can wield all four.

The thing has twice as many tentacles as a kraken and is half as smart. Maybe not even that much. It completely ignores me weaving around its body in favor of trying to eat my ship.

Not today, darling.

I dip between two massive tentacles and stop short at the sight of its massive mouth. A *mouth*, not a beak, as if I needed further confirmation. Krakens can be reasoned with. If they grow to ship-killer size, they're old enough to know when faced with a fight they can't win. They prefer easier prey than humans anyway. There is plenty to hunt in the cold, dark depths that won't rip you to shreds.

I'm still a sap, though; instead of immediately attacking, I project my voice through the water toward it. "Stop attacking my ship!"

I already know it won't work, but it gets the beastie's attention on me. It opens its mouth wide, exposing row after row of razor-sharp teeth nearly as tall as I am.

Okay, then.

I shove my hands forward, propelling air from the funnel and into its mouth. More and more and more, the force of it preventing the beastie from shutting me out. "Too late, darling." My body shakes from the energy drain, but we're not done yet.

The air fills it like a balloon, sending it toward the surface even as it keeps trying to eat me. It can't seem to figure out why the distance between us is increasing, which further proves that it's pure animal—if one of a truly monstrous size. It doesn't mean it deserves to die simply for existing, but it's eaten four trade ships in the last four weeks and shows no sign of slowing down.

It swipes a tentacle at me, and I have to take the hit because all my magic is devoted into propelling it upward and keeping enough air around my mouth and nose so I don't drown.

It's like someone dropping a ship on me. The tip of the tentacle is thicker around than I am. It slaps me hard enough that I see stars. I lose my grip on the magic bringing air to me—but not the air to the beastie.

The Cŵn Annwn are the biggest monsters in Threshold, the realm that connects all realms in existence, but occasionally one of the beasties wreaking havoc *does* need to be put down. It's always tragic, but again, that's *my* ship and *my* crew and *my* world. I'm not going to let a beastie keep eating people.

One final desperate burst of power overloads its natural weight and creates enough buoyancy to send its form surging to the surface. My body shakes as I keep it going up and up and up. I can tell the moment Bowen's power takes hold. The weight against my magic disappears.

I exhale slowly and start swimming. I'm far enough from the surface that I have to be intentional about my ascent. Deep pressure does a world of damage to the human body if not managed correctly.

By the time I shoot from the surface and use the water to propel me back on board, it's raining blood.

"Bowen!" Evelyn crouches on the deck with her hands over her head. "Did you have to *literally* rip it apart?"

Bowen looks a little woozy, which is worrisome in a man that large. "Sit down before you fall down." I nudge him with my fingertips, and he stumbles a few steps to sink to his knees next to Evelyn.

The rest of the crew is looking just as dazed. We've fought mermaids and other ships and all sorts of creatures we can't talk down, but I've never seen the *Audacity* covered in this much blood. It matches our crimson sails. In fact, I'm the only one who isn't red and covered in gore.

Well, I'm captain for a reason. It falls on me to snap everyone back to reality. I spread my arms and slowly circle. "Well done, chaps. Callen. Gable." I snap my fingers at the two, who straighten to attention when I name them. "Get the deck cleaned up as much as you're able. The rest of you, see what we can harvest of the beast. Evelyn will get shower schedules set up."

We might have the magic of indoor plumbing in the pocket dimension inside the ship, but the resources aren't infinite. We'll have to make port soon so I can refill our freshwater stores.

I turn to find my quartermaster, Poet, holding my coat. It wasn't spared from the carnage, now several shades darker than its usual crimson and dripping the same gore covering everyone else. I sigh. "Well, it was about time for a new coat anyway."

Poet shakes her head, her long dark hair flinging blood. She's a tall woman with light brown skin and a thick body that can carry three barrels to every one of mine. "You don't need an excuse to add to your wardrobe."

She's not wrong. I grin. "It's true, but this excuse is better than most."

"I suppose it is." She neatly sidesteps a surge of water Gable guides across the deck, concentration on zir face. Callen is next, slightly overlapping with zir path.

I glance over to where Evelyn is tugging Bowen to his feet. It looks absurd for the big man to be leaning on his short, curvy woman, but she's stronger than she appears. She keeps them both on their feet. "Before I get the shower situation figured out, I need to help Bowen," Evelyn says.

"I'm fine," he murmurs. Except his dark eyes aren't quite focusing.

"You're really not," she says tartly. She doesn't look much steadier on her feet, but Evelyn would have to be dead to not run her mouth. It's what I like about her. She frowns at me. "You look terrible, too."

I'm not about to admit that I'm fighting to avoid weaving on my feet. I can channel more magic than most elemental users, but even I have limits. All of us reached them today.

But I'm the captain, and the captain can't show weakness.

I dredge up a roguish grin. "Keep talking sweet to me, and I'm going to have to challenge Bowen for your heart."

She rolls her eyes and Bowen mutters under his breath as she turns them toward the hatch leading belowdecks. Poet snorts. "You done playing hero? You need to be looked over."

"I'm fine." It's more or less the truth. My ribs ache, but my breathing is uninterrupted so nothing's horrifically broken. "Save Orchid's tender ministrations for those who actually need it." Our healer is a miracle worker, and he believes in the cause. We might all be serving the same purpose—to undermine the

Cŵn Annwn and help the people and creatures who end up in Threshold by accidentally wandering through the wrong portal.

Poet sighs. "You'd tell me if you weren't."

"Of course I would," I lie. I want nothing more than to peel out of my wet shirt, but I suspect if I do so, Poet will come down with the vapors. There's sure to be a rainbow of bruises across my body. It's fine. I heal faster than most people.

The sea around the *Audacity* is red and chunky. Bowen might have been a captain at one point, but he's extremely good at following orders. Good enough that there's only carnage left of the beastie. I fight down a shudder.

This is Threshold and I sail under the banner of the Cŵn Annwn, for all that I find their policies loathsome. Each of their captains is a bigger monster than the next. It means *I'm* a monster—and Bowen, too. It's natural to wonder which of us would walk away if it came to a fight.

His telekinetic power is fearsome, but he's still human. He needs to breathe. The question is whether I could suffocate him before he tore me to pieces . . .

Cheery thoughts.

I motion to Poet. "Let's wrap this up. I hate the smell of gore."

A few months back, half the crew was killed in a hostile takeover—mine, notably—and we still haven't filled out our numbers. Even so, it only takes an hour before we're moving, cutting away from the frothing waters. The blood has summoned other predators, but they aren't our business.

I make the rounds, talking to my people, checking in, until I circle back to where Eyal stands at the helm. He's a tall, lean man with cool dark brown skin and blue locs—or he is normally; currently, he's the same shade as our sails.

Which means it'll be a bit longer before I can change out of these clothes. "You're going to undo all of Gable and Callen's hard work by dripping all over the newly clean deck. Go shower."

"Won't be time for that."

I narrow my eyes. "What are you on about?"

"We have company." He points, and I follow the motion to the horizon. I don't see anything, but that doesn't mean much. Eyal's got better eyes than most.

This day just got exponentially longer. "Trouble?"

"Hard to say." He squints. "Smaller vessel. White sails."

White sails don't mean much—the only ships that fly crimson sails are Cŵn Annwn warships. We're on the trading route between Drash and Three Sisters, so it might be a trader. Or smugglers. Neither fall within our purview.

Still, there's no reason to be foolish. I raise my voice. "Everyone, on alert. It's time to meet some new friends."

CHAPTER 2

Nox

A THREAD OF UNEASE GOES THROUGH ME AS WE GET close enough to pick out the details of the ship. It's easy enough because they're heading directly for the *Audacity*. They aren't attempting to pretend to do anything else.

"Orders?" Poet murmurs. She stands at my right shoulder.

I'm tired and itchy from the salt water drying on my skin, and I want nothing more than to get this over with, but that's just my impulsiveness talking. I know better than to listen to *that* voice. "Let's give them a nice warm welcome . . . at least until we know what they want."

Almost as soon as the words leave my lips, Gable yells from the bow. "It's Lizzie!"

"*Lizzie?*" I can't stop my shock. I thought for certain we'd seen the last of that murderous vampire. She ran off with Maeve ages ago. I fully expected her to find Maeve's stolen skin, retrieve her stolen family heirlooms, and then take a portal back to her world, never to return. She shouldn't be *here*.

Except she is. She stands at the bow of the small ship, her long dark hair trailing behind her in the wind of their passing. She's just as beautiful as the last time I saw her, but there's something looser in her body language. Interesting.

A second person joins her, and I stop thinking about the vampire altogether. Because I know this person, this woman. I know that tall frame and those broad shoulders, that tanned skin and handsome face.

Siobhan.

"Fuck," I breathe.

I haven't seen Siobhan in years. There was a time when she sailed more freely about, using her charm and smarts to convince more people to join the rebellion. But as our numbers increased, it became necessary to remove herself a bit, to *protect* herself. So she essentially went into hiding.

She should *still* be in hiding.

The fact that she's not is more than a little worrisome. I glance at Eyal. "Bring us close."

"Yes, Captain." He must sense my tension because normally he has a quip for every command.

None of the rest of the crew know how important Siobhan is to the movement to undermine the Cŵn Annwn's hold on Threshold—namely that she's the mastermind behind it. The fewer people aware of that fact, the safer she is. So why is she *here?*

Eyal brings the *Audacity* up next to the smaller ship, and the crew tosses a line over. Within a few moments, Siobhan is pulling herself over the railing and onto the deck. I expect Lizzie to follow her, but it's Maeve who joins us next, her red hair bright against her pale skin. She's paler than normal, appearing a little shaky on her feet. And *there* is the vampire, landing lightly next to her and wrapping an arm around her curvy waist, looking like a shark protecting a minnow.

I would enjoy that development a lot more if not for the way Siobhan stalks toward me, her long legs eating up the distance between us. She looks good, really good. She wears the years since I've seen her well, there in the laugh lines on either side of her wide mouth and the crinkles in the corners of her eyes that seem to suggest she's spent a lot of time laughing. And then she's before me, easily six inches taller than I am and widely muscled.

I would have preferred to conduct this reunion while not soaked and missing my favorite coat, but life rarely cooperates with my preferences.

Still, no reason not to make the best of it. I spread my arms wide, a monarch greeting someone who might be a rival and might be an ally. "Welcome to the *Audacity*." I cut a look over to where Lizzie glowers and Maeve smiles sweetly. "Welcome back, in your case. It looks like there's a story here, but there's one important question to be answered first. Your ship?"

"Leave it." Siobhan brushes that away. "It's got a beacon. One of my teams will pick it up."

Which means they came here for *us*.

I knew that, of course, yet hearing it all but confirms makes me twitch. "In that case, allow me to offer you the hospitality of my cabin."

Lizzie snorts. "Pass. Is our old room still open?"

"Indeed it is."

She turns, her arm still around Maeve, and heads for the hatch. No hesitation, no pussyfooting around. I've always appreciated that about the vampire.

I glance at Siobhan. "Maeve?"

"She was attacked during . . ." Siobhan sighs. "It's why we're here. She'll make a full recovery thanks to the miracle of vampire blood's healing properties, but that's the least of our problems right now."

That's what I was afraid of. "Let's get this over with." I reluctantly pull the remainder of the water from my clothing and send the little stream of it back into the sea. It leaves everything vaguely crunchy, but it's still better than being damp. Marginally.

I lead the way to my cabin, tucked behind the helm. Inside is part haven, part war room, but the latter seems to have taken over in recent months. It's certainly why Siobhan has sought us out. Sought *me* out.

The moment the door closes, she sighs as if setting down a great weight. I hate that I understand exactly what it feels like. I'm not carrying around as much responsibility as she is, but being captain means my crew's lives hang in the balance of every decision I make. As leader of the rebellion, Siobhan shoulders dozens and dozens of crews. Even I'm not sure of the exact number. It's safer that way.

"Okay, enough with the mysterious leader shit. What's going on?"

She smiles briefly. It's a good smile, a little crooked, and it warms her honey-colored eyes. "There's a reason you're my favorite."

"Now I'm actually worried. Stop flattering me and spit it out."

She hesitates, but finally says, "It's Bastian."

The name rocks me to my core and sends me stumbling back several steps. "Don't."

Siobhan's expression goes remorseful, but not so much that she stops speaking. "I wouldn't have come to you if I had any other choice. I'm aware of the bargain we made."

"Siobhan, *don't*." It's pathetic that hearing his name, fourteen years later, is enough to make me shake. Some wounds never truly heal and scar; they fester.

"They took him, Nox. I thought he was aboard the *Crimson Hag*, but when we brought down the ship in Drash's bay, he wasn't there. They transferred him somewhere along the way, and I don't know what to do."

No need to ask who *they* are. The Cŵn Annwn. But that doesn't make any sense. The Cŵn Annwn have a long history of abusing their power, but there are lines that even the foolhardiest captain won't cross.

I shake my head sharply. "Impossible. He's a fucking noble. His family would burn Lyari to the ground before they'd allow the Council to send him to trial for anything."

"Normally, you would be right. Not this time." She looks away. "He was caught using glamour."

My breath swooshes out of my lungs. "No. Not even he would be so reckless."

In a place like Threshold, we have more varieties of magic than I can begin to count, but the one that the Council universally banned as soon as they came into power is glamour. The Cŵn Annwn rule Threshold with iron fists and crimson sails, all in the name of *protection*. Unfortunately, there's no one to protect us from them. They don't like the idea that they could

be manipulated magically, so they spent the last few generations purging every single person capable of glamour from
Threshold.

Bastian is a throwback to some many-times-great-grandparent
who had that flavor of magic, but he's successfully hidden it his
entire life. When other children were being taught their letters,
he was being drilled in how he should never give himself away.
I swallow hard. "They'll kill his entire family. If not for possess-
ing glamour themselves, then for hiding him."

"Yes." Siobhan looks sick.

I've spent damn near half my life hating his family. They're
the reason he stayed in Lyari—the largest and most powerful
city in Threshold—when I left. If he wasn't the second son of a
noble family, loyalty ingrained in him right down to his bones,
he would have joined me and . . .

And *what*?

I still would have met Siobhan years later, and knowing
what's developed between them . . . It would have been heart-
ache no matter which angle I take. I shake my head. "No."

"Yes, Nox. Even if I didn't care for him as a person, he knows
too much about the rebellion. If he breaks, he and his family
aren't the only ones they'll come after. They'll hunt every member of the rebellion—including you and your crew."

I drag my hands through my short hair. She's right, but I'm
not prepared to admit it. "Find someone else, Siobhan. I understand the stakes, but you made me *one* promise when I joined.
One. Don't break it now."

"I wouldn't if I had any other choice." She sounds contrite
enough that I almost believe her. "There's no one else, Nox. No
one but you and this crew you've stacked too effectively. Be-

tween all the air- and water-users you have aboard and Bowen, no one can match your speed or your shields. The *Audacity* is the only ship that can catch them now—and the only one that can make a clean getaway."

I laugh harshly. "Now I know you're fucking with me. There's no clean getaway, Siobhan. If he was transferred between ships, then the Cŵn Annwn know he's valuable *and* that someone is coming for him. They'll have contacted the Council to report it. They'll have a whole fleet protecting the ship he's on. There's no coming back from this."

The only reason the rebellion has functioned so well is because we were beneath notice. A little mouse scurrying around, saving people in ones and twos, carefully skipping murdering some "monsters" we were set upon. If we're found out, we'll be annihilated. They have too much power. "It's over, then."

Siobhan takes my shoulders. "No. It's not. You can save him. I know you can."

Even knowing it's a mistake, I stare up into her handsome face, am captivated by the glow in her honey eyes. This is what drew me in all those years ago. Siobhan believes so strongly that it's like a force of gravity, drawing in those around her. She's asking the impossible, but with her determination bolstering me, it's difficult to keep fighting.

This is why she's so dangerous.

I sigh. "So be it. It will be a bloody funeral for us all."

CHAPTER 3

Siobhan

I F I COULD HAVE GONE TO ANYONE ELSE, I WOULD HAVE. AS
I told them, Nox has stacked the deck too thoroughly in their
favor. They have Bowen, who is one of the strongest telekinetics
I've ever encountered. They have a crew filled with elemental
users, which means the *Audacity* will emerge from any sea battle
victorious. They have a witch whom I haven't met personally
but have already heard stories of despite her short time in
Threshold.

Now that I've come with Lizzie and Maeve, they even have a
powerful and deadly vampire—and the selkie who holds her
leash.

I study Nox's sharp face. They're giving me little to read, but
too often my life depends on reading people who don't want to
be perceived. Nox is a challenge, but I have the advantage of
knowing the pinch point to this argument. "I understand you
and Bastian have a complicated history . . ."

They slice an elegant hand through the air. "No, we're not going to put a spin on this, Siobhan. When you courted me, talking of a rebellion and all the good things we can do for the people who need them most, I agreed on *one* condition. What was that condition?"

As much as I hate to admit it, they're right. A single condition and I've just broken it. "That I don't speak to you of Bastian." It went without saying that bringing Nox and Bastian into the same location was strictly forbidden.

A promise easy enough to make years ago, when Nox was just a clever quartermaster with ambition and Bastian was in *my* bed. I still don't know what went so wrong that both refuse to speak of the other, but weighing it against the lives of thousands . . . "If I had another choice, I would have made it."

"You do have another choice." They shake their head, the slightly longer top of their white-blond hair standing oddly on end. They look good, but Nox always looks good. Even whatever trouble they had here isn't enough to detract from that. Their lean features and pointed chin are a trap, the wicked gleam in their gray eyes the only indication of just how much trouble they're liable to cause.

"No one else has a chance of reaching them in time." I have to clench my fists to keep my claws inside. I never lose control of my form, but the stress of this clusterfuck of a situation is getting to me.

Bastian, what were you thinking?

I don't have answers. Bastian and I argued bitterly a few weeks ago. He was tired of all the secrecy and wanted to take the rebellion public, sure that the majority of Threshold would

follow us if they knew what we were fighting for. I called him a
naive fool and refused to even consider it. Too many people
would die. We're not *ready*.

When will we be ready, Siobhan? When will you stop letting your fear
control you?

His voice is so clear in my head, I nearly flinch. I didn't have
an answer then—still don't now—so I used words as weapons
to strike right into the very heart of him. And he . . . left. The last
time I saw him, he was standing aboard a trading ship headed
for Three Sisters, intent on bringing the leaders there around to
our cause. Three Sisters holds no love for the Cŵn Annwn and
their meddling, and Bastian is a charming fucker even without
his magic. If he could get Three Sisters on board, it would go a
long way toward forcing my hand.

I still don't know what went wrong to result in him using his
glamour—and getting caught. In all the years I've known him,
he's been so bloody careful to keep his magic contained. He
wouldn't have used it without cause.

Unless he was acting out of character because he was still
angry at me.

"Nox, please." I don't make a habit of begging. I tell people
what I want, and they make it happen. I've worked *hard* to ensure
my network is as expansive as possible so there's always someone in my corner wherever I go. So I'll never be desperate like I
was at nineteen, when my entire world was turned upside down
and I lost everything.

Nox curses long and hard. "You don't have to beg—I already
said I'd do it—but you've set forth an impossible task. We don't
know which ship has him or what route they'll take to deliver him to the Council in Lyari. I can hardly set up a single

ship blockade and check every Cŵn Annwn vessel that tries to pass."

At least I have an answer for *this*. "We don't need a blockade. We just need information." I nod at the magical map next to their desk. All Cŵn Annwn ships have one, a direct way of communication between captains and the Council. It's how they get their orders and update the status of their hunts.

Nox curses again. "It will break my cover."

"Yes." I can't pretend otherwise. "And if Bastian is taken before the Council, your name will be among those tortured out of him. Either way, they'll know you're a traitor. It's your choice how you deal with that."

"You are such a bitch sometimes." They laugh as they say it.

A growl slips free of my lips, the rumble in my chest almost vicious. "Help me, Nox. Don't make me beg." Again.

"I won't." They sigh and flop down into the chair behind the massive desk bolted to the floor. "As charming as it would be to see you on your knees, it would be undignified for both of us."

I ignore the bolt of heat that goes through me at their words. Nox flirts as easily as they breathe, and while rumor has it that a night in their bed is enough pleasure to last a lifetime, there's never been intent when they flirt at *me*.

Even if Bastian and I weren't exclusive, Nox would be off-limits. Their history with Bastian is thorny and painful, and allowing my attraction to Nox to bloom would hurt Bastian deeply. So I never have.

They slide their chair to the map. "Might as well get this over with." They spread their graceful fingers and press them to the edge of the map. "Nox of the *Audacity* here, ready to give my report."

A disembodied voice sounds almost immediately. "Report."

They glance at me, gray eyes considering. "We took care of the beastie."

"Classification?"

"Unknown. It was similar to a kraken, but more fish than squid."

"Noted. Please hold for your next target."

"No rest for the wicked." Nox rolls their eyes. "I actually have a question about the *Crimson Hag*. We've heard reports of her sinking in Drash's bay. What happened there?"

The voice ignores that. A few seconds later, they come back. "Travel to the sandbar in the west."

I frown, Nox mirroring the expression. "Excuse me?"

"Travel to the sandbar in the west. I will patch through coordinates, but I expect you're familiar with the location, as you've been sailing these seas for well over a decade." The voice is so prim it makes me want to sneeze.

"Lovely of you to notice my wealth of history and experience. What, pray tell, shall I do at the sandbar when I reach it? Find and fight some sand sharks?"

The voice goes colder. "We have no current reports of sand sharks in that area or any other."

"I'm aware," Nox snaps. "Now, stop playing with me and tell me what my full orders are."

"You will be acting as support and escort to the *Bone Heart* while they transport a highly dangerous prisoner to Lyari." The faint sizzling sensation of the connection fades, signaling the conversation is over.

The *Bone Heart*. That's going to be a problem. It's the one ship I've gone out of my way to avoid ever since Morrigan took over as captain. She's the only person who knows who I truly am . . . though she currently believes I'm dead.

There are seven members on the current Council that rules Threshold, each more corrupt than the next. Usually they're voted in by a ridiculously complex system that's rigged to ensure only a certain type of person is allowed to occupy one of their precious seats. Council members spend the rest of their lives as metaphorical dragons, hoarding their power and doing their best to never do more than absolutely necessary in terms of their actual jobs.

Morrigan is the exception. She has been a member of the Council for years now, and she's the youngest to hold the position. Rather than stay in Lyari and play politics, she became captain of the *Bone Heart* and has spent the intervening time carving out a fearsome reputation.

She's also my sister.

"No one does anything halfway in this mess." Nox curses. "Guess I don't have a choice after all."

I should have anticipated this turn of events. The *Audacity* has one of the best track records of all the Cŵn Annwn. It started because the last captain, Hedd, was a violent jackass who never met an enemy he didn't want to beat to death with his bare fists. Nox taking over has only cemented that reputation. Their success rate is nearly one hundred percent.

Of course the Council would want them playing escort to the ship carrying Bastian to Lyari.

"There's always a choice." I force my spine straight and any emotion from my face. "I can't make you."

"Don't pull that mystic bullshit on me right now. I'm not in the mood for it." They meet my gaze. There's so much in their gray eyes, old pain and resilience and determination. "I'll do this for you, Siobhan, because you're right: there isn't another choice. I'll get him back."

There's a ringing in my ears, and it sounds like someone screaming my sister's name while flames roar. Deep down, I knew I'd have to see her again someday, but someday was never *now*. A small, foolish part of me had hoped that someday would never come. My throat is so dry, I have to swallow twice before I can get words out. "Thank you."

"Don't thank me." They take a step back and motion for me to leave. "Figure out what you're going to do once you have him back to protect my crew and every other person who's pledged themselves to fulfilling your vision of a better world."

I walk out the door and back into the sunlight without answering. Because I *don't* have an answer. Not yet. The confrontation between the Cŵn Annwn and the rebellion has been coming from the moment I recruited my first person. Ten years ago, when I was filled with fury at an unjust system, I was sure that there would come a day when we would prevail, when Threshold would become the realm its people need, a place safe for *everyone* and not just those with crimson sails.

I'm not sure when things changed. There was no finite point where fear began to outweigh anger, no single loss that tipped me over into the shadow I am today.

I have people on most of the Cŵn Annwn ships at this point, reporting on their movements and bringing others into the fold. Most of the crew members aren't local to Threshold. As the hub realm between all realms, we get more than our fair share of people and creatures who take a wrong turn, step into the wrong spot, and tumble from their realm and into ours.

The rebellion does their best to see these people home instead of into the hands of the Cŵn Annwn.

If the Cŵn Annwn finds them? Well, they are given a choice: join the crew or die. It's the most efficient way they have of bolstering their numbers to continue to "protect" Threshold from monsters. Some of those refugees take to the murderous intent of the Cŵn Annwn naturally and embrace everything that's toxic and awful about them. Most don't. They're trapped and doing what it takes to survive.

I don't realize Lizzie is waiting for me until the vampire shifts from her position leaning against the railing. She's a fit woman with moon-pale skin, long dark hair, and eyes that flash crimson when she's irritated. She also doesn't believe in this cause. She's only here for her woman, Maeve. Up until recently, Maeve was just like hundreds of other locals who form a network of information that spans the realm. People who believe in a better world without the Cŵn Annwn's boots on their necks.

There's nowhere else to go for now, so I cross to the vampire and take up a position against the railing. "I'm surprised you're not belowdecks with Maeve."

"She's resting. Apparently my presence is not restful." Her lips shift into something that's almost a smile as she says it. They're two people who couldn't be more different—the soft and shiny Maeve, the violent and vicious Lizzie—but even I can't deny that the connection between them is real. She motions to the door to Nox's cabin. "Things didn't go well."

"'Well' is a matter of opinion." I shrug. In our handful of days together, I've learned to respect Lizzie's frankness, even if I find it irritating.

"Told you." Lizzie looks away, her brows drawing together

at the sight of the seemingly endless sea, not a spec of land in sight. "As I said before, I'll do whatever it takes to keep Maeve safe, even if we have to murder our way through the entirety of the Cŵn Annwn. I would appreciate an actual plan, though." She shudders delicately. "One that doesn't involve going into the water."

"I'll see what I can do." I survey the clear blue sky, not a cloud in sight. The *Audacity* has a handful of both water- and air-users, which means there's no risk of the ship ever being becalmed. The sails fill even as I watch, the gentle breeze coaxed into a strong wind by the two air-users on the upper deck.

The ship jerks beneath our feet and Lizzie goes a little green. "I'm going to check on Maeve."

I roll my shoulders and settle down against the railing to watch the crew. I've been on my own for a long time—and not only because everyone back in Lyari thinks I'm dead. When you're the mind behind an entire movement, anyone you spend time with will become a target alongside you. The only exception was Bastian, and look how that turned out. Our fight has to be the reason he was reckless enough to draw the attention of the Cŵn Annwn.

The first hard thing is done. Nox has agreed to help retrieve Bastian. There's still half a dozen difficult tasks remaining, but they can wait the few days it will take us to reach the sandbar that stretches from Ganabie to Exver, creating an impassable barrier to all but the shallowest hulls.

Later, I'll sit Nox down and come up with a plan.

For now, I'll let them stew and let the vampire and selkie rest.

CHAPTER 4

Bastian

U P UNTIL A FEW WEEKS AGO, THE CLOSEST I'D GOTTEN to a cell was reading about them in books. Now I'm in my third of the week. First in Mairi on Second Sister, where I made the mistake of letting my glamour slip in a fit of rage to protect a woman being harassed by two members of the Cŵn Annwn. Then in the relatively nice and clean brig of the *Crimson Hag*. Now in the significantly less nice and less clean brig of the *Bone Heart*.

I'm practically an expert at this point.

"Be a good chap and pass me that water," I say. Or at least I try to say. My gag makes the words a garbled mess. I'm not even certain the guard is there. I can't see due to the blindfold tight around the upper part of my face. My hands have long since lost sensation after being tied behind my back.

The only senses left to me are smell and hearing, and both are a torment. This cell hasn't been cleaned in my lifetime, and the acrid scent of filth never seems to get more mundane. I've always found the steady shoosh of the waves soothing, but I've never spent so much time in a brig where the only thing between me and the waves is a worryingly thin hull. The constant sound is agonizing.

Almost enough to distract me from how thoroughly I've mucked things up.

I want to blame Siobhan for being so stubborn and refusing to bend, which led to the final fight that broke us. That righteous anger only lasted the first night of captivity. Siobhan isn't the one who reacted emotionally and rushed into a situation without bothering to see who might witness me manipulating two Cŵn Annwn with a forbidden magic. She isn't the one whose frustration and anger made her sloppy.

Siobhan doesn't *get* sloppy.

Footsteps bring my head up even though my blindfold ensures there's nothing to see. I don't need to see to know who approaches, though. She's made a point of visiting my cell once a day.

Morrigan. Captain of the *Bone Heart*. Council member. The last member of her noble line after a fire killed her parents and—as far as she knows—her little sister.

"Truly, I'm embarrassed it's come to this, Bastian." Deft fingers pull my gag out. "Say the word and we'll get you cleaned up. I'm even willing to spare an entire cabin for you. There's a meal ready and waiting."

The same offer. It's tempting in the way all perfect things are tempting. I'd give my favorite ruby ring for a hot bath and clean clothes. Working with the rebellion sometimes means nights spent away from comfortable beds and long days between bathing, but for the most part, the role I'm meant to play is the one I was born into.

The noble second son, flitting about Threshold without a single worry in his head. All that messy responsibility and stress falls to my older brother, Liam. No one expects anything of *me*, except that I keep myself alive in case something terrible happens to the heir. At some point, there may be pressure to marry well and accumulate some children, but if Liam's wife manages to squeeze a few out in the next couple of years, even that won't be required.

Working with Siobhan is the first and only truly noble thing I've ever done. No matter how angry I am with her resistance to moving the rebellion forward, I won't betray her.

I close my mouth, doing my best to ignore how my jaw aches, and swallow. The gag only stays out as long as Morrigan talks to me. "You know, Morrigan, you're truly impressive. A Council member, a noble, and still you're out here on a ship, getting your hands dirty."

She laughs, low with a ragged edge that just makes the sound more attractive. "Compliments will get you nowhere with me when you smell like *that*."

I don't tense, but my pride takes a hit. I know I stink. Hard not to when I'm tied and trapped like this. "You could toss me in the shower and clear that problem right up." It's a pathetic attempt at flirting, but I've never been particularly good at it. When you have money and good looks, prospective bed part-ners tend to care less about the words coming out of your mouth than they do about where sleeping with you might get them.

Except Siobhan. Both of those features counted against me when it came to working with the rebellion, making it harder for me to move covertly.

And . . . Well, Nox was never one to be moved by a pretty face. Not when they're already the prettiest person in the room.

The old pain is comforting in its familiarity. I haven't seen them in fourteen years, not since they left Lyari on Hedd's ship. A choice I thought would end with them dead. We fought bitterly over it. Ironic, that. At twenty-one, we were both so determined to fix the problem from inside the system, and had wildly different views on what that looked like. Nox was sure the crews themselves could be turned with the right leadership. I firmly believed that the change had to come from Lyari to take proper root.

We were both wrong.

"Bastian," Morrigan says slowly. "Do me the respect of paying attention when I'm standing right here, enduring your presence."

I might hate her, but she's right. I can't afford to mentally wander right now. It's just hard to *think* with the pain radiating through my body and the hunger gnawing a path through my stomach. "Apologies, Morrigan. I'm not at my best currently."

"That could change in a moment." Her voice goes low and coaxing. "Your family doesn't have to be brought in for questioning if you simply tell us what you did to hide your glamour magic. It must have been difficult."

The same question from a slightly different angle. I try not to think about the fact that she's got to be lying—my family *will* be questioned. None of them have the same magic I do, but they did hide me. They know better than to tell the truth, though. It's a loss if I die, but I'm not irreplaceable the way my brother and parents are. "They don't know anything, which *you* know because I've told you that several times."

"Indeed." The faintest sound as she shifts. "But I do have a new question for you."

"I'd love to hear it."

She chuckles. "All you have to do is tell me about the woman you've been seen traveling with. We can discuss it over a meal after you've had a bath."

Siobhan.

She knows.

"A woman?" It takes everything I have to keep my body language relaxed, to keep my tone flippant. "You're going to have to be more specific. I'm something of a rake, you see."

Morrigan snorts. "That's what they say in Lyari—and only Lyari. It's interesting how your rakish tendencies don't leave the city's borders. Suspicious, even."

I sigh and slump dramatically against the bars. "You know, it's rude to suggest that I can only find bed partners who are familiar with the power my family wields. I'm not that kind of man."

Instead of marching away in a huff, Morrigan laughs. "I believe you, Bastian. I don't think you're that kind of man at all. I think you've hidden your glamour magic for far more sinister reasons than anyone else on the Council can begin to guess." Her voice lowers and comes closer. "What are you and your little girlfriend planning?"

"You can't have it both ways, Morrigan. Either I'm a rake or I'm not." I shrug. "If this is the best you can do, you're wasting both our time."

"Perhaps. Perhaps not." She grabs the back of my neck and shoves the gag back into my mouth. "In case you were holding out for a rescue attempt, it's not going to happen. Tomorrow, we reach reinforcements, and then it's a short twelve-day journey to Lyari and your trial. The Council is going above and beyond, of course. It's not every day they get to cut down one of the noble families' scions." She pauses. "Even a second son."

The cut stings despite being one that's been leveled at me my entire life. The spare, never the heir. I may not *want* to be heir, but being treated as an afterthought from the moment I was born was a constant ache.

It's only when Morrigan's footsteps retreat that I fully process what she said. Reinforcements. A trial. I knew it was coming, of course, but it's entirely different to hear those plans spoken aloud.

I'm not getting out of this alive.

The best I can hope for is to not take my family—or the entirety of the rebellion—down with me.

CHAPTER 5

Nox

"ARE YOU SURE ABOUT THIS?"

I look at the circle of faces gathered in my cabin. Poet and Eyal. Bowen and Evelyn. Lizzie and Maeve. Siobhan. Some of the most powerful people I've ever encountered, and I still don't know if it will be enough.

It has to be enough. "I'm sure. There's no way to do this secretly, so every single one of us will be branded as traitors. You're all here because you believe in a better Threshold, one not ruled by the Council and the Cŵn Annwn. If Bastian is taken to Lyari, then we'll be hunted. If we save him, then we'll be hunted." It should be Siobhan giving a rousing speech, but this is *my* ship and *my* crew. "I recognize that you didn't sign up for this, so if you want to sit this one out, I won't hold it against you."

Everyone gathered exchanges looks. Evelyn is the one to speak first, the adorable little witch with curves for days and a wicked wit. "It's really cute that you think we're going to fuck off *now*, as if we haven't discovered exactly how terrible the Cŵn Annwn are."

Bowen wraps an arm around her shoulders and tugs her back against him. "What she means to say is that I'm deeply invested in righting the wrongs committed during my time as captain of the *Crimson Hag*. We're with you."

I expected nothing less from Bowen. He's not exactly on a holy mission of redemption, but it's damn close. Evelyn is one of those people who seems like she was looking for a cause to believe in, and she's chosen the rebellion as hers. She's got good taste.

Maeve opens her mouth, but Lizzie speaks first. "She's in, so I'm in. Can't let my selkie get killed in your war." The vampire's droll tone almost makes me smile.

Maeve shoots her a sharp look. "I can speak for myself."

"I'm aware." Lizzie nudges her with her shoulder. "But we both know you were going to make a grand proclamation. I saved us both time."

Maeve rolls her eyes. "Fine. Yes. We're in. There. Nice, succinct. Happy?"

"I'm with you."

Gods, they make me sick. I much preferred the Lizzie before she went and fell in love with one of the sweetest women I know. The vampire was a necessary counterpoint to Bowen and Evelyn constantly making eyes at each other. In the days we've spent sailing toward the sandbar, it's become clear that while Lizzie will never be a ray of sunshine, she's deeply in love with Maeve.

Exhausting, honestly.

I wave a hand at Siobhan. "We already know you're invested in this suicide mission. Eyal?"

Eyal hesitates, looking around the room with his serious eyes. "I would heartily recommend coming up with an actual plan to minimize the chances that we all die horribly." He shrugs his shoulders. "But you already know my answer, Captain. It's the same it's always been."

From the time I was a small child, orphaned in Lyari by parents I don't even remember, all I wanted was to replace the gaping hole inside me. First with the group of street kids who watched each other's backs . . . and that's as far as their loyalty went. Then with Bastian, certain that I would always find a home in his arms. I had learned enough hard lessons by the time I joined Hedd's crew to know not to expect community *there*, but when I became captain, that desire, as hearty and annoying as a weed, sprouted again.

In reality, all being captain has done is make me increasingly aware of how much responsibility rests on my shoulders. I might have a true community now, but that community's safety is my responsibility. I lose sleep worrying about them. I am constantly considering different angles of approach to each battle we face in order to minimize the chances of them being hurt. I would rather take a hit than allow a single one of them to fall under my watch.

I can't help the fear that rises inside me at the war we're currently facing. Not a single battle with a definitive end point. An overarching conflict that only ends one of two ways: with them dead . . . or with us dead.

With that in mind, I turn to Poet. As quartermaster, she is the voice of the crew. "Surely you have thoughts, Poet."

She shifts from foot to foot. "I'm aware that you don't want to hear this, but every single crew member will follow you to the depths of whatever underworld you lead them to. We owe our lives to you—and the rebellion."

The pressure in my chest increases until I can barely breathe around it. I've spent my entire life searching for this, only to discover what a poisoned wish it is. Every time one of them is hurt, it hurts *me*. I worry. I . . . I swallow hard. "Okay."

Poet nods at Siobhan. "We know the cost of the Cŵn Annwn maintaining power. We're with you."

I've become adept enough at hiding my emotions that I simply give them all a rakish grin instead of demanding they all jump ship and find their way to the nearest portal until this is all over. "In that case, my darlings, you have work to do and I have plans to plan."

They file out, one by one, until it's only Siobhan left. Instead of following them, she closes the door and leans against it. "That was a rousing commendation of your leadership. You've done good work putting your crew together. They trust you implicitly."

"Shut up, Siobhan." I turn away, the effort of appearing cool and collected too much to maintain. "This is what you wanted. We're sailing into certain death at your behest. No need to rub it in."

"Nox." She sighs. "If I thought it was certain death, I wouldn't ask it of you. If there was any other choice, I swear I—"

"No, that's not what we're going to do." I spin back to face her. "What we're *not* going to do is pretend that you would make any other choice than the one you're making. You want Ba—" My voice breaks, and I mentally curse myself for being so affected, even all these years later. I clear my throat. "You want Bastian. You've always wanted Bastian."

"It's not the way you're making it sound." Siobhan shakes her head slowly. "There's never been one key to everything."

"Wrong. *You* are the key to everything." I finally make myself—*allow* myself—to look at her. She's beautiful in the way that mountains are, tall and broad and exhibiting the kind of remoteness that people can kill themselves crashing against. Not that she looks particularly remote right now, with her dark eyes lit up by an internal fire.

I know better than to let myself wonder what would have happened if I'd met her first. I know better, but I wonder all the same.

To distract myself from the toxic thoughts, I do my best to focus entirely on what comes next. "You shouldn't be on this ship when we get to the sandbar. We can risk me and the crew and even . . . Bastian. We can't risk you, Siobhan. Your strength is in your secrecy. If no one knows you're alive . . ."

"It's too late for that." For the first time since I met her, she actually looks defeated. "I came to you because you're the best shot we have. That doesn't mean we have a good shot, Nox."

I've never known her to be one to let impossible circumstances beat her down to dust the way they do to us mere mortals. When the rebellion was first getting off the ground about ten years ago, Siobhan and I worked together quite a bit. I try not to think about those days often, because we were so damned *young*. The very idea of the rebellion was exciting and filled with possibility, and I certainly didn't have any concept of what it would cost in pursuit of a better way.

Now look at us, worn to the bone and as weary as people twice our age.

Before I can think of all the reasons it's a terrible idea, I take her shoulders and shake her. "What did you tell me after our first fight?"

My shake barely moves her. She stares down at me. "How am I supposed to remember that? It was a lifetime ago."

No reason for that to sting. Just because she's been a figure who looms large through my life doesn't mean she feels the same way. She obviously doesn't. "We had gotten word about an entire family who ended up in Threshold by mistake. Hedd had his orders to scoop them up, and we were only days out from their location."

The memory lights up her eyes. "The Tu family."

"Yes."

"You didn't think I could make it there before the *Audacity*." She speaks slowly, her gaze distant. "You were afraid to risk me."

"I was." I still am. I drop my hands. "You told me that hope wins more battles than pure martial prowess. You told me that despair kills."

Her full lips curve, just a little. "That was rather clever of me."

"I certainly thought so. And you were right. You got there before the Cŵn Annwn and were able to see them home."

"I almost killed myself to make it happen," she murmurs. "I don't know if that's the moral we should cleave to."

If she were anyone else, I would use this opportunity to flirt, to distract with sex as much as with words. But she's not anyone else. She's Siobhan.

And she's in love with Bastian.

I just hope he treats her with more care than he treated me.

A hope that dims as I consider how he could have possibly been so foolish as to be caught after all this time. Everything else has changed in the last fourteen years; surely Bastian has changed as well. I shove the worry away. We'll rescue his goofy ass and then I'll get my answers.

For now, I have to inspire hope in the woman who's inspired me from the very beginning. I clear my throat. "It's time to bring the rebellion out of the shadows and change things once and for all."

"Easy to say. Significantly more impossible to pull off."

"One step at a time." I don't exactly know how we so effectively reversed roles from when we were young and fearless. I frown. "Are you manipulating me right now?"

Her smile, small as it is, disappears. "It's a fair question, and I'm not above doing so, but not this time. It's just . . ." She starts to turn away. I don't think, I just catch her biceps and keep her in place. Siobhan raises her brows. "It's been a full decade, Nox. And we haven't moved the needle even a little."

"We've saved countless people."

"Yes, and the Council has harmed countless more." This time, when she pulls away, I let her go. She walks to the massive window overlooking the wake of the *Audacity*. "Remove the current Council and the noble families will just elect new representatives. It changes nothing. We have to make an example of them and purge the rot that exists in the Cŵn Annwn."

It's nothing more than I've considered in the past . . . and no less impossible. "Even if that was the plan, how do you decide who to purge and who to pass over? The crews have spent years fighting monsters and terrorizing the population. One ship isn't an easy mark, let alone the whole fleet."

"I know." Siobhan's shoulders drop. "This isn't how it's supposed to be. The Cŵn Annwn—the originals—hunted monsters, regardless of the skin they wore. The monstrosity was the *intent* to harm, not what they looked like on the outside. This whole thing is wrong."

"I don't know if it matters what the originals did. They're gone. They've been gone for so long, we don't even have written history about them."

"I know." She drops into the chair in rough proximity to my bed. "But we have stories. *I* have stories."

Best not to think about the bed now. Certainly not in relation to Siobhan. I thought I had locked away my disastrous desire for her, but the longer she's on my ship, the harder it is to deny the truth. The desire never disappeared. I was simply lying to myself about it. The lie only worked as long as I didn't see her, and now it's crumpling around me.

I cross my arms over my chest, my tone snappish with my internal thoughts. "And those may be lovely bedtime stories for children, but what the originals may have been doesn't change what the Cŵn Annwn have become. They're more monsters than the creatures and people they hunt."

"Yes," Siobhan says slowly. "They are."

I frown. "I know that look. You have a plan. Why do I think I'm not going to like it very much?"

Siobhan laughs, the sound low and melodious. "Nox, you just spent all this time talking me out of a pit of despair and *now* you want to object?"

"Well . . . yes." But I find myself smiling a little all the same. "As for saving Bastian, it will be simple enough." I don't even stumble over his name this time. "Evelyn will create a shield around our ship—she's rather impressive at it—and the rest of my crew will be ready with fire, water, and air to defend the ship as we get out of there. Bowen will be standing in position to help with the extraction or the getaway, depending on how things go. The vampire and I will take the *Bone Heart*. We pulled off something similar saving Maeve a while back."

"Yes, I'm aware of how that went." Siobhan grimaces. "But the *Bone Heart* is not the *Drunken Dragon*. Morrigan is dangerous."

"I'm aware." Each ship sailing under the Cŵn Annwn runs like its own little territory, answering only to the Council. Some captains interact more regularly for coordinated hunts, but that's never been something I've opted into—and not only because I prefer to work without oversight.

Hedd, the last captain of the *Audacity*, felt the same way for similar reasons, though he wasn't worried about oversight preventing him from helping people. More that it would prevent *him* from doing whatever the fuck he wanted, usually in as bloody and violent a way as possible.

Even with all that, Morrigan's reputation is such that even Hedd avoided the waters where she's known to sail. She's vicious and inventive and the only Council member who actually has a crew and a ship.

Siobhan shakes her head slowly. "I know what Lizzie is capable of, but Morrigan sails with Ace and Bull now. Even without those two, she's the scariest person I've ever met."

I know all this. I just smile, projecting the bravado that's gotten me out of no small number of scraps over the years. "Honestly, Siobhan, I'm hurt. You don't think I'm scary?"

Siobhan clears her throat. "You're terrifying in an entirely different way."

It's tempting to read into that, but we're in the process of sailing to save her partner of ten years. I may be nursing something of an infatuation with the fearless leader of the rebellion, but I'm not fool enough to offer her my heart.

I stretch my arms over my head. "Well, she's not as good as I am. Guess I'll have to prove that to you."

I just hope it's the truth and I'm not about to get every one of my crew killed.

CHAPTER 6

Siobhan

WHEN ALL IS SAID AND DONE, NOX'S PLAN TRULY *IS* brilliant in its simplicity. Lizzie, Maeve, and I conducted a three-person assault on the *Crimson Hag* that damn near sank the ship and their formidable crew along with it. With Nox and their elemental magic in the mix, victory should be a sure thing.

But Morrigan isn't Miles. She isn't like any of the other captains in the Cŵn Annwn. She isn't like *anyone* else in Threshold . . . except me.

My younger sister, whom I haven't seen since the fire that killed our parents and was supposed to kill me, the better to clear the way for her ascension to power as the last remaining member of our family still standing. If she'd known I was alive, she would have hunted me through the realms until she stood over my dead body, sure that she'd finished the job.

After we save Bastian—if we're even able to pull it off— Morrigan won't stop coming after us until every single one of us is torn to pieces.

I know what Nox said about despair, but I can't stop myself from worrying as each day brings us closer to the rendezvous point.

"Stop moping. It's unbecoming of a leader."

I look up as Lizzie drops down next to me. She watches the crew move about with narrowed eyes. "Nox knows what they're doing. I'm aware that Morrigan is scary, but so are we. So buck the fuck up and put that intimidating persona back in place to inspire courage in the crew who are about to risk their lives for your cause."

As pep talks go, it's not particularly good, but after a few days in Lizzie's presence, I'm inured to her particular . . . charm. "I'm not moping. I'm plotting."

"Looks the same from where I'm sitting." She stretches out her long legs. "It goes without saying that Maeve will not be involved in any efforts to retrieve your little boyfriend a second time."

I follow her gaze to where the redhead is currently engaged in an animated conversation with the witch, her hands moving rapidly as she speaks. "Does she know that?"

"We've spoken about it," Lizzie says stiffly. "By the time we reach our destination, I expect to be victorious."

At that, I twist to look at her. She's glaring at the deck as if it insulted her personally. I don't know what it says about me that Lizzie in a foul mood amuses me greatly. "Does she know you intend to murder your way through Morrigan's crew? You know how Maeve feels about murder."

"Don't be smug." She shrugs stiffly. "With stakes as high as they are, she's willing to waive her determination to save every lost soul who crosses her path."

Love is so strange. It changes a person, and watching it happen in real time is admittedly odd. I can't help but think of all the ways I've changed since Bastian and I started our relationship. I want to say it's all been for the best, but now I wonder.

When you're happy, it's so easy to make excuses to remain *safe*. Even at the cost of others' lives.

I shake myself and push to my feet. "Nox has the ability to incapacitate the crew by restricting blood flow to their brains. You can turn their own blood against them. It's a good plan." There will be crew members who have shields their magic can't penetrate, though, and *that's* what I'm worried about.

"Yes, it is." Lizzie watches me closely. "And it doesn't require your presence on that ship."

"Gods, not you, too." I've had to sit through lectures by Nox, Bowen, and now apparently Lizzie about how the head of the rebellion shouldn't put herself at risk.

As if I haven't been at risk from the moment I was born. As if that risk hasn't increased exponentially now that I'm supposed to be dead.

But that's not something I can say, not without explaining why I take the Cŵn Annwn's perversion of the originals' vision so personally. A problem to deal with later, one we won't have to worry about if we don't successfully save Bastian from being brought before the Council.

The mood on the deck shifts, and I know without looking that Nox has emerged from their cabin. They don't say anything, but they don't need to. Their energy draws the crew's spines straight and makes the people want to please them, to say something to make them laugh, to bring a smile to their sharp mouth.

Even as I tell myself not to look, I can't help twisting in their direction. It's like turning to face the sun. Damn it, I can't let my continuing attraction to them muddy the waters. There's a reason I've kept my distance from them over the years, and it's not just because I fell in love with their ex.

If Bastian distracted me from the ugly parts that come with being leader of a rebellion, then Nox would have made me careless in a truly dangerous way. They are the kind of person the unwary can get lost in, and if I'd like to think I would never allow that to happen, the temptation to simply *live* for myself and no other . . . it's stronger than I want to admit. My entire life has been in service, first to my parents and then to the rebellion. I can't stumble now.

No matter how exhausted I am.

Even now, I'm having a hard time not going to them, not leaning on their strength the same way I did in their cabin a few days ago. I remind myself I am Siobhan, leader of the rebellion, and I cannot afford to falter . . . and yet I crumbled when it was just us.

I crumbled, and they didn't make me feel worse because of the weakness. They simply met my despair with a plan of action that has a solid chance of being successful.

They look particularly good right now, with their head held high and their crimson coat trailing behind them in the wind of our passage. Their pale skin seems made for the color, but I'd love to see them in anything but the hated bloody tone that represents everything wrong in this world.

Someday . . .

"Well, I can't fault your taste." Lizzie rises. "I'm serious, though, Siobhan. Trying to bully your way into that rescue attempt when we have an entire crew of people willing and capable of being successful is a silly, reckless thing to do."

It's a sign of how rattled I am that I actually snarl at her. "Since when do you actually consider yourself part of a crew?"

Lizzie doesn't blink, but her eyes flash crimson, a sure sign of her irritation. "I'm not Nox or Evelyn or even Bowen. *I'm* not going to argue circles with you. If you try to join the rescue attempt, I'm going to knock you the fuck out." She turns away. "It doesn't matter if you see me coming. You can't do a damn thing to stop me."

My fingers shift, claws shooting past my human skin. "Try to knock me unconscious and you'll see exactly what I *can* do."

"Children, children, let's not fight."

I didn't realize Nox was approaching until they slid between us. They don't flinch away from my claws or Lizzie's deep red eyes. They wear a small mocking smile, but their gaze is unrelenting. "Lizzie, this is *my* ship, and I'll thank you not to give orders to the people aboard. You've stated multiple times that you're only here for Maeve, which puts you outside the chain of command. Go find something to do."

Lizzie hesitates long enough that I think she might be spoiling for a fight, but then she shrugs and tucks away every bit of tension in her body. She smiles, flashing sharp canines. "Sure thing, *Captain*."

Nox waits for the vampire to walk away before they turn to me. "You're not coming, Siobhan. We can't risk you." They hold my gaze. "In fact, I don't even want you on deck starting tomorrow morning. We'll be close enough that we're bound to run into other ships. Most of them don't know what you look like, but it's still too big a risk."

I take a step toward them—and bounce off an invisible barrier between us. "Nox," I say quietly. "Are you shielding against me right now?"

"No." Their smile doesn't dim. They point to the side, leading me to look to where Bowen stands, his attention on us. Nox shrugs. "Your claws are still out. It's making my crew nervous."

Their crew.

Lizzie technically may not be part of it, but it's clear *she* is still more a member than I'll ever be. There's no reason for that realization to hurt. I chose not to sail with a crew of my own. It leaves me the ability to move swiftly without the need for votes or protests. The lack of a crew means less chance of people dying simply from being in my presence. It means there's less chance of my identity being tortured out of people. It's a *good* thing.

It just doesn't feel like a good thing right now.

I take a deep breath, and then another, doing my best to calm down enough to retract my claws. Most shifters talk about their other half as a separate personality inside them. That's not how I work. I am me, whether in human form, beast form, or something else altogether.

"Fine. I asked for your help, so I'll follow your lead. Even if it means hiding."

"Good girl." Their lips quirk when the insinuation in their words makes me blush. "Now, I think we can both agree that you've sulked enough. I have a task for you."

Nox

Several days later, we reach the sandbar right on schedule, catching sight of a trio of ships with crimson sails well before the sun sinks below the horizon. I study their positions. The *Bone Heart* will be the center one.

"You know what to do, Eyal," I murmur.

"Take us over to say hello." Eyal matches my tone, his sure hands easily guiding the ship in that direction.

The deck of the *Audacity* is mostly barren. It would be odd if there weren't any crew members around, so we have a few strategically cleaning the deck on the opposite side of the ship from where Evelyn has drawn her circle in preparation for the attack.

Lizzie lounges against the stairway leading to the upper deck. The only indication that her relaxation is a lie is the tension in her shoulders and her breathing coming a little faster than normal. The vampire might be able to decimate a small army with her power, but she's terrified of the sea.

It really just goes to show that she's smarter than she looks.

I nod at Eyal and then turn to Poet. "While I'm gone, you're in charge."

She shifts. "Don't look at me like that, Captain. I have no interest in your job." She jerks her chin toward the sails. "We have the alternatives ready to go. We just need the opportunity to change them out."

"Good." I roll my shoulders. "Are the others ready?" Three ships are about what we expected. It's a testament to Morrigan's reputation that the other two have anchored far enough away that I can't identify them on sight. It means they're close enough to assist in a pitched sea battle, assuming all three are in motion, but they're too far away to help easily tonight.

With the trios currently getting ready to launch a secondary assault on each ship, they won't be able to help at all. Our goal isn't to sink them, only to dismantle their ability to give chase.

As much as I hate the Cŵn Annwn and the horrors they enact, it doesn't change the fact that the first horror they carry out is in their recruitment. Most of the other crews are filled with people who just want to go home. Some end up embracing their new, bloody life. Most wither away and die before their time. A tragedy either way, and not one I want to contribute to if there's any other choice.

Morrigan's crew is the exception. *She* doesn't allow anyone on board who hasn't volunteered, and even then, she has more volunteers than slots to fill. It's why her crew is the best of the best—and it's why I have no problem eliminating any of *them*.

With that in mind, I turn to the vampire. "This won't be like last time. Most of them will have shields."

Lizzie shrugs. "So bring the big man and have him toss those with shields into the sea."

I open my mouth to tell her that Bowen needs to remain in reserve, but she's right. When you have telekinetic power on the level he does, he wouldn't even need to get past a single shield. He could just rip the ship apart and scatter the crew. "We'll save that for after Bastian is safe. If he drowns in our rescue attempt, we'll never hear the end of it from Siobhan."

"Siobhan. Right. You're definitely not *still* stumbling over his name every time you say it." Lizzie rolls her eyes. "I'm not a fool, Nox. You obviously have history. Is it going to get in the way?"

I clamp my mouth shut to keep from snapping at her. Lizzie is a predator right down to her bones. Giving her even a hint of weakness won't end well. "You have nothing to worry about." I motion for her to head to the agreed-upon spot on the deck where we'll approach the *Bone Heart*, and I cut around the stairs to where Bowen lingers with Evelyn. He's never far from her side these days, but he rarely gives me reason to complain. The man is a machine.

"Bowen, new job." I wink at Evelyn, which makes him growl under his breath. He's so *easy* to rile. "Our priority is getting Bastian off the ship. If we fail, I want you to rip it to shreds." Lizzie has a point, and I'm not one to cling to a faulty plan when there's a better—and less dangerous—option.

He flinches. "People will die."

"Not people, darling—Morrigan's crew, murderers and monsters to a person. But if you're so worried about unnecessary death, be careful when you're dismantling their ship." I pat his shoulder, but I can't quite make myself continue the facade of carelessness. It's getting harder and harder to wear this particular mask. "I wouldn't ask this of you if there was another option. We need all the advantages we can manage in order to have even the slightest chance of escaping. Otherwise, it's likely that we'll face heavy losses."

Am I being emotionally manipulative? Absolutely. Bowen is a paladin in a pirate hat, and his code of honor is honestly exhausting. Add to that a healthy dose of guilt for being part of the problem for so long and he's ripe to question every single order I make in an effort to negate harm.

I can't afford *another* argument with *another* strong personality on my crew. We're out of time.

Help comes in the form of the witch pressing her hand to his arm. "Bowen, you've told me yourself the stories of the horrors Morrigan has perpetuated."

He hesitates but finally nods. "I'll do it. If you fail, I'll dismantle the ship."

"Thank you." I turn to Evelyn. "Wait until my signal to put the shield up."

Her green eyes are alight with anticipation. How these two ended up together, I'll never understand, but she's good for him. I suppose he's good for her, too, what with reining in her more chaotic impulses. Evelyn grins. "Can't wait to see what you decide to make your signal."

"You'll know it when you see it."

"Oh, I have *no* doubt of that."

CHAPTER 7

Nox

DÉJÀ VU IS ONE OF THOSE CONCEPTS THAT HUMANS CAME up with to explain the unexplainable. At one point, we had a human on our crew who liked to go on and on about the theories behind the phenomenon. I never put much thought into it, but now, crouched on the railing in a fitted black suit that covers me from neck to wrist to ankles, Lizzie beside me looking green?

It feels just like the night we rescued Maeve.

It doesn't matter that we're not doing the exact same rescue plan. It's the vampire and I, intent on mass murder and rescue. I wink at her. "Ready, darling?"

"I will not hesitate to slit your throat and bathe in your blood." There's no bite to her words. She reluctantly takes my hand and steps up onto the railing as the *Audacity* closes the gap between us and the *Bone Heart*. We're close enough to see their crew gathered to watch, but too far for a normal person to jump.

Luckily, I am not a normal person. "Keep flirting with me, and Maeve is going to yell at you."

"Shut up," she hisses. She glances down to the inky waves lapping at the hull. "I really hate this."

"I know." I pat her shoulder with my free hand. "You're a very brave vampire, and I'm exceedingly proud of you."

"I *will* bite you."

"No, you won't." I pull her into my arms. "I won't let any sea monsters eat you. I'll even keep you from getting wet. Probably."

"You motherfu— *Godsdamn it*."

I step off the railing, taking her with me. It's harder to corral air than it is to manipulate water, but I've had decades of practice in making myself one not to be fucked with. It helps that Lizzie has gone still and stiff beside me. I gather the air between us, so we only drop about five feet or so before rising back to deck level.

"I *will* kill you. I swear to the gods I'll do it." Lizzie is speaking softly enough that she might as well be talking to herself.

It's just as well. I don't have any concentration left for words. I float us across the gap in about thirty seconds and drop us onto the deck of the *Bone Heart*. Lizzie is as agile as a cat. I'm ashamed to say my knees buckle a little, but I manage to keep my feet. Barely.

"You're late."

I straighten and turn to face Morrigan, the captain of the *Bone Heart*. She's a woman in her thirties with golden skin, hair just as crimson as the sails above us, and deep inky eyes that remind me of a skull. She's petite to the point of being delicate.

"Morrigan." I grit my teeth and bow. I fucking *hate* bowing, but if we have even the smallest chance of pulling this off, we have to get her guard down. And ideally encourage her to give us a tour of the ship right to where they're holding Bastian.

She approaches with deceptively long strides. One moment she's halfway across the deck. The next, she's before me. Her unsettling gaze lands on Lizzie. "A vampire is an unconventional choice."

I swear I can feel Lizzie tense, but she's a bloodline vampire, and for all her hissing and dramatics with me, she's not to be fucked with. When she speaks, her voice is cool and even. "One could argue that a Council member being a captain is an equally unconventional choice."

Morrigan laughs softly. "So they could."

I hold myself straight and still. Lying is always a fine line, especially when lying to someone as dangerous as this woman. "We're here to report in and see what you need from us."

She studies me for several long beats. "We have a prisoner who threatens the very balance of Threshold. We have reason to believe he's among a small group of people whisking intruders around Threshold instead of presenting them to the Cŵn Annwn for their choice. His allies nearly sank the *Crimson Hag*."

I very carefully don't look at Lizzie. "They sound dangerous."

"They're pests, but we have no way of knowing how deep the rot goes."

It's eerily similar to what Siobhan and I talked about only a week ago, albeit on the other side of the equation. Morrigan wants to stamp out the resistance and bring the Cŵn Annwn into full control of Threshold once and for all. The rebellion wants the corruption within the Cŵn Annwn to be purged and the islands to be given back to their people to rule as they see fit, rather than grouped together under one ruling body that doesn't represent anyone outside of Lyari.

We are not the same.

Morrigan laces her hands behind her back. "We set sail at dawn and take the direct south path to Lyari."

I raise my brows. "A risky route." There's nothing but sea between the sandbar and Lyari. The nearest islands are several days to the east and weeks to the west. There's no safe harbor in the event of a storm, and this time of year in this portion of Threshold, storms are plentiful.

"A direct route." She nods at the *Audacity*, gently bobbing a hundred yards away. "We'll take the point position in the morning, and I expect you on the starboard flank."

"Will do," I say slowly. Damn it, she's about to send us back. "We'd like to see the prisoner. There's a chance we may recognize him and be able to give you more information."

Morrigan smirks. "I hardly need common trash like you to tell me what I already know. The prisoner is Bastian Dacre, second son of the Dacre noble family."

The insult rolls right off me. The only people who care about bloodlines are nobles, and I couldn't give a shit what most of the nobles think. Except for Bastian. I raise my brows. "A noble helping . . . intruders?" Damn it, I almost called them refugees.

"I'm shocked as well." Morrigan doesn't move. "I've already spoken with the rest of the Council, and while they're reluctant to prosecute the Dacre family in Lyari, they're eager to remove this nuisance." She flicks her hand at me. "Now stop wasting my time and return to your ship. We'll sail at first light."

Damn. I guess there's no chance of getting to Bastian and fighting our way free from there. Oh well. It was worth a shot. I glance at Lizzie. "Now's as good a time as any."

To the vampire's credit, she doesn't hesitate. She tenses, and the people on either side of Morrigan go down. Morrigan herself doesn't, because why would anything be easy?

Morrigan's eyes flash as if reflecting light. "You *dare*?"

"Sorry about this, except not really." I gather my magic with a flick of my wrist and send a massive fireball into the main sail. I don't expect it to take—the sail will have been treated with magic to ensure it doesn't burn down at sea—but it should be bright enough to signal to Evelyn and the other teams that it's time.

Morrigan leaps for me, fingers morphing into long, vicious-looking claws, but Lizzie gets there first, intercepting the captain. "Go!" she yells as she ducks a swipe and kicks Morrigan in the stomach, sending her staggering back. "I'll take care of her."

Lizzie is one of the most dangerous people I've ever met, and I still hesitate. Morrigan is on another realm entirely.

"Go, Nox!" Lizzie takes a hit that opens a long line on her arm. She doesn't hesitate to pull the blood from her own body and coat her hands with it, forming claws similar to Morrigan's. With her longer reach and similar speed . . . she might stand a chance.

I can't afford to hesitate. The faster I get to Bastian, the faster this whole fight ends.

The crew is taking an interest now, rushing forward. Damn it. I sprint at them, and there's no time for finesse. I yank the air from their lungs as I approach. There's a way to do it without causing damage to the person I'm knocking out, but I'm not being careful right now. The force of the pull crumples their lungs in their chests, physical damage on top of suffocation.

They die.

At least some of them. Elemental magic is tricky, because it can get through some shields but not others. It truly depends on the person casting the shield. I can't get through Evelyn's shields, for example. Most of the Cŵn Annwn crews don't have the magic, control, or interest in that level of protection. Sadly, Morrigan's crew seems to have a disproportionately high number of people capable of repelling me.

A short gnome with purple skin and a truly impressive beard leaps at me, wielding a sword. My brain unhelpfully provides his name and role in the crew: Bull, the quartermaster.

Only to be stopped short a few feet away as if an individual hand reached out and grabbed him. We stare at each other in confusion—he certainly isn't responsible, and I didn't have a chance to even attempt an elemental shield—before he is flung backward and into the sea.

It takes my adrenaline-laced brain a second to understand what just happened. "Thanks, Bowen." I sprint the rest of the way to the hatch and muscle it open as pure chaos erupts around me. Despite my orders for the crew to remain out of sight, they've opened fire. Water and fire streak across the night sky to strike the enemies around me. Defending me. Protecting me.

I drop down through the hatch and into relative quiet. This warship is larger than the *Audacity*, but I'm familiar with the layout. There are only so many options when it comes to building ships, even magical ones. No one wastes pocket dimensions on the brig.

I suffocate the person running at me before I even register what I'm doing. The fight is barely audible overhead, but it *is* audible. A reminder that I have to hurry, that for every moment the battle continues, the greater the chances of someone on my crew being hurt. Of them dying.

Focusing on that isn't going to do anything but distract me when I can least afford it. I have to move. "Come on, Nox. *Focus.*" I step over the dead body at my feet and make my way down the narrow hall into a darkness that seems to have a strange weight against my skin. I almost make a small flame to see by, but that feels dangerous in a way I don't entirely understand. What the fuck does Morrigan do down here?

There are no answers. Just more uncanny darkness. I sigh and keep moving, following the increasingly rank smell of an unwashed body and chamber pot that hasn't been emptied any- time recently. Which just goes to show that Morrigan is too smart to be underestimated. I don't know if Bastian would break under traditional torture, but the man I knew fourteen years ago loved to be clean. From the scent currently trying to trigger my gag reflex, he and clean haven't been on speaking terms since he was taken.

I refuse to feel pity for him. *Refuse.* Even when I reach the first cell and reluctantly summon a small flame. It barely pushes back the darkness. The small hairs on the back of my neck rise as I begin to understand. He's huddled in the corner of the cell, hands tied behind his back, blindfolded and gagged. The magi- cal darkness dampens sound and ensures that even if he got the blindfold off somehow, it wouldn't make any difference. It's fucking nefarious.

Bastian looks *awful*. His expensive clothing is filthy, dirt and things I refuse to contemplate cover his skin, and his dark hair is so greasy that it shines against my small light.

"Oh, Bastian," I whisper.

He flinches. He catches the response immediately and straightens, but it's too late. I want to tell myself that he's expecting an enemy, not flinching because of *my* voice, but even I don't believe that stretch of logic.

"I'm getting you out of here." I hurry back to the guard I killed and search their body—something I should have done before walking past them—and come up with a key that must be to the cell.

When I return, Bastian is on his feet, tracking my footsteps even though he can't see me, can't speak. I ignore the shaking in my hands and unlock the door.

He's even worse off than I first realized. Bastian's body naturally favors a slighter build than someone like Bowen, but he's absolutely gaunt under his clothes. "Close your eyes." I barely wait a second before pulling off his blindfold and carefully untying the gag.

The key won't fit the bindings on his hands, but that's a problem to worry about later. The ship rocks violently enough to send Bastian tumbling into me. "Fuck. We're running out of time if Bowen is in the fight." I barely keep Bastian on his feet. There's no way he can get up the ladder and across a deck of battling crew members. If we try, we'll have done all this only for him to die violently.

Damn it, I need to *think*.

"Nox?" His beautiful voice is so raspy, it's almost unrecognizable. "Is this a trick?"

I ignore his question and avoid his deep brown eyes. Maybe it would have been better for Siobhan to do this part. Surely he'd be happy to see *her*.

The thought is so absurd in the face of what we're dealing with, I huff out a laugh. "Okay, change of plans." Siobhan told me the details of how they attempted to sink the *Crimson Hag*. We'll just do that in reverse and hope for the best. "This will do for a secondary signal to retreat."

"What—"

I suck every bit of moisture from the wood wall in front of me. It should lead out to the starboard side of the hull, which puts the bulk of the *Bone Heart* between us and my ship, but once we're in the water, no one will be able to catch us. "Behind me."

Bastian doesn't exactly obey, but I don't give him a chance to argue. I grab a fistful of his filthy shirt and jerk him behind my body.

The sea is always eager to comply with my magical demands. It's chaotic and violent, and the less finesse required, the more likely it is that things will go perfectly. "Take a breath and hold it." I wait for him to clutch my shoulders before I tug on the water sloshing against the *Bone Heart*'s hull. The boards in front of us creak ominously. "Once more should do."

"Nox . . ." He coughs. "This is a terrible idea."

"Just hang on." I yank on the water again, harder this time. The weakened boards buckle and creak. Water sprouts in the new gaps, more and more of it as the creaking gets louder. "Almost there." One last pull and the boards burst, the sea rushing in, eager to fill the new space in great, greedy gulps. It smashes against us, and I manage to get an air bubble around our heads just as the water closes in and slams us against the ceiling.

Bastian wraps his arms around my waist, as if he really thinks I'll let him be swept away in this mess. It pisses me off. He's been underestimating me from the moment we met, and I'm literally saving his ass right now, and he's *still* sure I'm going to botch the job.

"You're lucky I don't kill you myself, you absolute wanker." I wrap an arm around his waist and use my magic to propel us through the new hole in the ship. The moment we reach the sea, I'm tempted to breathe a sigh of relief. I know better, though. There's still so much that could go wrong.

In the seconds it takes us to shoot the hundred yards to the *Audacity*, I have half a dozen contingency plans in place in case our retreat is hampered. The other teams were scheduled to strike earlier enough that they should have returned by now. Bowen should be able to bring Lizzie back aboard.

Too many "shoulds."

Our momentum is enough to drive us past the surface and all the way onto the deck, where we land in an undignified heap. I shove Bastian's prone body off me and lurch to my feet. "Orchid! Get him belowdecks!" I don't pause to ensure my order is obeyed. "Poet! Report!"

Poet appears at my side as if by magic. She grabs my elbow and steadies me when our ship rocks violently to the side. "Both teams are back. We're just missing Lizzie."

"Is she—" *Dead.*

Poet saves me from asking the thing I very much do not want to ask. "Still fighting."

Thank the gods. That vampire is a nightmare to work with sometimes, but I like the little asshole. I don't want her to die.

A quick glance around finds Bowen, his massive form braced against the railing as he moves his hands, fighting to dismantle the *Bone Heart*. I rush up to him. "We've done enough. Get Lizzie and we're leaving."

"Impossible to pull Lizzie without pulling Morrigan, too," he grits out. "They're moving too fast."

I see what he means immediately. The women are a blur of violence, their strikes coming so quickly I can barely follow them. Blood coats the deck around them, but neither shows any sign of slowing down. Bowen has mostly cleared the deck, but that doesn't help us get the vampire back.

"I'll go," Maeve says.

I grab the back of her shirt and haul her away from the railing. "Absolutely not. You go over there, Lizzie is going to get distracted and Morrigan will rip out her heart." I can't pause to feel guilty for the way Maeve's face goes gray in response to my words.

"Bring them both." Siobhan nudges Maeve back even farther and takes her place next to me. "I'll separate them, and then you can toss Morrigan as far as you can throw her."

There's no time to ask her if she can do this, if she's really considered what it will mean for Morrigan to see her, to know Siobhan is potentially the leader behind all this. There's no going back after this. There hasn't been a way to go back since we set ourselves on this course.

I nod at Bowen. "Do it."

"Okay." His shoulders bunch, and the chunk of deck under

the fighting women's feet rips away, taking them with it. In the space of two heartbeats, it reaches us and lands on our deck. Through it all, Morrigan and Lizzie never once miss a beat.

Later, I'll be impressed. Right now, I'm too worried that I don't have the energy needed to keep fighting. I'm already weaving on my feet from the transport to and from the *Bone Heart*, to say nothing of breaking a massive hole in the hull.

But I'm the captain, and the captain has to take their hits to protect the crew. I lift my hands, dragging my magic to the fore to attack. Siobhan beats me to it. She launches herself forward, a shot of movement toward the fighting women.

She hooks Lizzie around the waist—taking a swipe along her arm in the process—and tosses the vampire backward. Another time, I'd enjoy Lizzie's surprised squawk of protest. Right now, I'm too focused on the danger Siobhan just put herself in.

Morrigan looks up and her eyes go wide at the sight of the other woman. "Siobhan." There's a thread of . . . familiarity there. Not just in her knowing the name, but as if they have history.

Siobhan unsheathes her claws. "Sister."

CHAPTER 8

Siobhan

I LAUNCH MYSELF AT MY SISTER, THE TORMENTOR FROM my childhood who made my life a living agony. Sixteen years since I've seen her in person, nearly half my life, and somehow she's still larger than life, for all that I tower over her. I kick her in the chest, sending her sliding back across the deck.

She stops herself with her claws sunk deep into the deck and looks up through her hair at me. Her eyes go wide. "Impossible."

Now is the time to attack, to do my best to rip her throat out before she can do any more damage. To remove the threat of her, once and for all. But my feet feel like they've grown roots, sinking deep into the ship and deeper yet to the very bottom of the sea. "Leave," I say hoarsely. "Leave and I'll let you live."

Morrigan quickly gets over her shock at seeing me alive and grins. I know that expression. It haunts me still. "I think not." She launches herself at me. She's even faster than when we were teenagers, her movements lacking the faint friction of a body still growing.

She hits me with the force of a tidal wave. I stagger back a step, using every ounce of my speed to stay ahead of her strikes. One wrong move will disembowel me, and then this will all be for nothing. Morrigan will kill every member of the crew. She'll kill Bastian. She'll kill Nox.

That knowledge has me pushing back, forcing her away from the people on deck with my larger size. She's fast, but I think I could be faster. It's been so long since I've fought for my life against someone who was just as strong, fast, and deadly as I am.

Morrigan opens up a gash on my thigh. "Still leaving your left side open, I see." She's panting, which is a small victory . . . or it would be if I wasn't bleeding already.

I feint to the right and deliver a vicious punch to her side. "Still . . . too confident."

"We'll see who's too confident." Her claws flash, growing longer yet, and her eyes shine eerily in the light of the lanterns on deck. "Time to finish what I started with that fucking fire."

Overhead, the sails fill and the deck jerks beneath our feet. I'm expecting it, so I roll with the movement. Morrigan isn't. She stumbles. A tiny drop in her guard—one that won't last long—but it's enough. I punch her in the face and kick her in the chest, putting every ounce of my strength behind the strike. A burst of gale-force wind sends her hurtling back to flip over the railing and into the sea.

"Go, go, go!" Nox roars. "Gable, get Callen and boost us from the water."

"Too fast and the ship will break apart!" someone yells.

"No, it won't. Go!" And then Nox is at my side. "I don't ex-pect the ships to give chase right away, but I'm not taking any chances. I need you to help Orchid get Bastian to my cabin and clean him up as best you can. There's food there, too. He looks like he needs it."

There's no time to question them, to ask if they really want us in *their* cabin. But of course it makes sense. We need to know what Bastian told Morrigan. "Okay."

Nox is already turning away, hollering orders to other members of the crew. They're glorious like this, fresh from battle and without a single ounce of hesitation.

I move on unsteady feet to where Bastian is on his knees, watching Nox with glazed eyes. To the best of my knowledge, they haven't seen each other since that mess back when we were barely more than kids. It was after the fire that drove me from Lyari, and though Bastian has told me the broad strokes, it's clear from both of their reactions that time hasn't healed this particular wound.

As I move closer, he finally focuses on me. "Siobhan."

"Bastian." I scoop him into my arms, ignoring his attempted protest, and hurry to Nox's cabin.

Orchid, the healer for the *Audacity*, meets me at the door. He's as tall as I am and reed-thin, his cloak and veil obscuring his features—except for his silver eyes. "Let's get him in and I'll look him over."

Closing the door muffles the worst of the racket from the crew rushing about to follow Nox's commands. I bypass the desk and try very hard not to look too closely at the bed. My destination is the door that leads into a narrow but relatively roomy bathroom. I set Bastian on the toilet.

Orchid nudges me out of the way. "Injuries?"

"Siobhan," he says.

"Let Orchid get you patched up and then we'll get everyone the information they need to know."

He searches my face, completely ignoring Orchid. "You don't have to treat me like one of your rebels. Not *me*."

In fact, that's exactly what I have to do. I want to pretend that the only reason I fought so hard to get him back was because of what it would mean for him to stand trial in Lyari. That it had nothing to do with how my heart refused to beat when I thought about him in danger.

"Please answer Orchid's questions," I finally say. "You're injured and we can't do *anything* until that's resolved."

"Fine." He drops his gaze. "The bindings on my wrists may have caused permanent damage. I'm malnourished, but not starved. Some small scrapes and bruises, but nothing more serious than that."

My heart leaps into my throat and lodges itself there. The Cŵn Annwn had him for a couple of weeks, and that's more than long enough to cause irreparable harm. All because I refused to consider changing our operation. I glance at Orchid. "How can I help?"

He nudges Bastian to rotate away from us so we can see the bindings on his wrists. The skin of his hands is tinged with blue. Orchid makes a worried sound. "I'll need to get something to cut these off."

"I've got it," I say roughly. I shift two of my fingers. The bindings were done by an earth-user, fusing the metal around his wrists. I've undone bindings like this before, and gods know I'll do it again. My claws can cut through damn near anything. The metal parts easily, freeing him.

"That's a start." Orchid nods at me. "I would appreciate if you'd stand over by the door so I have room."

Orchid's people reside in Drash, and as a culture, they're incredibly closemouthed about their magic. They don't overtly shun the Cŵn Annwn's rule, but they hardly welcome it, either. It's passing odd that Orchid chose to sail on one of their ships, even if it *is* Nox's ship.

I don't want to take my eyes off Bastian, but there's no way Orchid would hurt someone under Nox's protection. It still takes several seconds before I can make myself turn away and face the door. Orchid might not have explicitly asked me to do so, but I hear his sigh of relief all the same.

"This won't feel good," he says quietly to Bastian. "But it will heal your internal damage and allow me to check for any unknown injuries. May I put my hands on you?"

"Yes," Bastian rasps.

I clench my fists and hold my place, fighting not to turn around when Bastian makes a faint pained noise and something pops in his body and then pops again. It's not a fast process.

Healing magic is a tricky thing, regardless of what being or culture is doing it. Most healers only encourage the body to do what it does best. Some methods, like a vampire's blood, override the body's normal processes and *force* it to heal.

The universe craves balance, no matter what realm a being inhabits. Most healing pulls on the body's reserves—both healer and patient. Things like vampire blood work well in the short term but lose efficiency over time, a neat little quirk to encourage vampires to create more of themselves, since their

birth rates are notoriously low. All immortals have that problem, to avoid overrunning every realm in existence with their
progeny.

I'm doing a poor job of trying to distract myself from what's
going on behind me. I can smell blood and something sour—
his wrists are infected. Bastian breathes heavily as Orchid
works on him. It feels like a small eternity before Orchid exhales slowly. "That's the worst of it. Have a small meal and drink
water consistently—in small sips—to help your body continue
to heal itself."

"Thank you."

Orchid shifts, and that's my cue to turn back around. He
nods to me. "I appreciate the privacy. I'll check on him in the
morning, but I need to look over the rest of the crew. There were
a few minor injuries that need my attention."

"Of course." I move out of the way to let him pass.

It's only when he's gone that I realize how much his presence and the immediate threat bolstered my courage to face
Bastian. Now, with him sitting there staring at me with his
pretty, dark eyes, the small cowardly part of myself that I never
let see the light is whimpering for a retreat.

"You came for me." He searches my expression. "Or was it
the rebellion that came for me?"

The urge to protect my heart is nearly overwhelming. It
hasn't been very long since we threw hard and vicious words
at each other, since he called me a coward for not wanting to
push the rebellion into direct confrontation with the Cŵn
Annwn.

He's right. I am a coward. We can't take back what we did
tonight. Morrigan knows I'm alive, and she's smart enough to

wonder what else I might have been up to for the last sixteen years. "You're getting your way. They know about us now."

"That's all you have to say to me?"

No. The things I want to say to him are climbing over themselves in the back of my throat, choking me. "Bastian—"

"Never mind. It's worse than you think." He moves stiffly, trying to pull his shirt over his head. "After I clean up, we need to talk to Nox about next steps."

"I can—"

"I've got it," Bastian snaps. "I'd like some privacy, please."

There's nothing to say, and even if I tried, I would no doubt make it worse. It was never difficult with Bastian. He's charming and beautiful and, from the moment we met, it was so *easy* to be around him. I took that for granted. Apparently I'm still taking that for granted.

I slip out of the bathroom and close the door softly behind me. Things were so much simpler when I was just a shadow among thousands upon thousands of them. One piece helping coordinate the others moving to a greater purpose.

I can't stay in Nox's bedroom, waiting to see which one of them will walk through the door first. Not to mention . . . Bastian is more likely to eat the provided food if I'm not around to stand over him. I slip out onto the deck and move to the helm, where Nox is perched, their coat streaming dramatically out behind them.

I glance around. The sandbar and other ships are nowhere in sight. It's difficult to gauge exactly where we are, but I think we're heading northeast.

Nox doesn't take their gaze from the horizon. "Orchid says he'll make a full recovery."

"That seems to be the case."

"Is he still angry with you?"

I blink. "Excuse me?"

"That's why you're out here with me instead of in there giving him a bath, right?" They shoot me a wicked grin. "Unless you actually prefer *my* company, in which case . . . I can be convinced."

I know they're just flirting to keep the attention away from *their* relationship fallout with Bastian, but I can't help the image that springs into my head in response to their words. Of them in my arms, their gray eyes alight with wicked mischief. I can't help wondering how they'd taste.

"Stop trying to distract me from the fact that you're just as bothered by his presence aboard as I am." I clear my throat. "He's still angry with me, yes. Angry enough that if I stick around, we'll end up fighting. He needs to eat."

"As good an excuse as any. As to the other?" They shrug. "We're ancient history."

"Nox." I don't have to glance around to ensure we're not being overheard. There's no one close enough, and all of them are intent on their goal of getting us as far away from our enemy as possible. "Pretend with others. Don't pretend with me."

They sigh, their shoulders slumping. "You don't get to demand that kind of intimacy from me, Siobhan. I believe in your cause and I believe in *you*, but some scars don't heal—they fester. I would love to say that I'm a gracious and lovely person who doesn't hold a broken heart against my ex fourteen years later, but it's not the truth. I love a grudge as much as I love my ship. And he's the one who taught me that."

Because Bastian hurt Nox so intensely. I only know the basics of what happened: that Nox wanted Bastian to come with them when they left Lyari, that he chose his family over them. Bastian avoided saying more than that about Nox, and Nox's only condition to joining the rebellion was that I never talk about Bastian.

And now I need to get them both to agree to work together.

"Morrigan isn't going to give up," I say finally. "Especially now that she knows I'm alive." I still haven't processed *that*, but I have no intention of thinking about it too closely anytime soon. I may have been using a vast network of people to undermine the hold the Cŵn Annwn have on Threshold, but we intentionally kept to the shadows.

I'm terrified of what it means to step into the light.

"I'm aware." Nox finally looks at me, eyes narrowed. "Just like I was aware that Morrigan had a sister—but I was under the impression that her sister died in the same fire that killed her parents about two years before I left the city."

If I close my eyes, I can still see the flames licking up the curtains. "Our parents died in that fire. I chose to use it to escape Lyari."

Nox's hands tighten on the helm. "You lied to me."

"No, I didn't. I just didn't disclose all the information." When they open their mouth, I hold up my hand. "Come on, Nox. I'm the leader of the damned rebellion. You knew when you signed on that you weren't getting my life story and every detail about me."

"That's true." They sigh. "It's also true that it would have been nice to know that you were a noble."

"It doesn't matter." Even as I say it, I know it for a lie. It would matter even if I wasn't sister to Morrigan. It *especially* matters because I am.

The look Nox gives me says as much without them uttering a single word. But this is *Nox*, so of course they have more to say. "Morrigan wasn't likely to let us abscond with Bastian without a prolonged and violent chase. Now that she knows *you're* on my ship? She's going to come at us with everything she has."

I want to argue with them, but everything they've said is true. "You're right."

"I usually am."

Eyal walks up, giving us both a wary look. "You need to get some sleep, Captain. You're weaving on your feet."

"I'll hold until we're clear."

Eyal shakes his head. "I spoke with Poet. The teams we sent did a good job of sabotaging the rudders of the support ships. Even if their respective crews have someone with a helpful flavor of magic, it will take a few hours to fix. If they don't, it will be a lot longer." He motions behind us. "The *Bone Heart* will also take some time to repair after Bowen and you tore holes in the deck and hull. I can keep us on course while you rest. We're running our air-users in shifts so there's always someone fresh in case we need to pick up the pace."

Nox smiles faintly. "You seem to have thought of everything. What do you need me for again?"

"You know we're lost without you." Eyal nods at the helm. "Sleep. I will send someone to wake you if there's so much as a peep of wrongness."

I recognize a losing battle when I see one. It takes Nox a few seconds longer to admit defeat. They release the helm and step back. "I suppose a few hours won't hurt." They nod at me. "Come on. We need to know what Bastian told them—and if he picked up any useful information during his time aboard the *Bone Heart*."

It's only as I fall into step next to them that I fully register the fact that we're about to walk back into the room where Bastian waits.

There's no avoiding the coming conversation.

CHAPTER 9

Bastian

I'M AS SHAKY AS A NEWBORN, BUT I MANAGE TO GET CLEAN without having to call for help. I don't think my pride could manage it, which is pathetic considering Siobhan and Nox just launched the rescue mission to end all rescue missions to save me. Hiding in the bathroom instead of facing them sounds like a wonderful idea, but having *them* come to me here is unthinkable.

All this to say, I'm a damned mess.

I step out of the shower and dry myself off as quickly as possible. Which is right around the moment when I realize I don't have any clothing that I can bear putting back on my body. I would happily burn the outfit I spent the last however many days wearing.

For lack of a better plan, I wrap a towel around my waist and step carefully through the doorway into the bedroom. Someone has left food for me on the table, and with no one to witness, I fall on it like the starved creature I am. There's no space for decorum when my stomach is an ache that makes me woozy. I clean the tray and sit back, exhaustion setting in. Even though I bloody well know better, I inhale deeply. It smells like Nox in here. I don't know how fourteen years aren't enough to banish the memory of them.

And then the person themself walks through the door, dressed exactly as they were when they saved me, from head to toe in crimson, their blond hair spiky on top from the salt of seawater. They stop short when they see me, and even though I've seen better days, their cool gray gaze still skates over my bare chest and lingers where my hand grips the towel.

Then they step aside and Siobhan enters the room. Her presence should be enough to cool the tension that rose between us, but somehow it only makes it worse. She looks between us and then walks over to perch on the edge of the desk. "Well?"

"You left Bastian without even giving him some clothing?" Nox carefully skirts past me to a chest on the other side of the bed. They dig through it for a few seconds and come up with two sets of clothing. The black set gets tossed to me.

I catch it against my chest with my free hand. "Rumor has it that you only wear crimson."

Nox ignores me and walks into the bathroom, shutting the door firmly behind them. Leaving me and Siobhan alone. Again.

I stare at her. I wish I were a better man who could put past concerns behind me in the face of this rescue. I'm not. "You went to Nox."

"I went to Nox." She crosses her arms over her chest. Her gaze is steady, but I know her as well as I know myself. She never would have broken her word to Nox if she wasn't desperate, and she was only desperate because I put her in that position. "What happened? You're not usually careless with your magic, and even if you were, you should have been able to talk yourself out of any mess you ended up in."

She's right. I'd done exactly that in the past. "There was a woman—a girl, really—being threatened by two Cŵn Annwn in Mairi. It was a few days after we . . . went our separate ways." I clear my throat. "There was a third I didn't see, and they had a mental shield that my magic couldn't penetrate. By the time I realized, it was too late and they'd broken my hold on the other two."

"Bastian." The censure in her tone snaps my spine straight.

Guilt is a live thing inside me, because I *did* fuck up, but I'm still so damned angry at her. I don't know how to reconcile the two. Instead, the feelings amplify each other. "Have you changed your mind?"

Siobhan slashes her hand through the air so quickly it's almost a blur, her movements jerky and just as furious as I feel. "*That* is what you want to ask me right now? You were so certain you were right, and the first thing you did was get scooped up by the Cŵn Annwn, which *perfectly demonstrates my point.* We only saved you by resorting to lies and manipulation—and then running the first chance we got. That won't work again. It isn't possible to win an all-out war."

I should know her words by heart at this point. I practically do. I shake my head. "I made a mistake, and a costly one at that. I'm aware. That doesn't change the fact that I'm right. Even though they didn't know about the rebellion before, they're bleeding us with a thousand cuts. The war isn't even out in the open, and it's already a war of attrition."

"Yes," she says bluntly. "It is. How much worse will that be when they realize the size of our network? *We* don't have a fleet to fight them with. They'll cut off our informants, cut off our supply chains, and then kill us at their leisure. At this point, I don't even think we could escape through the portals into other realms because they would chase us down just to prove a point."

I want to say such a thing is unprecedented . . . but it's not. There have been dozens of times over the years when the Cŵn Annwn slipped into the very realms they're supposedly protecting in order to kill those they call monsters. If they discover the rebellion, we'll be lumped in with the so-called monsters. "You can't let fear guide you."

"There's nothing new to add to this conversation. We disagree, and it's clear we won't reach peace now . . . or ever."

"Or ever," I repeat numbly. "So that's it, then."

The bathroom door opens before she can reply, revealing Nox in their new crimson clothing, their blond hair spiky from the shower. I can't think about *that* too closely, or I'll be remembering how good Nox looked naked and wet and . . . Fuck, I'm remembering it.

Nox looks from Siobhan to me. "So. It's like that."

"You agree with me," Siobhan snaps. "Don't pretend you don't."

"I did." Nox shrugs. "Morrigan changes things. She's not a fool like so many of the other captains—or Council members, for that matter. Now she knows you're alive *and* she knows we're working together. She's not going to stop."

"Then kill her. You're good at that."

Nox laughs bitterly. "As if it's that easy. Morrigan is more powerful than I am—and more deadly. Our only option now is to run." They turn to look at me. "The real question is if there's anywhere left to run to."

"Yes." Siobhan sighs. "Bastian, we need to know what you told Morrigan."

I blink. It takes my exhausted brain a few seconds to understand what she's saying—what they're both suggesting. "You think I broke."

"Torture will do that to a person," Siobhan says gently.

I thought I couldn't get angrier. It turns out I was wrong. I sit there stiffly and look from one of them to the other. "I didn't tell her anything. She knew about the glamour. She . . ." My breath catches in my throat. "She threatened my family, but I think the Council was pushing back against the plan to arrest them." I meet Siobhan's honey gaze. "She already knew something was going on, that I'd been spotted in the company of a woman, that people were disappearing instead of being brought to the Cŵn Annwn."

Siobhan and Nox exchange a look, and it strikes me all over again that they have a relationship that has nothing to do with me. Nox joined the rebellion *despite* my presence. They and Siobhan spent plenty of time together in the beginning, enough to build a true friendship.

Enough to build . . . more?

Nox sighs. "Well, fuck."

Siobhan scrubs her hands over her face. "There's something else. Something you both need to know before we go further. You can't underestimate Morrigan."

"Obviously." Nox waves that away. "Didn't I just get done saying that she's dangerous?"

"She is. More than you know." There's something almost

like panic in her dark eyes. She looks from one of us to the other, her shoulders dropping in defeat. "She is—I am—Cŵn Annwn."

I blink. "No, you're not. You've never sailed for them."

"I don't mean those *pretenders*." She makes a motion like she might spit, but aborts it halfway through. "I mean the true Cŵn Annwn, the ones those fucking parasites stole their name from. Most of the records about the originals have been lost over the centuries, but they *did* exist. I'm proof of that."

I run her words back, but they don't make any more sense the second time through. "But . . . that doesn't make any sense. You're from a noble family that has been in Lyari for generations. If your ancestors were the real Cŵn Annwn, then why doesn't anyone know it? Why hasn't Morrigan used that fact to propel her right to the top of the Council instead of sailing about, playing pirate?"

Nox rolls their eyes. "Because they would have been wiped off the face of Threshold. You think the Council is going to let anything threaten their death grip on Threshold? Not even Morrigan can stand against them alone."

I open my mouth to deny it, but . . . they're right. The Council bets on being the most powerful thing in Threshold, able to command thousands of ships. It's an uneasy balancing act, though, because at this point most of the crews are filled with refugees.

There *are* volunteers, of course, but no one comments on the fact that Lyari locals are disproportionately represented among them. The people of Lyari see it as something noble and exciting. The rest of Threshold, though? All the islands that never asked to be under the Council's rule? All the people who are terrorized by the unruly crews? They don't volunteer. They never have.

More than that, the original Cŵn Annwn have risen to become something akin to gods for us. There are statues of them in Lyari, people pray to them—though it's fallen out of favor in recent generations. If the originals were able to just . . . show up . . . it would change everything. The Cŵn Annwn would be forced to stop co-opting their name and reputation, perverting it in the pursuit of more power in order to provide *protection* no one asked for.

Nox drags their hand through their hair. "Look, we all know how little I like the idea of war, but tonight changed things. We can't keep running, Siobhan. We sure as fuck can't hide. The only thing left to do is to decide how we fight."

Siobhan drops her head into her hands. "I hate this. More people are going to die."

Nox and I exchange a look of perfect understanding. It's strange how even with all the distance and time between us, I still *know* them. Siobhan won't come around tonight, but the fact that she's not arguing means she *will* come around. Now's the time to let her think, to process, to come to the same conclusion Nox and I obviously have.

We're going to war.

"That's enough for tonight," Nox finally says.

Siobhan doesn't speak another word; she just storms out of the cabin and slams the door behind her. I should follow her, should try to talk to her. Her instinct to dig in her heels has kept her alive for a long time, but she's hurting and our history means I know what to say to fix it. Or at least push it away until it's manageable.

But Nox holds up a hand before I can make a move. "We might as well get this out of the way to avoid things being awkward. Are you going to have a problem taking orders from me?"

I can't stop myself from smirking. "When have I ever had problems taking orders from you?"

"Don't do that." They hold my gaze until it's uncomfortable, their pale eyes giving me nothing. "Don't flirt with me as if we don't have a particularly painful history. It's cruel."

I duck my head before I can think better of it. "I'm sorry. I never wanted to hurt you."

"And yet." There's a wealth of history in those two words.

"Yeah." I sigh. "And yet."

"I have one question, and I would like an honest answer."

I already know I'm not going to like it—and that they won't like the answer—but I nod. "Sure. Whatever you need to know."

Nox parts their lips, hesitant in a way that hurts my heart. The Nox I know, both personally and, later, through reputation, is never hesitant. They are bold and brash and fearless. They finally say, "How long?"

I know what they mean, but I can't stop myself from parroting their words. "How long?"

"How long after you told me that your life and home and everything were in Lyari did you sail away from the city with Siobhan?"

I suck in a harsh breath. It's the question I didn't want to hear because the answer will hurt them, will add to the pain I've already caused them. "It wasn't like that."

"I don't really care *what* it was like. I heard all your arguments on why you couldn't leave your family behind. Even after all this time, I could probably recite them from memory." They meet my gaze steadily. "I want the answer."

I hate this. I hate that little fool I was, who didn't appreciate or acknowledge how valuable the person he cared about was. "I was afraid, Nox. I was twenty-one, and it all felt very exciting when we dreamed about a future together, paving our own way, but I knew my family would cut me off."

"Bastian." They say my name on a sigh. "Please."

Ancient history has no business hurting as much as the confession rattling around in my chest. "A year."

"A year," Nox repeats. "I see."

There's so much I could say. I could tell them that the moment they sailed out of port, I was waiting for them to return so I could right the mistake I'd made in letting them leave. That as the weeks ticked into months, I realized that I *couldn't* fix anything. That my cowardice had ruined everything. So, when the opportunity came to travel to Mairi to look after one of my father's business interests, I jumped at it.

Except instead of magically finding Nox again, I met Siobhan in a pub one evening after long negotiations. In the weeks that followed, I secured the deal for my family, and then decided to stay with Siobhan, to help her realize the dream she held of a free Threshold.

None of that will change the hurt I caused. The harm. "I'm sorry."

I actually see Nox putting their charming mask back into place. They grin, but the expression doesn't reach their eyes. "We're all sorry about a lot of things."

"Nox—" I don't know what I'll say to try to take away the pain I've caused.

They don't give me the chance. "Siobhan is scared," they cut in. "It's understandable. She's been hiding her entire life, and we're asking her to go against the training that's kept her alive and the rebellion running smoothly."

"Yes," I say slowly. The change of subject is clunky, but I'm not cruel enough to force the issue. Nox asked their question and I answered it. They don't owe me a single thing; certainly not forgiveness. "But hiding won't work anymore."

"No, it won't." Nox sounds exhausted. As if realizing it at the same time I do, they give themself a shake. "Go talk to Poet— she's the large woman who looks like she tosses kegs for fun. She'll give you a room assignment and see about some extra sets of clothing so you don't have to walk around in mine."

I like wearing your clothes. I always have.

I don't say it. I may not be a genius, but even I know that would hurt them unnecessarily. "Okay."

When I don't immediately move, they shake their head. "Go, Bastian." They speak softly, but there's no give in the words. "We have plenty to talk and argue about in the morning. We all need our rest."

It's a clear dismissal. I move slowly toward the door. "I'm sorry, Nox. For everything."

"We all are."

CHAPTER 10

Nox

I DON'T BOTHER TO CHANGE AFTER BASTIAN LEAVES MY cabin. No matter what I told him, I won't be sleeping tonight. I hurt too much for the sweet embrace of oblivion. Which just goes to show I'm a fool.

Instead, I wait long enough to ensure our new guest will be safely tucked into his room, and then I slip out the door and onto the deck. We're still racing away from the inevitable pursuit, and the few air-users on the deck are entirely focused on their task and, aside from short nods, pay little attention to me.

I'm not in the mood for company, so I make my way to the stern. There's a little space between the railing and some supplies we have strapped down, and I tuck myself into it, letting the wind and waves of our passing soothe me as little else can.

The sea may be a cruel mistress, may be as changeable as any force I've encountered, but she's not selfish and petty and shortsighted in the way we humans are. Her cruelty is pure in the way only an element can be. Fire, air, earth, water: they have unique personalities, but they're all beautifully uncaring and beyond our human concerns.

It's good to be reminded how small we are in the grand scheme of things. Humans, monsters, others, we could be wiped off the face of Threshold tomorrow and it wouldn't matter. The sun would still rise and set, the tides would still be called by the moon, the storms would still sweep across the sea, the fire would still burn as easily as it warms.

I close my eyes and breathe the salty air deep.

Things were always going to change, this conflict was always coming, but I was fool enough to think I'd have more time. I've only been captain for a few months, after having spent more than a decade under Hedd's tender mercies. It was difficult doing my part for the resistance while trying to corral that asshole, and I had been looking forward to more time to actually make a difference.

Which just goes to show—I should be careful what I wish for.

A slight creak of timbers has me opening my eyes as Bowen sinks carefully next to me. There's not much space, so his broad shoulder brushes mine. I sigh. "Did you draw the short straw to come talk to me?"

"Eyal is busy keeping us on course, Poet is dealing with the new addition to the crew, and Evelyn decided I would be a better choice than Lizzie."

I make a show of shuddering. "Threatening me with the vampire. That's just rude." I like Lizzie quite a bit, but it doesn't change the fact that I'm feeling too raw to deal with her brutal honesty. "What about Maeve?"

"You don't get Maeve without the vampire attached to her hip." He braces his wide forearms on the railing. "What's going on, Nox?"

I almost tell him to mind his own damn business, but the crew will have to find out the change of plans soon enough. No matter what Siobhan and Bastian—and I, I guess—decide, we can't force the crew to do anything they don't want to do. I have no interest in forcing them. Which means a vote.

"Up until this point, the rebellion has functioned in secrecy. Siobhan is the head, and she coordinated all the moving pieces to do the most good with the least amount of danger. Bastian being taken captive . . . and then our rescuing him? It changes things."

I expect impatience, but all he gives me is a steady look. "I know."

"We can't run. They'll hunt us through any realm we attempt to take refuge in, and running would put others in danger. The movement is too big; it won't stop just because we disappear. It will get more disorganized, which will mean more people will be caught, tortured, and killed. The fight has to come out into the open, but Siobhan doesn't see how we can win. They have the numbers and the power on their side, no matter how stacked this particular ship is."

He stares out into the darkness. "This was going to have to happen eventually. A system like this—corrupt from the top to the bottom—can't be fixed from within it. I believed it could at one point, but I was wrong."

"I know." I sigh. I hesitate over the reveal of Siobhan's ancestry, but ultimately this is Bowen, a former captain, and one of the most honorable people I know. I . . . want his input. "There's one other thing. Siobhan is a noble and sister to Morrigan. She's been believed to be dead for sixteen years, but now Morrigan knows the truth." I take a deep breath. "And they're both descended from the original Cŵn Annwn."

Bowen whistles under his breath. "A lot of hefty secrets."

I don't have it in me to be the charming captain in this moment. That particular mask feels too constricting right now. "Yeah."

"So she's descended from the originals." He doesn't look at me as he speaks. "Even if the people believe that, do you think it will change things?"

"I don't know. It would have if she was the only one left, if we could spread word faster than the Cŵn Annwn could suffocate the truth . . . but she's not the only one."

He nods. "Morrigan."

"Morrigan," I agree. "And the fact that they were a noble family, hiding their bloodline. The rest of Threshold has a very understandable distrust of Lyari nobles. Even if she shifted fully in the middle of every village in the realm, there would be plenty of people who wouldn't be swayed. The Cŵn Annwn won't risk it. It's in their best interest that this rebellion doesn't have a true hero to follow."

"A problem no matter which way you look at it." Bowen, the giant of a man, one of the most powerful beings I know, shudders. "Morrigan isn't going to stop coming until Siobhan and the rest of us are dead."

"Or unless we kill her first." I lean back and look at the stars overhead. We're moving fast enough that I can almost believe *we* are the ones standing still and they're streaming around us. "Some of the baddest motherfuckers in Threshold have tried to over the years. They've all failed." I was never foolish enough to attempt it. I know when a fight is a losing one.

Just like the one before us. "I don't see a way through, Bowen. The rebellion is far-reaching, but its strength is in its secrecy. The Cŵn Annwn are so fucking powerful."

"There's an . . ." Bowen trails off and shakes his head. "I'm sorry. My memory of the time before Threshold is filled with holes. Or, more accurately, more hole than anything else. No matter how hard I try, that time is a giant blank."

"I know. I'm sorry." Bowen was scooped out of the sea like so many people. The main difference was his age. He was young—too young, honestly—but that ship's captain at the time, Ezra, was as good a person as you could be sailing under the Cŵn Annwn. He was a true believer, but for all that, he kept his crew in line and never let a local be hurt under his watch. That's more than most captains do.

Bowen shakes his head, hard enough that it's as if he's sure he can shake out the information dancing just out of reach. "There's a legend," he says slowly. "I can only catch the edges of it, so I'm not sure if it's from Threshold or . . . before."

"Bowen, it's okay." I pat him on the shoulder. We don't always get along, but he's been invaluable since he joined the crew. "Don't strain yourself."

He's still staring out into the darkness, brows furrowed. "How is the Wild Hunt called?"

I blink. "Excuse me?"

"The Wild Hunt. Evelyn talked about it at one point." He scrubs his hand over his face. "The Cŵn Annwn, the originals, used to run with it, at least in her realm. A great magical hunt that swept across the land. Anyone caught out on nights like that were taken."

I shiver. That sounds just as dangerous as any individual element if left to run rampant. "That's not part of *our* legends." Evelyn and Lizzie both come from the same realm, one where the magical folks operate in secret and most of humanity is mundane. Still, since Threshold connects to all realms, it stands to reason that some of our histories would overlap. At least if they *were* histories instead of legends.

"No, I guess it isn't." He shrugs. "Siobhan and Morrigan might be the last of the originals, but what if they're not? We've always been taught that the originals are unknowable and untethered to our world. What if it isn't true?"

I smile despite myself. "You sound like Evelyn right now." There's nothing the witch loves more than questions. It's delightful and aggravating by turns.

"I suppose I do."

"It's something to chase down." I pat his shoulder again and shift back, breaking the contact. "I'll talk to Siobhan about it in the morning."

"Good." He glances at me. "Try to get some sleep tonight. You're no use to anyone if you fall over from exhaustion because of all the brooding."

That surprises me enough to laugh. "You can't have the market cornered on brooding, darling. It's rude."

"Yeah, yeah." He turns and starts to move away, but stops before he takes two steps. "I meant what I said, Nox. We're with you. All of us."

I wait for him to walk away to speak. "I know," I whisper. "That's what I'm afraid of." I believe in the cause. Deeply. I always have.

It's just my luck that I've finally found the community I've spent my entire life searching for . . . only for every single member to be in immediate and fatal danger. Just in time for both Bastian and Siobhan to be aboard, both so damn magnetic that I've fled my own damn cabin to escape thoughts of them.

I shake my head. Guess I didn't do a particularly good job of escaping. What's done is done, and Bastian is ancient history. It just doesn't *feel* like ancient history with the man himself on my ship, disrupting things with his presence. And Siobhan? She's a future that was never mine to have. Not when she and Bastian have been together for well over a decade at this point.

They met a year after he watched me walk away. A fucking *year.*

That's no time at all in the grand scheme of things. I exhale slowly. I shouldn't be mad all this time later. Life on Hedd's ship wasn't particularly pleasant even after I worked my way up to be quartermaster at record speed. And Bastian was a noble-born second son who had never worked a day in his life. It would have ended in disaster.

Knowing that doesn't allow me to rationalize out of the hurt I feel knowing he *did* leave his privileged life on Lyari. For Siobhan. Not me.

I give myself a shake and head back to the helm. Eyal is there, just like Bowen said. I nod at him. "Set course for Barth."

He raises his brows. "Barth is closer than I'd expect you to want to be after our quick escape."

"I know." It's less than a day from where I estimate us to be now. "Morrigan will expect us to head to the farthest side of Threshold. This time of year, Barth should have a dozen islands in close proximity. We'll be able to lose them there, even if they somehow follow us." There are countless ways to track . . . "*Fuck.*"

"What?" Eyal lifts his voice as I dodge past him toward my cabin. "Nox?"

I ignore him and duck into my cabin. The desk contains the magic that allows communication between the Council and the *Audacity*. It also allows them to track our movements. If Morrigan hasn't already reported our treason, she will soon. We need the desk gone and gone now. There's no fucking *time*. I was a fool for not thinking of it immediately.

As tired as I am, I draw forth the last dregs of power within me and concentrate on setting the desk aflame—without letting it spread. Fire is a fickle creature, more temperamental than the others. Most elemental users only control one, so I've never been able to get a satisfying answer out of the others if they feel like their element has a personality. All four have had personalities to me since the beginning.

Hot and hotter, draining my power at an exponentially faster rate than normal. The desk is spelled, resisting my efforts. "Burn, damn it." I flick open the small window, diverting power I can't afford to use wind to whisk the smoke out of the room.

The space wavers before my eyes, but I muscle down and focus harder. If we have a chance at all of escaping, we need this thing gone. There's a pounding between my ears that feels like someone is ringing a bell right next to my head, but I ignore it.

Finally—*finally*—the desk crumples. It takes even more effort to catch every spark and divert it out the window. I should get the pieces of the desk, too . . .

It's the last thought I have before everything goes gray and I slump to the floor.

CHAPTER 11

Siobhan

WHEN I CIRCLED BACK TO TALK TO NOX, I EXPECTED them to argue, to shut me down, to do anything but collapse the moment I stepped through the door.

"You bloody little fool!" I take a step forward to rush to them, but the moment they go down, the carefully controlled fire in the ruins of what used to be their desk flares back to life. "Damn it." I lean out the doorway. "Water-user! Get in here! Fire!"

Two people rush in. I belatedly recognize Callen and Gable. They move as a coordinated unit, one pulling water from the sea and the other "catching" it and sending it in a controlled burst onto the desk. Within seconds, the fire is gone.

Which leaves Nox, passed out on the floor of their cabin. "Medic!"

The call is passed down the line. I go to my knees next to Nox and carefully turn them onto their side. Their chest rises and falls in a steady rhythm, and best I can tell, their heartbeat is steady. I recognize this even before Orchid arrives in a rush and then curses under his breath. "Magical burnout."

"You *bloody fool*," I snarl. "Couldn't ask for help. Had to do it all yourself." I scoop Nox up, hating how slight they feel in my arms, and look around. The fire may be out, but the soggy mess of the desk and stink of smoke permeates the room. It should be easy enough to clean out in the morning, but that would require hauling people out of bed and . . . Nox shouldn't be alone right now.

Orchid sighs. "This has happened before regularly enough that I can say with the utmost confidence that Nox will be fine in the morning. They just need sleep and a hearty meal when they wake."

This happens regularly enough . . .

Oh, I am going to *strangle* them when they wake up. Despite all current evidence to the contrary, Nox isn't a complete fool. They must know that every time a person experiences burnout, it runs the risk of their magic reserves not replenishing fully. And that change is *permanent*. "I'm taking them to my cabin."

No one bothers to argue with me as I sweep out of the room, across the deck, and down the hatch to the crew's quarters. Bastian sticks his head out of his door as I pass. "What's . . . Is that *Nox*?"

"Magical burnout," I say shortly.

I should have expected him to follow, but somehow I'm still surprised when he catches my door before it can shut and slides into the room. I do my best to ignore him and lay Nox out on my bed. They look better already, some of the color returning to their pale skin.

"What were they thinking?" Bastian mutters. "We're on a

ship full of magical people and they just had to . . . What were they doing?"

"Burning the desk that communicates with the Council." A smart thing to do, but that doesn't mean the way they went about it was smart. They could have asked for help from one of the dozens of people capable of it. Instead, they ran themselves into the ground to do it themselves. "Stubborn ass."

"They always were more likely to take on too much rather than ask for help." Bastian sinks onto the edge of the empty bed, apparently having no intention of vacating the room anytime soon. He looks up at me. "Siobhan, talk to me. I know you're furious. I am, too. But we can't move forward if we're all being strangled by the past."

"You left me." He's right, but I still choke on the words. "We had a fight, and yes, it was a nasty fight, but you *left* me."

"You know that wasn't intended to be permanent."

He sounds so sure, but doesn't he know by now that there are no guarantees in life? Our current situation is proof of that. Maybe he intended to return . . . and maybe he didn't. Maybe he was finally sick of our differing outlook about the future. "I don't know that."

"Siobhan." He sighs. "I'm sorry. I know this isn't what you wanted, and if you *had* wanted it, this isn't how you would have chosen to reveal yourself. We have to make do with what we have. The rebellion is out there, whether we want it to be or not."

He's right, but that doesn't make the truth easier to swallow. This was always going to happen, but I worked damn hard to ensure it didn't happen before we were ready. "We've saved so many lives," I whisper.

"Yes." Bastian doesn't move, hardly seems to breathe.

It makes it easier to say what I need to say next. I close my eyes, taking solace in the darkness. "I'm scared."

"I know." The words are barely more than a whisper. "We're all scared."

And just like that, the words are pouring out of me. "I'm not supposed to be scared. I'm the leader of the damned rebellion. There are *thousands* of people putting their lives in my hands, trusting me to take care of them. I can't—"

"How does one call the Wild Hunt?"

I stop short and look down to where Nox's eyes flutter open. Just like that, all I'm thinking about is them. I go to my knees next to the bed. "What the fuck were you thinking, overstretching yourself like that?"

"I wasn't . . ." They lift a hand to their brow and wince. "Going under again soon. Don't panic." Their words gain a woozy affect and their eyes slide shut.

It takes everything I have not to shake them awake just to reassure myself that they're okay. From the tension radiating off Bastian, he's harboring similar feelings. It's only when Nox's breathing evens out again that I rock back on my heels and sigh. "They're so damned dramatic."

"To the bitter end." Bastian moves to sit back on the edge of the bed. "What did they mean? About calling the Wild Hunt?"

I shake my head. "I have no idea." The words make something toll in my chest, and I rub the back of my hand over my sternum. "We'll ask them when they wake up, I guess."

Bastian nods slowly. He pats the bed next to him. "Might as well sit down."

I almost tell him to get out. My pride has the words pressing against the inside of my teeth, but I forcibly swallow them back down. The truth is that I don't want to be alone, counting Nox's steady breaths for the rest of the night. I don't know how to heal the fissure of hurt between me and Bastian, but he's been my closest companion, my lover, for years. It's so simple to climb onto the bed next to him and let my shoulder rest against his.

How many times have we sat like this? I don't know. I couldn't begin to count. The familiarity helps as much as anything, bringing relaxation with every inhale. I don't mean to close my eyes, but I stir sometime later to the sound of Bastian snoring lightly, my head propped on his shoulder. I'm as much a fool as anyone, because instead of moving away, I allow my eyes to close and sleep to take me once again.

Bastian

The night passes quickly enough. Despite my exhaustion and newly full stomach, I don't sleep for long. How can I, when I'm watching Nox and Siobhan, certain that if I close my eyes, they'll stop breathing?

It's foolish. Magical burnout is dangerous, but it's on a spectrum ranging from taking a forced nap to death, and it's clear Nox is nowhere near death—even if they're actively endangering their power supply. I can actually watch the color return to their face and chest. They'll be fine.

Siobhan is another story, but nothing as simple as a good night's sleep will help what ails her. I don't know how to tell her that she doesn't have to do it alone—or at least how to tell her in a way that she'll actually hear. We were part of a rebellion up to this point. Now we're in a war.

Nox's question from earlier rings through my head. *How does one call the Wild Hunt?* I know the term, of course. It's not necessarily part of our history here in Threshold, but as part of my duties to the rebellion, I have encountered people from more realms than I can begin to count. In our time together, those people talked—especially when they encountered familiar terms in an unfamiliar world.

The problem with myth is that it's ancient history to the point of fiction. We can look for clues in the stories passed down in various realms, but they've evolved over the generations to be almost unrecognizable. There's not going to be a handy solution in those stories . . . but it can't hurt to gather as much information as I can before these two wake.

Or maybe that's just an excuse to move, to leave the room where I feel so damned helpless. To divorce myself from the agonizing moment between exhale and inhale of the slumbering pair.

I slip out of the room and head down to the kitchen to grab another quick snack—and watch the crew come through. It's right around time for a normal shift change. I don't know how Nox runs their ship, but shifts are common on every ship I've been on. It's a reasonable assumption that they do the same here.

Sure enough, roughly fifteen minutes after I take a seat in the middle of the room, people start filing in, wiping sleep from their eyes and muttering greetings. I didn't get the best look at folks last night for obvious reasons, but a quick count tells me that Nox isn't running a full crew. There are some familiar faces from the rescue, but the only one I know for sure is the vampire. I grab my food and move to sit at the table she shares with two plump women—one with fiery red hair and pale skin full of freckles, and the other with slightly less pale skin, short blond hair, and a network of tattoos on her chest.

"Lizzie, right?"

The vampire stares at me blankly for long enough that a smarter man than I would retreat. At least until the redhead smacks her lightly. "Stop it. You know there's no murder on Nox's ship."

"Fun to picture it, though." Lizzie takes a sip of whatever is in her cup. "What do you want?"

I glance at the redhead and then smile when I recognize her. "Maeve. You're the selkie from Viedna who was a key informant. You did good work."

She blushes prettily. "Thank you." Then she smacks Lizzie again with the kind of flirty familiarity that speaks volumes. "Be nice. He almost died."

"How many people have died because of the rebellion?" The vampire surveys me with the kind of derision that I've only witnessed in my parents' eyes. "You're noble. Playing captive must have been the first time things didn't go your way."

I don't argue with her. There's no point. I've been hurt and harmed and gone without plenty of times since leaving Lyari, but there's a thread of truth in Lizzie's accusation, because I always had a cushion of family money to fall back on, at least in theory. All I had to do to access it was go home.

"Lizzie," the blonde says playfully. "You're scaring the poor man."

"No, I'm not."

They have a sense of history that's interesting. I remember reading about the vampire. Siobhan was particularly interested in her in Nox's reports. She and Maeve obviously have some kind of relationship going, but she and the blonde just as obviously have history. "You're not from Threshold."

"What an astute observation," Lizzie mutters.

The blonde rolls her eyes. "I'm Evelyn." She holds out a hand.

I take it and give a light shake. "Bastian. Nice to meet you."

"Lizzie and I come from a different realm, though the portal back to it is shattered now due to some . . . unfortunate circumstances." She beams at me, her charisma nearly knocking me out of my seat. "I suspect you know that, though, because Siobhan knows and you were traveling with her."

Traveling with her. That's quite the tactful statement, especially considering that Siobhan can barely stand the sight of me these days. "Yes, I'm aware of you." I lean forward and prop my elbows on the table, ignoring the faint hiss from Lizzie. She's a prickly one, and although I'm not fool enough to underestimate her, from the lack of fear or concern from the other two, I assume she's simply posturing. "I wanted to ask you a question that Nox voiced. We know the Cŵn Annwn run through many realms' myths, but I'd like to know yours."

Evelyn's smile doesn't change, but her pretty green eyes sharpen. "Bowen said he mentioned the Wild Hunt to Nox last night."

That must have been what got them thinking about it. "How does one call the Wild Hunt in your world?" I don't even know why the question matters, only that Nox felt it important enough to wake up from bloody magical burnout to ask. The very least I can do is investigate their words while they're still out.

"I don't think they *are* called." Evelyn frowns a little. "They show up in myths and stories over an entire continent in my realm, so it's possible that there's an answer to that I'm not aware of, but to the best of my knowledge, they run either randomly or based on a moon cycle or time of year."

Maeve taps her fingers on the table. "There are a lot of different calls that go on during a mundane hunt, though. It's not silent, regardless of whether it happens in the water or the forest. Horns, drums, the kinds of instruments that can relay orders over long distances without shouting."

"Sure, in a normal hunt." Evelyn shrugs. "This is a magical one. In some myths, they're perfectly silent; in others, it's a giant party. Whatever the original experience that spawned the myths, each culture has taken its own spin on it, which might be important or might just be how myths work."

Their words wash over me as they continue discussing it, but little penetrates the sudden flurry of my thoughts. Horns. Drums. We don't have much use for mundane methods of hunting things in Lyari, where the Cŵn Annwn are plentiful and all the noble families have some kind of claim to magic.

But there *is* a horn. It sits on a magically protected stand hidden deep in the library in the center of Lyari, on the ground floor below the Council's meeting chamber. Technically, the noble families have access to the library whenever they like, but I have only visited a few times on one errand or another for my father. The horn is massive enough that I don't think I could lift it, twisted and curved unlike any other I've seen before, the carvings in its surface inlaid with gold and jewels and spells for a purpose I couldn't begin to guess.

I wonder if Siobhan knows about it? I wonder if *Nox* does . . .

CHAPTER 12

Nox

I WAKE TO A FIERCE POUNDING IN MY HEAD THAT NOR-
mally suggests I had an *exceedingly* good time the night before. Unfortunately, that's not the case right now. Not when I
can taste blood on my tongue and feel like I've been chewed on
by a dragon. Magical burnout is such a bitch.

"Good. You're awake."

I open one bleary eye to find Bastian perched on the bunk
across from me. I'm not in my cabin, but I recognize this one as
on the ship. Of course it is. Where else would I be? I heft myself
up and have to close my eyes again to fight against the way the
room spins. I'll have to take it easy today, but I should be feeling
better by the time lunch rolls around. None of that explains
why he's sitting here, watching me sleep. "What are you doing
here?"

"Siobhan needed food and didn't want you to be alone." The
words are right, but he's practically vibrating with excitement.

"You know the library in the same building as the Council chambers? The one where they keep all the dangerous and illicit texts?"

"Why the fuck would I know about that?" I press my fingers to my throbbing temples. "Why are you asking me about that right now?"

"Nox, *focus*." Bastian's voice rings with sincerity. Of course it does. He's perfectly sincere at all times, even when he's breaking your heart. In the gentlest way possible, of course, as if that doesn't make the situation a thousand times worse. "The library. There's a giant horn in a case. Do you know what it does?"

The way he's asking me, he obviously has some kind of idea, but I can't *think*. "When I lived in Lyari, I avoided the buildings where the Council reigns supreme. People like me weren't welcome in the area. I have no idea what you're talking about."

"Oh."

I open my eyes to find him visibly deflating, his excitement draining away. I *hate* that I want to draw back my sharp words, to find a way to soften them. I take great pains to shield the worst of myself from people. Partly because captains who rule by fear are only captains until someone comes along who's brave enough to slit their throat. Partly because it's just . . . easier.

But Bastian knew me before I learned those lessons. So of course he draws out the ugly bits I'd rather keep hidden. I sigh. "Why are you so excited about a horn?"

"Horns and hunts." He doesn't quite vibrate in enthusiasm, but it's a near thing. "You asked us how to call the Wild Hunt.

We don't have a Wild Hunt in our histories, but plenty of realms do—and in a lot of them, the Cŵn Annwn are involved."

"Yes, I'm aware." I barely have a memory of waking up to slur out the question Bowen posed to me last night. "But what you seem to be suggesting is that we sail to Lyari, break into the library, bypass the nasty magical traps that are no doubt around that horn, and . . . blow it? Just to see?"

He wilts a little more. "When you put it like that, it doesn't sound like a particularly good idea."

My headache makes me want to snap at him, but damn it, that's not entirely fair. I rub my temples harder. Orchid is going to berate me for pushing myself too far, but if I let him lecture me until he runs out of steam, he might brew me one of his potions to combat the headache so I can *think*. "*Why* do you think it's a good idea?"

"Siobhan isn't wrong," he says soberly. "A war will have great cost. I still think the cost is worth it for freedom, but if there's another way, we need to try it. No matter what she believes—what you believe—of me, I don't want any unnecessary loss of life. If there's a way to direct the Wild Hunt, we could potentially have the originals on our side. That's the kind of thing that turns the tide of a war."

At this point, I can't shy away from any potential options. "It's something to look into, I suppose." We don't have much in the way of better plans right now, but if we're trying to stay one step ahead of Morrigan and the rest of the Cŵn Annwn's fleet, sailing right into the heart of them will get us all killed.

"Nox."

The seriousness in his tone makes me look up despite my

determination not to. Gods, he's even more beautiful now than he was when we were barely more than kids. Suffering and hardship leave a mark on people, and usually it's an unfortunate one, but there's something about the new lines branching off from his eyes that speak of a maturity he didn't have when I was foolish enough to love him. He's grown up.

We both have.

That should mean the spark that flared to life between us as teenagers, meeting in secret and dreaming of a life spent together, is gone. We're not the same people we were fourteen years ago. I don't even recognize that naive child any longer, for all that I was forced to grow up fast to stay alive. The truth is that trauma is no substitute for actual life lived. Some lessons can only be taught through decades.

Obviously I haven't learned my lesson when it comes to this man, though. Not if I still feel the tug under my ribs whenever I look at him. "What?"

Once he's sure he has my full attention, he quietly says, "You know that every time you burn out magically, you risk it being the last. And even if it's not, you risk permanently diminishing your magical reserves."

Guilt lashes me, so fierce that it steals my breath. I worried him, which means I worried *everyone*. "I'm aware." It's still worth the cost. My crew are fucking exhausted, and there doesn't promise to be relief on the horizon. We made a clean getaway from Morrigan, but it took too long for me to remember the desk. At any moment, we could be running for our lives again. Better that I be laid out, risking my deep reserves, than one of them experience the same thing.

"Your crew needs you. *We* need you." He leans forward suddenly, not near enough to touch, not by a long shot, but close enough that it would take little effort to mirror his movements, to bring our faces close, to . . .

I shake my head—and then immediately regret the motion when my headache blooms in response. "I. Am. Aware." I shove to my feet, only wobbling a little. "I don't need a lecture from you, Bastian. I'll talk to the crew and apologize for worrying them, but I don't answer to you. Not anymore."

"Nox."

I stop in the process of turning to the door and look down at him. "What?" It's absolutely absurd that he can still hurt me with just a look in his deep brown eyes. I'm not the ignorant little fool I was when I followed him around with hearts in my eyes, dreaming of a future together. I've suffered in the time since, have sacrificed so much in order to do even a little good, have learned so many more important lessons at more ruthless hands than his.

For a horrible moment, I think he's going to apologize again, that we're going to go round and round and round and never escape the cycle of hurt and anger. Instead, he surprises me by saying, "You're not alone. You weren't even before Siobhan and I came aboard. You don't have to be the one to shoulder it all. I know you care about your people and want to protect them, but hurting yourself hurts them."

His words steal mine away. I can do nothing but stare at him until the door opens behind me. I feel Siobhan there, and a part of me hates that I can tell the difference between her and the others in my crew even without looking.

She shuts the door firmly. "You started without me."

"We were just wrapping up." Bastian sounds just as tired as I feel, and why not? He doesn't look like he got much sleep last night, and he certainly wasn't well rested while under Morrigan's tender care.

I turn to Siobhan, but looking at her isn't any easier than looking at Bastian. She's so close that I can feel the warmth radiating from her strong body, that I have to crane my head back to meet her honey gaze, that my mind skips right to other activities we could be doing with a little less space between us.

It's a testament to my shakiness that I'm thinking about kissing instead of the dozens of other more pressing issues. I take a careful step back. "I got my lecture, thank you very much. I'll be a good captain in the future and not scare you poor folks."

Her lips thin with displeasure. "Don't patronize me."

"Wouldn't dream of it, darling." I have no real defense against these two, so I lean hard on the mask that protects me—or at least has historically. The rakish captain, humor and flirtation as a wall no one can climb to get to the real me. I'm just . . . not so certain it will do the trick now.

Sure enough, Siobhan doesn't move from where she blocks my exit. "We have perhaps a day's lead on Morrigan, and that won't hold indefinitely. Eventually even *your* crew will tire."

I thought as much earlier, but I can't help bristling at the implication that I would *ever* put my crew in unnecessary danger. "I'm aware. Which is why I already spoke with Poet about how to structure the shifts to keep everyone safe. You let *me* worry about *my* crew." I jerk a thumb over my shoulder. "Or are you ready to chase a wild hare like Bastian here, and want me to sail to Lyari to blow a damn horn?"

"A horn?" Siobhan frowns, her gaze flicking over my shoulder to Bastian. "What are they talking about?"

"I was speaking with Evelyn earlier when I grabbed food, and something she said got me thinking. Horns and drums and the like are used on mundane hunts." As he speaks, he becomes more animated, excitement written all over his gorgeous face. "There's a horn in the library in the Council's building. It might be a way to summon the originals."

"It's a long shot," I cut in. "You're operating on a lot of assumptions. It might just be magically protected to preserve it because some ancient asshole liked it a lot. There's no reason to connect it to the Cŵn Annwn."

"Except it's in the Council's building, and the Council controls the Cŵn Annwn."

I open my mouth to keep arguing, but he has a point *there*, at least.

Siobhan frowns harder, seeming to ignore us. "I don't know anything about a horn or the Wild Hunt, but my parents used to tell us a bedtime story about our history and how the ancestors would come if we called, but we'd only get one chance to ask a boon. You think there's some truth to that? That the horn might be the way we summon them?"

"I think . . ." He glances at me and sighs. "Nox is right. We don't have enough information. Certainly not enough to set course to Lyari right now." He half lifts his hands and then lets them fall back to his thighs. "But I thought it might be worth looking into."

I expect Siobhan to close that door firmly in his face, but she just crosses her arms over her chest and her gaze goes to somewhere far beyond this cabin. It's eerie, as if she can really see something that is lost to both me and Bastian. I glance at him, but he's watching her closely, as if this isn't new or unexpected.

Finally, she exhales slowly and gives herself a shake. "Dia might know. She's lived a particularly long life, and she's connected with Threshold on a level not even I can match. She has a particular interest in the originals and the old gods that most people have forgotten."

I glance between them. "Dia? As in the former navigator of the *Crimson Hag*?" She was a member of my crew for a very short time, but I dropped her on First Sister weeks ago.

"The very one." Siobhan is still frowning. "I'm not entirely certain where she is now. She's not one to linger in a place for long, not with her vow compelling her to join another crew."

I hold up my hands. "Hold on a moment. *Dia* is a member of the rebellion?"

"Not in the way you mean." Siobhan huffs out a sound that's almost a laugh. "Dia's loyalty was always to Ezra, and then by extension to Bowen. When the crew voted Bowen out, she left as well. But she's no friend to the Cŵn Annwn. She told me to come find her when I was ready to actually *do* something."

"Why didn't she stay with Bowen?" Bastian asks.

Siobhan shrugs. "Who can say? That woman moves to the rhythm of her own tide. But if anyone has an answer to that riddle, it's her."

"We don't even know if that riddle *has* an answer that can help us." I almost hate to pull their enthusiasm up short, but it has to be said. "We're operating under some rather large assumptions. We don't know if the originals even exist, if the Wild Hunt is actually connected to them, and we certainly don't know if they'd be sympathetic to our cause if they *do* exist and it *can* be summoned. It's far more likely that even if we could find a way to summon them, we'd just be bringing a destructive force into Threshold with no way to stop them."

That sobers them both. Bastian nods. "So, we go to Dia and ask. If she knows the answer to those questions, then we'll create a new plan. If she doesn't? Then we'll create a new plan."

"That's not what—"

"Nox," Siobhan says quietly. "We're going to be hunted to the ends of Threshold and beyond. Even if we could gather all the members of the rebellion, it will be a slaughter if we attempt to meet the Cŵn Annwn in battle. We have to find a different way."

I don't tell them we should run. It was never really an option, and even if it was, neither of these fools would take it. I suppose I'm a fool, too, because I'm going down with my crew, one way or another. "First Sister is on the other side of the realm. Our chances of making it there without encountering the Cŵn Annwn are nonexistent."

Siobhan and Bastian are so different, but their expressions are identical. Stubborn, hopeful, bent on this course of action. I'm captain of this ship, which means the final decision should be mine, but that's a naive thought. The truth is that a good captain weighs the needs of their crew against all their hard-earned knowledge.

I don't want to admit that Siobhan's right, but she is. We can't beat the Cŵn Annwn in a straight battle. They have the numbers, the firepower, and everything else in their favor. Without some kind of trickery, we don't stand a chance.

Even with my crew on steady rotation running themselves into the ground, it will take well over a week to reach First Sister. Morrigan may not have as many air- and water-users on her ship, but she's got all the power of the Council behind her. She'll catch up with us sooner or later, and I'd wager everything I own that it will be sooner than I'd like.

I sigh. "So be it. To First Sister we go."

CHAPTER 13

Siobhan

I T'S BEEN A VERY LONG TIME SINCE I'VE SAILED ON A SHIP this size. Bastian and I spent time on a smuggler ship for about a year after leaving Mairi. It was in those months that the realization of how poorly things work in Threshold became clear. Because the *Brune* didn't trade in alcohol or treasure or anything of that nature. They traded in *freedom*.

There are no laws prohibiting travel between the islands of Threshold. Each island is—theoretically—left to govern themselves. But while that might be technically true, the fact remains that the Cŵn Annwn have a tendency to bend the laws to suit themselves. Being caught out on open water with crimson sails in the distance is the stuff of nightmares for most citizens of Threshold.

And so we helped people—for a price. We would run circuits north and south, then east and west, through Threshold, transferring people to their destinations while under the relative safety of sailing on a Lyarian ship. *Strange* how the Cŵn Annwn never plunder the capital city to bolster their numbers.

In that year, the rebellion was born. I could see *so clearly* how much good we could do if there were more than one ship doing the work, if there were a network of safe people and safe houses to take refuge in.

During the first few years after leaving the *Brune*, Bastian and I spent a lot of time apart, carefully courting people to our cause. It was in that time that I met Nox and so many others. But as the years passed, it became clear how vital secrecy was in order to keep people safe.

That secrecy demanded Bastian and I isolate ourselves. Me more than him, honestly. Up until his arrest, he kept up the fiction of being the feckless second Dacre son. Publicly he oversaw his father's interests in Three Sisters. Privately he used his connections to secure funding and all manner of support for the rebellion.

And all the while, I kept to the shadows. I got used to it over the years. Which means that, as nice as it is to be among Nox's crew, helping switch over the sails to a mundane white, it's a bit overwhelming. Everyone moves in a seamless rhythm that I'm a half step behind on no matter how hard I try.

The crimson sails are rolled up and deposited into a subsection of the deck that's been magicked open. Not standing in the bloody shadow of the Cŵn Annwn sails helps the pressure in my chest, but I'm achingly aware of the fact that my sister catching us will result in the deaths of many of these people—if not all of them.

Morrigan isn't the type to leave survivors to spread the tale of rebellion. Our parents taught her that lesson well; better to leave no witnesses than to risk exposure. It's a lesson I internalized alongside her, but instead of killing anyone who witnesses me in my hound form, I simply . . . don't shift. Not all the way.

My sister may be violent to the extreme, but she's no fool. She doesn't shift fully, either. All of Threshold would have heard about it if she did. A partial shift could be attributed to any powerful shifter, but our hound forms are not normal by any stretch of the imagination. We're too large, too fluid, too uncanny. No one looking at us would mistake us for a normal shifter.

And the Council and Cŵn Annwn would never allow a symbol like that to exist, even within their control. They'd kill Morrigan, Council member, noble, or no. They'd certainly kill *me*.

A soft grunt has me looking over my shoulder. I immediately wish I hadn't. Bastian is in the middle of the deck, helping Evelyn do something to the warding circle drawn there. In the heat of the afternoon, he's removed his shirt and . . .

Longing hits me so hard, it roots my feet to the deck. His light brown skin gleams in the sunlight, practically begging to be touched. I know what the lines of his muscles feel like beneath my fingertips, how they flex when . . .

He grins at something Evelyn says and then laughs aloud, the sound reaching me even over the length of the ship. My hearing is better than most, and gods, I want nothing more than to move closer, to catch whatever they're talking about that's so amusing, to soak up some of the sunlight Bastian seems to carry with him wherever he goes. No matter what happens, he bounces back *so fast*.

"You should talk to him."

I heard Nox approach, but can't seem to tear my gaze from Bastian. "There's nothing to talk about."

"Siobhan." There's amusement in Nox's tone, but beneath it something infinitely more complicated. "You clearly love him as much as he loves you."

"Love is the least of the elements that keep people like us apart."

This time, Nox does laugh. It's got a bitter edge, so unlike them that I finally manage to tear my attention from Bastian. They hold a hand up to shield their gray eyes, and if Bastian seems to be finding his feet quickly, Nox has recovered even faster. Their skin is as warm as the light flickering over the waves, their short blond hair ruffling in the wind of our passing.

"What's so funny?"

"Oh, nothing." They shrug, a small smile still playing at their lips. "Just that we're likely on a suicide mission. It's incredibly silly to let a little argument get in the way of whatever happiness you can claim before Morrigan rips out all our throats."

Despite my best intentions, my hand goes to my throat. What Nox describes isn't enough to kill *me*. My sister already tried it, when we were barely more than children, years before the fire. A *sparring* accident, according to her. My parents believed her, despite my fear over her ferocity. I don't know if things would have been different if they'd realized how much she wanted to be heir, no matter the cost.

The scars are all but gone, courtesy of my healing ability, but the memory remains unblemished no matter how many years pass in the meantime. "We're not going to die."

"Sure we are, darling." They're doing a damn good job at

playing the careless captain, but they can't quite manage to banish the strain lingering beneath every word. "Everyone dies eventually. Even gods."

I cross my arms over my chest. "If what you say is true, why not rekindle *your* romance with Bastian?"

That gets a reaction. They flinch. "Excuse me?"

"It's only a conversation gone wrong, a single fight, right?" I'm being cruel, but no less cruel than they were. "More time may have passed, but don't lie and tell me you feel nothing for him. I see the way you watch him when you think no one is paying attention." I know exactly how much Bastian still cares for Nox. He knows he did them wrong, so he's respected their very clear boundary of not wanting to see him, but his feelings are clear in the rare times when he speaks of them.

Maybe those short conversations are when I started to *see* Nox. The charming pirate, yes, always, but they care so bloody deeply. More than they want the world to know.

"Oh, sure." They wave a careless hand. "I'll just take him to my cabin and fuck him right now. That's what you want, correct?" The edge in their words is even more pronounced. Nox shakes their head. "I might as well fuck *you* instead. At least we don't have the messy history."

I turn fully to face them. I've never been able to afford to tread carelessly with my lovers. My strength can bring more pain than pleasure if I lose control—and there's always the risk of losing control. Bastian and I found ways around it, and while we never spent much time in the beds of others, the specter of Nox was there often enough that I laugh in their face. "We don't have a messy history? Come now, Nox, I never took you for a liar."

"Compared to Bastian, we don't."

I lean closer and lower my voice. "We have a messy history *because* of Bastian."

Nox raises a brow. "Are you propositioning me?"

I can't help the bolt of pure need that sears me at the thought of doing just that. But I'm not ruled by my desires. I can't afford to be when so much hangs in the balance. "Nox, I swear to the gods." I look up at the clear sky as if it might offer me some advice. Even if it did, I wouldn't take it. "Sleeping with you while Bastian is among the crew would be the height of cruelty. You have too much unfinished business."

"Hmm."

I lower my gaze and freeze. No one can sneak up on me, but Nox has shifted to stand directly before me. It's only when I note that they're taller than normal that I realize they're using air to raise themself above the deck. Truly, their control is staggering. It leaves me breathless. "Nox," I finally manage, voice choked.

"Do you think about sleeping with me, Siobhan?" Their voice has gone low, sultry with just a hint of growl. "Or more accurately, *not* sleeping? If I had you in my bed, I wouldn't waste time being unconscious."

My jaw works, but it's as if I haven't spoken a single word in my life. "Wha—"

"I have thought about it, you know—you and I. How could I not? But you're right," they say softly. "It *would* be cruel. And while I may be accused of many things, I'm not unfair with my bed partners. Not even him. Certainly not you."

They pivoted too quickly. I'm still scrambling to keep up. "You don't even *like* me that much."

"Darling, sex has little to do with liking as long as there's some mutual respect and a dash of trust." Their smile is so wicked, it makes my knees shake. "You're a big, strong woman with muscles I'd like to sink my teeth into. You're also honorable enough to make me want to strangle you on a regular basis. Of course I want you."

I am no blushing maiden, unused to frank propositions, but this isn't . . . right. Nox and I have spent a lot of time together over the years, and they've never come on to me, let alone come on this strong. I reluctantly take a step back, and then another. "You'd use me to hurt him."

Their smile falls away slowly enough that I suspect it was real, rather than a mask. "I'd use you—if you want to call it that—for pleasure through my last days in this realm. If it stung him in the process, it makes no difference to me."

Instead of reassuring me, their words just prove my suspicion correct. "That's the first time you've lied to me."

Nox turns away, changing the subject. "We'll barely make it to First Sister with our current supplies. Before you came aboard, we hadn't planned on a prolonged escape, and my crew is running through resources faster than anticipated. It's vital that Morrigan has no idea where we're headed."

I don't argue that we don't have time to resupply. Magic has a cost. Burnout is a risk for anyone with even a drop of magic in their blood, but there are different risks depending on the flavor of magic. Elemental users, in particular, are prone to magical burnout. There's something about the way they wrestle the very elements into submission that burns their physical resources first. It's incredibly dangerous, but once an elemental user is experienced, there are ways to prolong their usage and hold off burnout by ingesting food and water in increased quantities. "I'll find Dia when we arrive, and the crew can re-supply."

"I don't need your permission to do so."

I sigh. "Nox, you're swinging wildly from one thing to an-other. I realize having Bastian on board isn't ideal because of your history, but you know damn well that I value your crew and want them taken care of as well." I step into them, close enough that they have to crane their neck to meet my gaze. "And if I come to your bed, it will be because you want *me*. Not because you want to hurt *him*."

They lick their lips. "Why not both?"

"That's not good enough for me." I hadn't realized I'd draw this line in the sand until I said it. Bastian and I tend to be mo-nogamous as such things go. Even when we're fighting, it's al-ways been us against the world. I won't touch Nox without talking about it with Bastian first, and probably not even then. Not when doing so would hurt him. It feels cruel, and while I know Nox can be cruel, this is their pain talking. "I don't do things halfway, Nox. It's all or nothing." I don't know how to hold things—or people—lightly. I never have.

They study my face for several beats and finally nod. "Then it's nothing. Now go. I have things to do."

Disappointment sours on my tongue, but did I really expect anything different? I refuse to think too closely about it as I turn and walk away. We have bigger things to deal with than my confused heart.

I just . . . I didn't expect any of this.

CHAPTER 14

Nox

AFTER SEVERAL DAYS OF ENSURING THAT WE ARE MOV-
ing at as quick a pace as possible, I finally crash. Truth be
told, I should have left the *Audacity* in Poet's tender care after the
first day when Morrigan didn't appear. But I'm nothing if not a
control freak, and so I wanted to ensure that we put as much
distance between us and Siobhan's sister as possible. My crew is
full of capable people who are the best at what they do, but I
refuse to ask anything of them that I won't do myself.

And it's entirely possible that I'm an arrogant asshole in addition to being a control freak.

I shut myself away in my cabin and barely take the time to
shower before collapsing face-first into my bed. I've never had a
problem with sleeping, but this evening it eludes me despite my
best efforts. I can't help thinking about Siobhan, about the tension between us. It's always been there, unacknowledged, but if
I've been a fool in love before, I have no intention of being one
again. Or at least I didn't. Falling for the leader of a secret rebel-

lion whom I can see only once every season or so is a recipe for a broken heart, and so I refused to allow myself to even dream.

But now she's on my ship. And somehow the flawed, human version of Siobhan is even more attractive than the caricature of her that I had put on a pedestal. She's not perfect, and that's fucking irresistible to me.

And, if I'm being honest with myself, with not a single person to witness except the shadows of my room, I can admit that the feelings for Bastian haven't dissipated. It feels particularly pathetic to be pining after a man who left me in the dust so long ago. But if my perception of Siobhan has changed, I can't quite ignore that my perception of Bastian is in danger of shifting as well.

At eighteen, at twenty-one, he was reckless to a fault. It thrilled me even as I feared for him, and when you're that age, fear and thrill are practically the same thing. Now, though? Now he's grown up. I don't know why that surprises me. I'm hardly the same person I was all those years ago. But the Bastian in my head was caught outside of time, unable to change or evolve or grow up. Even though I've been avoiding him since he came aboard, I can't ignore the fact that he *has* changed. And I don't know what to do with that.

I'm still mulling over the problem as I slip into sleep's sweet embrace.

Only to be woken what feels like fifteen seconds later by Poet's tense voice. "Captain, we need you." She doesn't say anything else, but she doesn't need to. There's no point in wasting breath when we have a wealth of shared experience between us. There's only one reason for her to have woken me up.

Trouble.

As soon as Poet opens the door, yells from the crew reach my ears. It's hard to parse the specific words, but I don't need to. We're in danger. I barely pause to pull on a long tunic that covers me from neck to mid-thigh before I rush out of my cabin to find out what all the fuss is about.

I find Poet with Eyal at the helm, him gripping the wheel with white knuckles, his expression tense and carefully blank. "Report," I say as I come to stand next to them.

Poet doesn't take her eyes from the horizon. "Crimson sails spotted. Three of them."

I turn to look, even knowing I won't see anything. My eyesight is better than most, but it can't compare to a shifter's or some of the other magical people we have aboard. "Damn it. I thought we'd have more time before Morrigan found us."

"Not Morrigan." Eyal shakes his head. "They're coming from the wrong direction. From the east instead of behind us."

The east, which is the horizon before us. Fuck. By my count, we still have another day or so before it's safe to turn north and follow the line of islands that create the trading path across Threshold. I had no intention of following that path closely, but turn too soon and we're at the mercy of the storms that rage through the northwestern part of the realm this time of year. With a fully rested crew, I might be willing to take my chances, but we're all operating on the edge of exhaustion. A storm could very well kill us.

The Cŵn Annwn will kill us even faster, though.

"Fuck." I scrub my hands over my face, trying to think of a different option. There's none. Turning to the south takes us away from our goal, and at this point time is of the essence. Obviously Morrigan reported to the Council at least some of what happened when we took Bastian back. It is a testament to my reputation—and that of my crew—that they've sent an additional three ships to bring us down. If this trio fails, no doubt the Council will send the entire fleet, or near enough to it. We can't afford to waste any time.

I rotate to stare north, as if that would tell me our chances. I must have slept quite a while because the first fingers of dawn are lightening the sky, chasing away the stars. There's a clear sky, calm seas. That should reassure me, but it only reinforces my suspicion that things are about to go horribly wrong.

"Captain?" asks Eyal.

"I'm thinking." I scrub my hand over my face again. No good options. Well, we've faced no good options before. I straighten and turn back to them both. "North. Now. We can't afford to sail any closer to the ships trying to pen us in. Especially when we don't know which ships those are." Between Siobhan and me, I'm confident that we have information on most of the ships in the Cŵn Annwn's fleet. We just need to know who we're dealing with, and then we can form a proper plan to flee or attack.

Really, though, fleeing is the only option. An attack will slow us down, and even if we survive, it will cut the distance between Morrigan's pursuit significantly. That's more dangerous than anything.

Eyal nods. He's tense as he guides the ship north, a slow turn that causes our sails to dip before the crew readjusts and they snap full again. Within seconds, we're skimming over the surface of the waves.

The awful feeling in my stomach worsens. We have a fight on our hands, one way or another. "I'm going to check on the crew. Give me a few."

"Might want to tell them to batten things down," Poet says, eyes on the sky. "I suspect we're in for a rough ride."

"Poet." I inject a level of charm into my voice that I certainly do not feel. "Keep talking like that and I'll think you're sweet on me. A little bit of optimism never hurt anyone."

Her only response is a tight smile. It's enough. I go. It feels like so much of my time as captain is spent choosing between one bad option and another even worse option. Understanding that doesn't make me have any more sympathy for the late Hedd, but damn if my stress level hasn't risen significantly since I have an entire crew's safety resting on my shoulders.

An hour later, Siobhan finds me in the process of tying down whatever I can find on the deck. In the time since we turned north, the wind has picked up, slamming at the ship from side to side, causing it to shudder even with my crew's best efforts. Despite that, Siobhan moves easily. Her long hair whips about her face, obscuring her features. Every few seconds, the light catches her eyes and they shine eerily in the growing light. "Why are we headed north?"

I could remind her that I'm captain and I don't have to answer to her, but she's the leader of the fucking rebellion, so I guess I do. I open my mouth, but pause when I realize that my foul mood is going to make me come across as an absolute asshole. If Siobhan were anyone else, I wouldn't bother to censor myself, but I can't completely forget the thoughts that circled my mind while I lay in my bed. So I swallow hard and moderate my tone. "We have another three ships closing in. They're trying a prolonged pincer move. If we didn't turn, we'd end up in between six ships, and while I'm good, not even *I* am that good."

She frowns down at me and then twists to look east, where the sun is a bloody orb in the sky. I can barely see the ships our lookout spotted, but Siobhan goes tense. "How did they recover the *Crimson Hag* so quickly? We broke a hole in that ship that should've sunk it."

"Magic, darling. What else?" In the short time between the attack on the *Crimson Hag* and Siobhan and the others finding our ship, I received no word of what happened on Drash. So I have no idea what magic they pulled to bring that ship out of the bay and patch it up in such a short time.

Siobhan sighs. "I don't have to tell you that the storms are probably going to rip this ship into a thousand pieces."

"Nope."

"Even with your crew, we can't—"

"I know," I cut in gently. "But it's a choice between a certain death and a less certain death. We have to take our chances."

She hesitates as if she might keep arguing, but finally nods. Because she's a leader, too. She understands that sometimes there are no good decisions, only bad ones measured in mere inches' difference. "What do you need from me?"

I'm tempted to tell her to go belowdecks and stay safe until this is over. It's a selfish desire. I should know better than to try to hide away those I care about to keep them safe, but I can't stop myself from trying over and over again. It's never worked before. It certainly won't work now. Siobhan is a warrior. She's going to be in the middle of the approaching fight, regardless of whether our opponent is the Cŵn Annwn or a storm. Or, if we're unlucky, both.

I pat the large crate that I've just finished tying down. "Help the crew lash down anything they can find. Things will be challenging enough without someone getting knocked overboard because of carelessness now." That should be enough to keep her busy, but I find myself continuing to speak. "And keep an eye on Bastian."

She pauses in the midst of reaching down to check my knot. "Bastian?" Siobhan frowns as if I've presented her with a puzzle that she doesn't quite understand the parameters of yet. "You hate Bastian. If we're not worried about the Cŵn Annwn getting him, it would make your life significantly easier if he went overboard. No one to blame that way."

I blink. Despite everything, a slow smile pulls at the edges of my lips. "Siobhan, are you trying to manipulate me into admitting something about Bastian?"

The blush that rises to her tanned cheeks is confirmation enough. She's even more attractive when she blushes, and if I didn't have a dozen dangers facing us, I might be tempted to coax her into my cabin and see just how far that blush extends.

I hadn't realized that I'd already made the decision to seduce her. I've always been awful with timing when it comes to these things, but never quite so bad at timing as this. Then again, if we're sure to die, why not go out in style?

"Not a manipulation, but . . ." She huffs out a strained laugh. "Okay, you caught me."

I don't point out that she's furious at Bastian and has been since before we saved him. Love is a complicated thing, and it still shines between them with a strength that I swear I can actually see, even when they're fighting. They'll figure this out as long as they survive to see the end of it. That should make me jealous, I think. I'm deeply attracted to Siobhan, and I respect her strength and canniness. And Bastian? Well, there was a reason I loved him, and a reason that when he broke my heart, that pain has echoed through every year that I've lived since.

I'll worry about the lack of jealousy later. Right now, I need to keep us all alive. "Just watch over him. Please."

Her faint smile fades. She nods. "Okay, Nox. I'll watch over him. I promise."

CHAPTER 15

Bastian

I'VE BEEN ABOARD COUNTLESS SHIPS OVER THE YEARS, but never one as tightly run as the *Audacity*. We're sailing into all but certain death, and the crew hasn't panicked once. Instead, they move about with fierce expressions and determination in their eyes. It's a testament to Nox's leadership skills and the community that they have built that no one panics. Personally, I feel like panicking. There's nothing I can do. I've never felt so helpless in my entire life, which is saying something, because my sole purpose as the Dacre spare is to exist should something happen to my elder brother. I don't know what that could be termed if not helpless.

Siobhan sticks close enough to me that there's no way it's coincidence. I wipe the salt spray from my face and turn to her as we finish tying off the last set of supplies. "Did someone tell you to babysit me?" Even as I ask the question, I realize there's only one person on this ship who would dare give Siobhan an order. "Nox did, didn't they?"

"I would've looked after you even if they hadn't." With a frustrated grunt, Siobhan twists her hair back and does something to it to keep it out of her face. "I hate this. If we were on land—"

"I know." I smile but nothing's funny. "But we're in Threshold. Land is in short supply. We always knew that our battles would be fought at sea."

"Don't be reasonable at me right now. I don't appreciate it." Just like she has dozens of times before, she turns to look in the direction of our wake. I can't see much in the growing darkness, but Siobhan has never had a problem seeing over long distances. "They're gaining," she says shortly.

"But how?" I shift a little closer and lower my voice. The last thing I want to do is accidentally insult any of the crew. "We're moving faster than we have any right to be. The air-users have been filling our sails for days now, and more so since those ships were spotted. Even if they have their own air-users, they shouldn't be moving faster than we are."

"I don't know." She looks so grim as she says it that I want to hug her. Only the knowledge that she wouldn't welcome the embrace keeps my feet planted and my hands at my sides. Siobhan shakes her head. "I know most of who they have crewing those ships. They have maybe four air-users between the three ships. This is something else."

Unfortunately, in Threshold, "something else" often signifies the kind of trouble that people don't survive. Fuck. "I suspect part of the problem is that our crew has been working themselves to the bone." Another gust of wind comes from the north, so strong that it pushes me back half a step and Siobhan has to catch my elbow to keep me steady. I glare into the darkness.

It's far too early in the day for that kind of dark. I don't like what it signifies.

"It's the storm." Nox walks up to us, their expression pinched. "Captains who want to keep their ships stay out of these waters at this time of year. Unfortunately, we don't have that option."

I can't help drinking in the sight of them. Soaked to the bone, with their clothing and hair plastered to their body, looking more tired than I've ever seen them, Nox is still so devastating that they take my breath away. It's possible they're even more attractive like this, because as worried as they are, they're still in complete control.

I swallow hard. "We've dealt with storms before."

Nox snorts, the sound almost lost in the howling wind. "Normal storms, yes. But these aren't normal storms. Can't you taste it on the wind?"

I almost stick my tongue out to see if I can actually taste what they say, but Siobhan speaks before I have a chance to make a fool of myself. "This is going to be a problem."

"Welcome to my world." Nox spreads their arms. Even in the midst of crisis, they are still a showman. "I would love to say that the storm will slow down the ships in pursuit, but there's no guarantee. This territory is fickle."

I don't tell them that territory cannot be fickle. As they said, this is Threshold. We all know better. I've done plenty of research over the years on all the little quirks and nightmares that our realm has to offer. Even with that knowledge, I'm coming up blank about this so-called magical storm. I frown. "I've never read anything about this."

Nox gives me a look that I can't quite define. "You've been

sailing around Threshold for well over a decade at this point. I would assume you've learned that not everything can be found in a book."

"You're patronizing me and I don't appreciate it." I scrub at my face, but it's a wasted effort. The salt water is *everywhere*. "I understand there's plenty of both good and bad things within Threshold that never make it into books for one reason or another. But that doesn't negate the fact that if there are ship-killing magical storms in an entire section of the world, someone would've written about it by now."

Nox shrugs. "There are only a handful of islands out here, and most of them are uninhabitable to humanoid beings. Your valued scholars never bothered to come this way once they decided they'd witnessed everything there was to see."

Siobhan crosses her arms over her chest, her body easily shifting with the shuddering of the ship. "You're not wrong, but neither is Bastian. This should have been reported."

Nox rolls their eyes. "You are both too experienced in this world to be so naive. The storms started appearing a few years ago, and anyone who sails close to this route learned quickly to avoid them. There's no reason they would've spoken about that to scholars or even the Council."

They're still being patronizing, but at least this argument makes slightly more sense. Most of the books written on Threshold are practically ancient at this point. Some Council long ago invested significant time and effort in mapping all of the permanent islands and shifting ones as well as they could, and cataloging every people, animal, and resource available on said islands. I know that there's a trio of small islands north and west of our approximate location, but as Nox has said, they're uninhabitable to anyone who breathes oxygen and likes their gravity to follow the expected rules.

I shift to stare north just as a lightning bolt shatters the sky. It's a deep purple that makes me shudder. "That's not—" The boom of thunder drowns out whatever I would've finished saying. So loud that it rattles my bones. I shudder. "What the fuck?"

Nox opens their mouth to answer, but a call trails down from the crow's nest. "Captain! Behind us!"

All three of us waste no time sprinting to the upper deck to look where directed. I had seen the trio of ships in the distance, mere specks, when I was up here earlier helping Siobhan lash things down. Before, they'd been so far away that only someone with her eyesight would be able to pick out the details. Now they're significantly closer. Worse, another trio of ships has appeared in the distance. Still too far away to detect the color of their sails, but I don't need shifter eyesight in order to understand that it's Morrigan and the other two ships sailing with her.

They're gaining as well.

"Better and better." Nox tilts their head back, closes their eyes, and seems to go to somewhere deep within themselves. It only lasts for a handful of seconds, and then they snap to attention. "I don't see a way out of this." They shake their head, expression almost wondering. "This might be the end for us."

Siobhan grips their shoulder and leans close. "Don't you dare. There's always a way out." She gives them a little shake. "We could turn west and try to shake them as soon as we exit the edges of the storm."

"Won't work. The wind will try to drive us south again, right into their tender embrace." Nox shakes their head even harder.

"Okay, that was enough melancholy. You're right. There's a way. We just need to figure out what it is."

Nox turns a slow circle, eyes narrowing. "One of the shifting islands should have shown up within the last week. It's maybe half a day's sail from here. Northwest, I think. It will only be there for another week, but if we make port there, we can ride out the worst of the storm."

Siobhan frowns. "That would be a great idea if we didn't have six ships wanting to blow us into a thousand pieces. Making port will just trap us."

"Then it's time for a bit of trickery." Nox grins. "I'm sure we can pull something out."

But Siobhan doesn't look convinced. "We're not the only ones who are aware of that island. Morrigan will be as well, and no doubt at least a couple people on the other crews. Even if we could somehow shake their line of sight, that's exactly where they'll assume we went. It might take them a little longer to get there, but they'll still come. And there will still be the storm to reckon with."

As they argue semantics, a reckless plan forms in my mind. No one's going to be a fan of this, but it might be the solution to our problems. I clear my throat, but they ignore me, too intent on finding a solution. So I go to them and lean close so they can hear me. "What if they only *think* we go to that island?"

"What do you mean, Bastian? That's the only place we can go." Siobhan motions vaguely in the direction they'd been speaking of. "If we head anywhere else, all it will take is a sharp eye at lookout to find us."

"Not if they're already following us."

The confusion on Siobhan's face clears, replaced by worry. "You've never gone that far before, or created a glamour that large. There's no telling if it will work. Even beyond that, you are still recovering. You'll send yourself straight into magical burnout."

Nox's brows pull together. "Correct me if I'm wrong, but you seem to be suggesting that Bastian can create a glamour from absolutely nothing. But that's impossible. You can only alter the perception of what already exists."

"There's a reason glamour was outlawed," I manage past the knot twisting in my throat. When I knew Nox—when I loved Nox—I was still young enough to fear my heritage. I suppose I still am. But I've learned a lot since then. Away from Lyari, I've had the opportunity to test myself and develop my skills in a way I never would've been allowed to by my family. I don't know if I can do what I'm promising, but I can damn well try. The alternative is too terrible to contemplate.

Nox is no fool, though. They watch me closely. "The concerns Siobhan raises are legitimate."

"Yes." There's no point in arguing. What I'm suggesting is incredibly dangerous. For me. And for everyone else if I fail. "But we don't have another choice, at least not a good one."

Siobhan starts to argue, but Nox holds up their hand. "Even if you created a duplicate of the *Audacity* and sent it in a different direction, they would still see two ships. They're not foolish enough to throw all of their power into following one and letting the other sail off unmolested. Unless . . ."

"You can't seriously be considering letting him do this. It will kill him."

Nox smiles bitterly. "If he doesn't do this, we all die." They turn to me and, for the first time in far too long, there's actual respect lighting their gray eyes. "I need a little time to coordinate, but I think I can take care of the visibility issue. Go get something to eat and rest. I'll come find you in about an hour."

We watch them walk away. Siobhan turns to me and takes my shoulders. "Bastian, please."

I don't remind her that there was always a decent chance neither of us would survive our mission to bring a better world to Threshold. I don't tell her that this is a sacrifice worth making. She knows. It's a testament to her love for me, even with all the broken words between us, that she would rather save me and risk us all dying than allow me to risk myself. "I love you, too." I pull her into a tight hug. "But I have to do this."

CHAPTER 16

Nox

E VEN AS I GO THROUGH THE MOTIONS OF PUTTING TO-
gether a reckless plan that will facilitate the *Audacity* hiding
from view long enough for Bastian's glamour to draw our pursuers away, I wonder if it's even possible. Obviously I was aware
he could cast glamour, but apparently I was a fool for assuming
the only person he could cast it on was himself, or possibly use
it to influence the perceptions of another person interacting
with him. It never occurred to me that he could create something from nothing with enough detail to fool a large group of
people.

I'm still not entirely certain he can do it, but we don't have a
better choice, so I have to assume he will be successful. Otherwise, we're going to have a fight on our hands in a setting where
we can least afford it. The farther north we sail, the more violent the seas become. Lightning is now a regular occurrence,
the thunder coming so quickly that it's almost impossible to get

two words out between booms. Everyone who isn't strictly vital has been sent belowdecks. The pocket dimension that holds the crew's quarters will eliminate the worst of the potential seasickness, but if the ship goes down, the entire crew goes down with it.

The thought leaves me sick. In every other confrontation, I've been able to see half a dozen ways out. I've been aware that my power, or the power of my allies, is enough to ensure victory. Maybe not victory without losses, but victory nonetheless. I don't have that assurance currently.

In the hour it's taken me to gather the necessary crew members and go over the plan, the *Crimson Hag* and her two sister ships have closed the distance enough that I can pick out some of the individual members of their crew. Not close enough to see their expressions or faces, but I'm familiar enough with them that I can tell that that bastard Miles is at the helm, his green-scaled skin wet with rain.

I stop next to Bowen. If he were another person and I were a different captain, I might squeeze his shoulder and reassure him that his former crew will not take us. He doesn't want to hear that, though. Not from me. Likely not from anyone, excepting potentially Evelyn.

"You could always sink them," I offer.

He gives me the disapproving look I anticipated. "Because that worked so well when Siobhan attempted it. Even if I blew a hole in their hull, they obviously have the ability to patch it without going down. And if they didn't? You would have me condemn an entire crew for their captain's poor decisions?"

An entire crew who voted Bowen out a handful of months

ago. It's clear that as much as he no longer wishes to sail beneath crimson sails, that vote of no confidence still irks him. His crew was his family, and they left him on a beach and sailed away, all for the crime of not wanting to murder a mother dragon and her hatchling.

"No," I finally say. "The entire reason we're doing everything that we're doing is because a good portion of the Cŵn Annwn crews are filled with people who wouldn't have consented to participate if they had another option. I'm not above sinking them if it means saving us, but our current plan should negate that necessity."

He takes a breath and nods slowly. "Do you think it'll work?"

I have no fucking idea, but I'm the captain, and the captain must always be in control, so I smile and wink at him. "Of course it'll work. They have no reason to expect what we're about to attempt. If I didn't know Bastian could do this, then I doubt anyone else does. They will follow his glamour." I just hope he can hold it long enough for us to escape.

I've brought every air-user on the crew to the deck and stationed them in small groups where it will be most effective for them to direct their wind. It's impossible to ignore how exhausted they all look, even with the short shifts I've had them on. We can't keep up this pace for more than a couple more days without someone suffering magical burnout. This will be our one chance to make a clean getaway . . . at least until we encounter the next crimson-sailed ship. I'm already exhausted just thinking about it.

Evelyn approaches, her blond hair plastered to her face. It doesn't make her less pretty, of course. Especially because she looks like she's having the time of her life, a wide grin on her lips and her green eyes twinkling with mischief. "I have the amplifying circle in place. All it needs is a drop of your blood to activate. You'll have to move quickly, though, because the rain will wash the circle away even with my preparations." At that she frowns a little. "The water repellent in the spell should have protected it, but I had to put up a secondary shield in order to even finish it."

"Magical storm, magical side effects." I shrug. "I'll move quickly, though. If I'm not able to get the fog up before the circle dissolves, then we have bigger problems than the Cŵn Annwn."

"I'll hold the shield until you're ready."

"Thank you." As nauseating as it occasionally is to be in the presence of Bowen and Evelyn and their sickly sweet love for each other, they are both so fucking useful. The witch has more spells than I reckoned, and they're all adaptable to whatever situation we're in. "If you're ready, Bowen, I'll get Bastian."

The big man gives a tight nod. "I'm ready." Without another word, he strides across the deck and up the stairs to the upper deck, Evelyn a half pace behind him. The upper deck is where she put the amplifying circle, the better for me to be able to see what I'm attempting to obscure.

I take a few moments to touch base with each group of airusers. They're all grimly determined, shoving their fear down deep. We've been in places of crisis before, and while this is particularly devastating, fear will get you killed out here on the sea. Hope is everything, and determination even more so. They won't falter.

Next, I head to my cabin to gather up Bastian. He's been waiting there with Siobhan, and he damn well had better be resting. I step through the door but don't move farther in, aware of how my wet clothing drips onto the wood. Bastian sits in the center of the open space, his legs crossed and his hands resting loosely on his knees. Most of the people that I encounter in Threshold have magic inherent in their blood and family histories. Evelyn is one of the few ritual casters who combines natural skill with ritual. I'm not sure if Bastian's meditation will help the magic or is meant to settle his nerves, but now isn't the time to ask. "We're ready."

Siobhan looks like she's still trying to come up with a different solution to this problem. I don't know if it's worry for him or simply the feeling of being helpless that she's so unfamiliar with, but it's clear she's uncomfortable with the whole situation. She puts a good face on it, though. "Where do you want me?"

A testament of her trust—and the potentially fatal outcome of this race against time—that she's content to let me lead for now. I manage a smile for her, even if I can't come up with reassuring words. "You're with me on the upper deck."

There's not really anything for her to do, but I am achingly aware that ordering her to stay in a cabin is the equivalent of tormenting her. I would feel the same way in her position. She's more than capable of staying safe on deck despite the storm.

Bastian rises easily to his feet and stretches his arms overhead. It takes me an extra second to register the fact that he's wearing my clothes again. A thrum of pure pleasure, inconvenient and horribly timed, courses through me. Damn it, I hate that I still want him. I hate that I still care about him. There's a small part of me that's almost grateful for the life-and-death situation we find ourselves in, because it's an excellent distraction from my treacherous heart. He was careless with me, and yet there's a part of me that wants to wipe away all of our history and start again.

I never considered myself a romantic fool, but these two seem to bring it out in me.

We step onto the deck and are immediately slapped in the face with intense rain. I curse and hold my hand to shield my eyes. "Damn storm."

"It will work in our favor," Bastian calls over the howling wind. "The more wind and rain, the easier to obscure the details."

He's got a point. I squint into the darkness. "I'll create fog to further obscure their vision, and Bowen will orchestrate a large wave to hide us from view temporarily. That's your opportunity to create the glamour of a second *Audacity*. Send it north and west, cheating west a little, and hopefully they'll follow." If they don't, we're going to have a fight on our hands.

"Okay." He rolls his shoulders and then cracks his neck. "I can only create glamour on line of sight, so I'll need to be in the crow's nest."

One of the most dangerous places on this ship right now, with lightning still flashing far too regularly for my peace of mind. That it hasn't hit us yet is more a testament to the storm playing with its prey than to anything else. "I don't know if that's a good idea."

His expression goes stony and stubborn; nothing like the charming playboy I once grew to love. "Then we might as well prepare for a fight, because all this effort will be for nothing.

You don't even like me, Nox. What do you care if I die while saving your crew?"

Siobhan opens her mouth, but I find myself speaking before she has a chance to. "Don't be a stubborn bloody fool. Of course I don't want you dead." I point at Siobhan. "Change of plans. You go with him. You heal fast enough that you can survive a lightning strike. If it's coming, you take it over Bastian." I don't like giving the order, would take that responsibility if I could, but not even I can heal as quickly and thoroughly as Siobhan can.

Bastian flinches. "What? No! I don't want anyone else to be—"

But she's already nodding. "Consider it done." She takes Bastian's shoulder and leads him toward the netting stretching up to the crow's nest. It's not the most challenging climb under the best circumstances, but these are hardly that. I'm not worried about him falling; even if his strength fails, Siobhan's won't. She'll keep him safe.

I don't even bother to pretend I only want him safe in order to save my crew. How my mighty pride has fallen in just a few short days. It would bother me more if we hadn't spent most of that time on the brink of death. I watch them climb for a beat and then hurry to the upper deck. Bowen stands tall next to the shielded circle, Evelyn at his side. She's already starting to demonstrate signs of strain from holding the shield over the amplification circle. This magical rain is a real bitch and a half.

I take a breath and do a quick internal dive into my magical stores. They're still not fully replenished. Normally after experiencing magical burnout, I spend a few days babying myself. Resting a lot, eating plenty of food, drinking lots of water. There hasn't been the opportunity for any of that. Oh, I ate, shoving food into my mouth between hurried meetings with my crew. And I managed to catch a few hours of sleep earlier, but my stores are not as full as I'd like them to be.

I nod at Evelyn. "Stick to the plan even if I go down."

She looks like she's about to argue, but I step into the amplification circle and then it's too late. It's time.

CHAPTER 17

Siobhan

As bad as the storm was on deck of the *Audacity*, up in the crow's nest it feels ten thousand times worse. I keep a fistful of Bastian's tunic in my grip as I haul him over the edge and we hunker down in the relative shelter. I hadn't thought Nox was being dramatic when they said we very well might be struck by lightning, but up here, it's certainly believable.

I don't ask Bastian again if he can do this. We've come too far for that question. Instead, I ask, "What do you need from me?"

His light brown skin has gone a little green, but his expression is determined. "I need you to hold me steady so I can put my full concentration behind the glamour. I won't be able to react in time if the ship tilts."

"I won't let you fall." After some consideration, I grab a length of rope left from whoever was up here last and wind it through the rough slats in the wood. I loop one arm through the secured rope and one around Bastian's waist, pulling his back to my chest. We've stood like this a thousand times, but that was before. Before the fight, before the rescue, before everything changed. I'm achingly aware of everywhere we touch and all the words we threw into the space between us, hurt and angry. We might very well die tonight, and there's so much left unsaid.

"Siobhan . . ." I can barely hear Bastian over the shriek of the wind and rain, but his tone says his thoughts have mirrored mine.

"I'm sorry. I've said it before, but I truly mean it. You were right. You've been right this whole time. I've let my fear get in the way of what needs to be done. I'm sorry I held the entire rebellion back, and I'm sorry that I punished you when you rightfully called me out on it."

He half turns so that he can see my face. Amusement lights his dark eyes despite our circumstances. "Is this a deathbed confession? Are you trying to ensure there's nothing left unsaid between us since we're probably going to die?"

His humor centers me the way nothing else could. I drag in a breath, some of the weight pressing down on me disappearing, and give him a little squeeze. "We're not going to die. I won't let you fall, and Nox will ensure the ship remains safe. Between the two of us, that's as close to a guarantee of survival as you can get in these circumstances."

"I suppose it is." Slowly, inch by inch, he relaxes back against me. It feels so good that it's almost enough to distract me from things happening below us. Bastian won't form the glamour until we're hidden from view, and Nox and Bowen seem intent on making that happen. Even as I watch, an uncanny fog appears above the water, perfectly resistant to the rain, and spreads like wildfire. Within seconds, it covers nearly a mile's distance on either side of the ship and rises until I can no longer see the sea in our wake.

A sliver of fear goes through me. "They're spending too much magic."

Instead of arguing, Bastian tenses. "Has Nox used an amplification circle before? Surely they know that it drains your magic faster than normal."

Since I didn't fucking know that, I highly doubt Nox does. We're not witches or sorcerers to rely on ritual to accomplish our aims. Elemental magic is as instinctive as my shifting forms. The worry inside me turns to something that's almost like terror. "They'll die."

Bastian moves before I can, slithering out of my grip and giving me a light push. "Go. I can handle this. Get them out of that fucking circle."

Even though I should argue, I don't. His fear amplifies mine. "If you fall, I will find whatever underworld you go to and drag you back. Do you understand me?"

He hooks the back of my neck and tows me down for a quick kiss. "I wouldn't have it any other way. Now go!"

I go. But only after ensuring he's looped his arm through the rope. It's not as strong as I am, and I should stay to ensure he's okay, but the fog is still increasing, and even through the storm, I can see how waxy Nox's complexion is. That little fool is drawing too much. Again. I don't trust their crew to know their captain's limits. Nox is too damn good at ignoring best practices and concern, at playing at being untouchable. Their crew won't anticipate how close they are to the kind of burnout that results in death . . . but I will.

I make it halfway down the rigging before impatience takes hold of me and I jump the rest of the way. It's a fall that would break a human's bones, but I land easily and roll forward to eat up my momentum. And then I'm sprinting up the stairs and shoving my way through the thick magic coursing through the amplification circle. Evelyn tries to get in my way, but I dodge around her. "Get the wave going. Now!"

Bowen frowns but obeys. Concentration and tension roll through him, and the ship dips as the water rushes out from underneath us and rises in a massive wave from our wake. Higher and higher until surely it must be taller than Bastian's position in the crow's nest. In the back of my mind, I wonder why we don't just try to drown our pursuers and be done with all this, but there will be space for questions after we survive this.

Nox is only going to survive this if I pull them out of this godsdamned circle. I loop them around the waist, my fear a live thing inside me when they don't resist. Nox has been fighting since the moment they first drew breath. I would stake my life on it. And yet they're almost perfectly limp as I sweep them into my arms and jump out of the amplification circle. The moment we leave it—or, more accurately, the moment Nox's magic stops sustaining it—the circle dissolves, the rain plastering the chalk in foamy, milky rivulets over the deck.

Nox's head lolls on their shoulders, and they blink up at me. "I wasn't finished."

"You almost killed yourself, you bloody fool."

They blink again, slower this time. "You're being very dramatic right now."

"After we survive this, I'm going to tie you to your damned bed until you get some rest and refill your reserves properly."

"Kinky." But the word has none of their customary charm and flirtation. Instead, it's slurred and almost undefinable. At this point, they're lucky I don't kill them myself.

I turn, not entirely certain of my plan, but I stop short when I see a perfect replica of the *Audacity* rise out of the fog next to us. And I do mean perfect. Bastian has re-created the crewmen rushing about on deck. I see my doppelgänger arguing with Nox's twin. He's even replicated the mended tear in the mainsail.

I knew Bastian was powerful. I knew glamour was powerful. I've seen him use it to influence people, to protect those who cannot protect themselves, but I've never seen him use it like *this*. And he doesn't even have an amplification circle in play. "Holy shit."

Nox cracks their eyes open and curses softly under their breath. "At least he accurately portrayed how sexy I am."

"Of course he did. He still loves you," I say absently, my mind awash with the impossibility of this display of power. As Bowen's wave carries us skimming faster and faster forward, the glamoured version of our ship angles northwest while we cut to the east. I'm having a hard time gauging if the phantom ship is moving at accurate speeds or not, but with magic in play, who's to say what's accurate and what isn't? The storm and fog and waves further obscure the details. Surely this will work. It *has* to work.

Nox shivers in my arms. "Report! Someone give me a fucking report!"

Poet sprints up. She's smarter than the rest of us, because she's done away with her shirt entirely, wearing only a breast band and pants. The rain clings to her light brown skin and plasters her pants to her muscled thighs. "We'll know soon enough if they're following the glamour. We just have to put some more distance between us to ensure they take the bait."

"Put me back in the amplification circle."

"Absolutely fucking not," I snap. "Even if the circle still existed—which it doesn't—there's no way I'm letting you pull a stunt like that. You're already half dead—go back in and you'll be full dead."

Nox struggles, and it's a testament to their weakness that they have no chance of breaking free. I don't even have to tighten my hold. "Better me than the entire crew and ship. Put me back in."

"Negative, Captain." Poet motions frantically, and two crew members that I recognize but don't know the names of rush forward. "Siobhan is right. The amplification circle is gone, but we can take what you've done and continue it."

"It's too much. They'll harm themselves from trying."

Poet and I exchange a look of perfect understanding. There's absolutely no chance I am letting Nox back in that circle, even if the circle still existed. The fact that it doesn't should be comforting, but this is Nox we're talking about. They are so incredibly stubborn that they might go so far as to demand Evelyn create another one. I'm not going to give them a chance.

Poet turns and rushes toward the upper deck, the pair of crew members with her. Within a few minutes, the fog thickens around us again, so deep that I can't see anything more than a foot away from the edge of the ship. It strikes me that we might be ruining Bastian's chances to continue his glamour, but when I look up, I realize that the fog doesn't quite reach the top of the crow's nest.

I don't know what to do. As the leader of the rebellion, I've always had an answer. It's worrisome that the moment we have a proper confrontation and a true threat, I fall apart. But Nox doesn't. Bastian doesn't. Even the damn crew keeps it together better than I can. I've never felt more like an impostor than I do in this moment, standing in the midst of frenzied action while everyone else does what's necessary to keep us alive.

"Oh, get that look off your face. You can be a hero next time." Nox pats my cheek gently, and then their hand lingers there. "And don't think for a second I missed that horrific lie about Bastian still loving me."

I glance down at them, fully aware they're creating a distraction. I'm grateful for it, though. "I only speak the truth."

"Another lie, Siobhan." They smile a little, but their gray eyes are somber and serious. "We're all sure to die before this is over. The only question is whether we survive long enough to bring lasting change . . . or if we go down as a footnote in Threshold's history as fools with stars in their eyes, wishing for a better world."

"We've already created change. Bastian was correct. It's not enough. We need to take more direct steps, but it doesn't change the fact we've done so much good over the years. We've saved so many lives, communities, and given people a cause to believe in."

Nox's eyes flutter closed. This time they don't open again. They go limp in my arms, only their steady breathing reassuring me that they will be okay. The fact that they had the presence of mind to distract me even while fighting for consciousness humbles me on a level I'm not prepared to deal with.

Maybe I truly am an impostor, powerful only through an

accident of birth. Yes, my family trained me in everything from leadership to commerce to community. Yes, I've done good work, but there are so many better leaders among the rebellion. Bastian and Nox primary among them.

Why the fuck do they even need me?

CHAPTER 18

Bastian

I DON'T HAVE CAUSE TO STRETCH MYSELF MAGICALLY ALL that often. Small glamours are easy enough to pull off, but anything large runs the risk of exposure. My parents trained me to control my magic to prevent it from accidentally slipping free, but even since joining the rebellion, there hasn't been much opportunity to see what I'm truly capable of.

The risk was too high with the possibility of endangering Siobhan and the rest of the rebellion. A valid fear, because all it took was one mental shield that prevented me from using my magic and it all ended.

I'm pathetically grateful Siobhan wasn't swept up alongside me when I was taken captive. She would consider it the preferable option, certain that she would be able to fight her way free, but it's more likely that they would have taken us both, and gods forbid the Cŵn Annwn realize exactly what a treasure they held in their hand. I may be noble by birth, but I'm not delusional about my role within the rebellion. I play support. End of story.

Even now, as I fight to maintain the image of the phantom *Audacity*, sailing so far away that I can barely make it out, I'm aware that I'm replaceable. I have been since the moment I was born, first to my family and then to the rebellion. It's strange something that stung so sharply with one situation is almost comforting in the other. I *chose* to follow Siobhan. That's the difference.

The duplicate *Audacity* is far in the distance now, reaching the edge of my range. I grit my teeth and pour more magic into the glamour. I can see the ships following it, phantom shapes in the fog. "Just a little longer . . ."

A soft breeze, warm and deeply unlike the wind lashing at my face and hair, caresses the shell of my ear. "Bastian, you can release the glamour now."

"Okay." I let it go with a whoosh that slams into me and has my knees knocking together. Every muscle feels strangely liquid, my bones brittle, my head swimming in a way that has nothing to do with the violent rocking of the ship. I cling to the edge of the crow's nest, determined to keep my feet. If I go down now, I'm not sure I'll be able to get back up again. Siobhan has enough to worry about taking care of Nox without adding taking care of me to the equation.

I glance down at the deck, my gaze instantly drawn to the woman in question. She stands tall and strong, cradling Nox in her arms. Nox looks so damn small, and the care Siobhan takes with them, holding them close even as she speaks with Poet, makes my chest ache. I've held Nox like that, too, what feels like a lifetime ago.

I'm a greedy, unforgivable bastard. No matter how much I love Siobhan, I cannot fully exorcize my love for Nox. Even going without seeing them for fourteen years, that emotion never went away. I've heard all the stories of their exploits, how they worked their way up through Hedd's crew until they became quartermaster, about everything they've done since becoming captain. They were already impressive when we were young and foolish and filled with so many dreams that the world was eager to crush. Now they're on another level entirely.

An invisible massive hand wraps itself around my waist. Before I realize what's happening, I'm lifted neatly out of the crow's nest and brought down to the deck next to Siobhan. The moment I touch down, my knees truly do give out, and I collapse at her feet. I catch sight of a haggard-looking Bowen on the upper deck. He nods to me and then allows Evelyn to guide him down the stairs to the hatch where the crew's quarters lay.

Our sails are filled with so much air that the masts' creaks can be heard even over the wailing of the wind. It sounds like the screams of lost souls, if I believed that sort of thing. I don't know that I do. Death is one giant unknown, and while various islands in Threshold have different cultural and religious beliefs, I've always found the mystery to be more attractive than answers. I rub my hand over my face. "How is Nox?"

"Unconscious, but they were running their mouth before they passed out, so I suspect they'll be fine." Siobhan shifts Nox into a singular muscular arm and holds out a hand to pull me to my feet. She puts a little too much strength behind it and I actually elevate several inches before landing hard on the deck again. If she hadn't kept hold of me, I would be right back where I started. She winces. "Sorry. I'm a little distracted, too."

"Understandable." Things were so much easier when we thought we might die before the end of the day. No need to have tough conversations in those circumstances. The danger hasn't passed entirely, but it's abated enough that we'll probably live to see another day. A pair of crew members scramble up the rigging to the crow's nest; they'll keep watch for the Cŵn Annwn.

We've done all we can do.

Poet approaches, looking just as harried as she always seems to be. Her frustration is apparent in every word she speaks. "Take the captain to their cabin. Both of you stay there with them and ensure they get their rest and manage some food when they wake up. Keep off the deck in the meantime. You look like you're about to pass out, and I don't have time to worry about one of my people tripping over you."

Then she's off, shouting instructions to the closest group of air-users. Siobhan and I exchange a look, and I can't help a brittle laugh. "It's kind of nice being treated frankly."

"Poet certainly has a way about her." Siobhan turns, seeming reluctant to release me, and starts toward Nox's cabin.

Now's the time to retreat to my bunk. No matter what we said, there's a lot of mess left between us. Caretaking for Nox may create a bit of a bridge, but there's still so much left unsaid . . . and things said that can't be taken back. I called her a coward. The shame that brings me now cannot be overstated. Siobhan is well within her rights to toss me right out of her life.

We're doing the thing. We're going to fight the Cŵn Annwn

and the Council and everyone who would see us fail. I know what Siobhan thinks will happen as a result—that every single member of the rebellion will die—and maybe I'm naive, but I can't help the hope that blossoms in my chest. By all rights, the Cŵn Annwn should have found us out years ago. We've been operating in the shadows for a very long time, and they never noticed.

If we can succeed in that, who's to say we can't succeed in this as well? Especially if our hunch about the horn pans out.

"Bastian. Are you coming?"

My body makes the decision for me, trotting along after Siobhan. Inside Nox's cabin, the sound of the storm abates so abruptly that I have to stop and adjust to the heavy silence. It's strange to look out the windows and see the rain, wind, and waves and yet feel so separate from it. Lightning spears through the sky more rarely, but that's the only indicator I have that we may be moving away from the storm. I glance over to find Siobhan pulling Nox's tunic over their head, and I immediately spin back around to present my back.

"Bastian." She sounds so exasperated that I have to fight not to wilt. "They can't stay in their wet clothing."

"I understand that." But I don't turn around. I haven't seen Nox without the shield of cloth since the last night we spent together, and I don't think they'd thank me for witnessing their vulnerability when they're not conscious to decide if I should be in the room or not. Just because I've seen them naked before doesn't mean that permission survived our breakup.

There's still the faint rustling of cloth for several more moments before Siobhan finally says, "It's safe to look now. I have them under the covers."

I turn around reluctantly to find that she's done exactly that, carefully tucking the sheets high over Nox's chest. Which is right around the moment when I realize both Siobhan and I are dripping water all over the floor. "We're going to have to clean up all this mess."

"Without a doubt. Do you want the first shower or should I?"

"Lady's choice."

Siobhan rolls her eyes, but some of the tension that's been riding so intensely in her shoulders has disappeared. "In that case, I don't want to be wet and cold a moment longer than I have to. I'll be quick."

I pause long enough to remove my boots and jacket and pull my shirt over my head. That leaves me in my pants only, which is still decidedly miserable, but at least I'm a little bit warmer. If I had Nox's fire magic, theoretically I could dry all of our clothing in moments, but in reality I'd probably just burn the clothing off by accident. From what I've heard, controlling glamour is so much easier than working with the elements. I'm simply tricking the minds of anyone who witnesses my magic into believing that something's there that isn't. In a one-on-one situation, I can even fool their senses, but it's still a trick confined to their brain. Not reality.

The elements, though? They exist in a space outside of magic. Elemental users can coax or bully or persuade bits of the larger whole to obey their will, but it's not without cost. Nox has proven that twice already in a handful of days. I'm exhausted and worn out and won't be able to practice any magic until my inner well refills, but I'm nowhere near the level of burnout that Nox seems to be experiencing.

Worry worms through me. Even if magical burnout doesn't

kill the affected person, it's entirely likely that if Nox does it enough times, they'll lose access to the deeper parts of the well of their magic—if not *all* of their magic. The fact that they continue to risk it?

The captain takes care of everyone, but who takes care of the captain? Nox finally has the community they've been seeking since they were a child, but they still seem determined to hold themselves back, to shoulder all the burden so their people don't have to.

Even as I tell myself they wouldn't want my proximity, I can't help drifting closer to the bed where they lay. There are shadows under their eyes and lines bracketing their mouth, even in sleep. "You push yourself too hard. You always have."

"And you don't push yourself hard enough . . . except that doesn't seem to be true anymore, does it?" Their eyes flutter open but they don't otherwise move their body, pinning me in place with those pale gray orbs. "We're clear?"

"At least for now. With the storm and the fog and the wave, it will take them some time to figure out they're no longer chasing us, but a ghost. The glamour's gone, but the elements will work in our favor."

"Good." They shift and frown. "I'm naked."

There's no excuse for the bolt of heat that goes through me at their frank words. I have to actually turn away to hide the physical evidence of my desire—desire they didn't ask for and wouldn't welcome. I clear my throat. "Siobhan's work. I didn't look. I know that would have been crossing a line. No matter what else you believe of me, please believe that I don't want to hurt you. I never did."

"I know." Nox sighs, sounding more tired than I've ever heard them. "We really were nothing more than children, playing pretend at a future that we could barely conceptualize. It's easy to feel big things at that age, to be sure that the world will end because of a broken heart."

I have no right to respond to that. Something I am aware of even as I open my mouth to speak. "Just because we were young doesn't mean those emotions were false. I loved you with everything I had. My fear of my family cutting me off was just greater. I'll never stop apologizing for that."

They give a faint chuckle. "Bastian, please. You just saved the lives of myself and my crew with magic that defies comprehension. I don't think there's anything left to apologize for."

As tempting as it is to leave it at that, I can't. It wouldn't be right. They're trying to let me off the hook, but I don't deserve it. "That is not the same, and you know it. I may have learned a lot in the intervening years, may have grown up as much as the rest of us seemed to, but I didn't save your crew because I feel bad for what happened with us. I did it because it's the right thing to do. It was the only way any of us had a chance of surviving."

"I know." They smile sadly. "But the fact that you've put up with my . . . messy emotions? That speaks volumes. Maybe I was too quick to cut you out of any future I might have."

They make such massive jumps that I have a difficult time following them. "Are you saying . . ."

"They're saying they still want you, Bastian." Siobhan appears in the doorway to the bathroom wearing nothing but a long shirt that had to have come from a different closet than

Nox's. The only person I can imagine it fitting is Bowen, and I don't like the thread of jealousy that spears me in response to that thought. It's absolutely illogical in every way, shape, and form.

Nox gives that raspy laugh again. "Correction, darling. I'm saying I want you both. It's complicated."

CHAPTER 19

Nox

I N THE DAYS THAT FOLLOW MY ILL-ADVISED PROCLAMA-
tion, both Bastian and Siobhan move carefully around me as
if attempting to cage a wild animal. They're not wrong to do so.
I still don't know how to feel, how to handle my pride battling
with my desire. I want to blame my reckless words on being
woozy from overusing magic again. The truth is significantly
less convenient.

I *do* still care about Bastian. My friendship with Siobhan has
always had the potential to deepen. And that scares the shit out
of me. I know the cost of loving someone whose future isn't
their own; for better or worse, Bastian ensured I learned that
lesson the hard way. He may have shucked some of the hold his
family had on him, but he replaced it with the rebellion. Siobhan is the damned leader of the rebellion. I will never come
first for either of them, no matter the circumstances.

Maybe I could live with knowing that, could find a way to

navigate those treacherous waters now that we're all in our thirties instead of barely more than children.

But we don't have any kind of assurance of a future, let alone a future with the time to indulge in personal relationships. I could die. Worse, *they* could die. It would hurt me now to lose them. If I let them any closer?

It might destroy me.

The crew is more and more on edge with each day that passes as we journey toward Three Sisters. I don't have the words to reassure them. Every moment that we sail north and east and north again, we're all on high alert for crimson sails on the horizon, every person working their ass off to keep us afloat in the storm. Bastian's glamour faded away when his concentration did, but the storm would have helped confuse things. With any luck, Morrigan and the others are still out there, sure that their prey is just out of sight. But I know better than to wager our success on luck alone.

The Three Sisters are a trio of islands at the very end of the north–south trade route. I never like coming here. It reminds me far too much of Lyari. Only Mairi on Second Sister is a true urban sprawl. Third Sister is the smallest of the trio, and only a few hardy souls live out there on the windswept rocks. First Sister, on the other hand, desperately wants to be something it's not. Its capital city, Kanghri, seems like it's filled with all the undesirables from its sister city, Mairi. The people of Kanghri are forced to crouch on one side of the narrow straight and watch the glittering, glowing city that they'll never be welcomed into. It sets the stage for resentment and hatred, which means it's only a matter of time before the Three Sisters go to war with themselves.

If I had any choice, I never would have come here. The trade route is heavily patrolled by the Cŵn Annwn. The only reason I can figure out that we haven't seen any since our desperate flight from the storm is because we came in at an angled approach that didn't bring us past any ports. But that will change. Sailing into the bay is a huge risk, far too much for me to agree to.

Eyal stands next to me as always, his expression a perpetual frown these days. "What angle of approach do you want to take?"

"We can't risk using any of the official ports." I recognize the stubborn look on his face, but cling to my patience with both hands. "It's the only way, Eyal. We'll anchor the ship just offshore of First Sister, and two small teams will take a pair of boats in—one to find Dia and one to resupply. I know the crew needs a break and could use some time ashore, but it's not safe for us to disperse. We need to be able to run at a moment's notice."

If I could have risked it, I would have turned south the moment we were clear of pursuit, but I left the old woman in Kanghri, so that's where we need to look for her. The more time we spend running, the greater the opportunity the Cŵn Annwn have to create a net to trap us. If the horn truly is the way to end this war before it properly starts, then we can't waste any time doing exactly that.

"Yes, I'm aware." Eyal waves my explanation away. "The part of the plan I'm getting stuck on is where we anchor in a shallow surf with violent currents. We'll either be washed ashore or thrown upon the reef. Neither option does much for our chances of survival."

I haven't had what the spoiled nobles in the capital city

would call an easy life. I've fought from the moment I first drew breath, and never more so than once I realized how unfair this world really is. With all that said, the last few days have been some of the most exhausting I've experienced. It's so challenging to pull forth a charming smile and inject cheer into my weary tone. "Come now, Eyal. Maybe that would be true of other ships, but this is the *Audacity*, with you as the navigator and Poet as quartermaster. I have no doubt that you will make easy work of it."

He's used to my shenanigans, so he's not convinced. I didn't truly expect him to be. He props his hands on his hips and gives me a long look. "Coming in through Third Sister would be safer. Those beaches are significantly less dangerous, and the island is all but uninhabited."

"That's true, but Third Sister means we have to travel through the bulk of First Sister to get to Kanghri—which makes a quick getaway all but impossible." I shrug, tension riding high in my shoulders. "I don't like this, either. With any luck, we'll be in and out of Kanghri within a few hours, with the *Crimson Hag*'s old navigator in tow. I just need you to hold steady until then."

Eyal nods. "Be quick, then. Otherwise, you'll only have wreckage to return to."

"Dramatic to the bitter end, aren't we?" My smile fades away. "We'll see each other through this. I promise."

"Don't go making promises you can't have any hope of keeping." He narrows his eyes. "Who are you taking with your team?"

That's the question, isn't it? There's absolutely no chance of taking Siobhan and Bastian with me. Bastian was just picked up from Mairi a relatively short time ago, and there's enough cross-over between the two cities that it's too large a risk. The Cŵn Annwn have a habit of putting out notices to ensure that the civilian population does the dirty work of tracking down their targets. At least when those targets are of the humanoid variety.

Monsters are easy enough to find.

"I'm inclined to leave Lizzie here with you." It will do double duty of ensuring Maeve stays safe, which will please the vampire, and protecting the ship. Lizzie can hold off a small army on her own if she's not holding back—or at least a small army of people with limited magic. When it comes to Morrigan and the heavy hitters on her ship, even the vampire would only last ten minutes at the very most. But ten minutes is a small eternity in a battle, which makes her invaluable. "Dia knows Bowen and Evelyn, so I'll likely take them with me and leave everyone else. We'll move faster with just three."

For a moment, it seems like Eyal might continue arguing with me, but he finally nods. "Those two will keep you safe and watch your back. We'll do our best to ensure you have a ship to return to." He eyes the islands in the distance. "Best to circle around Third Sister. No reason to give the bloated rich in Mairi even a glimpse of us if the north is our goal."

"Sounds like a plan." I clasp him on the shoulder and then move along. Poet and I have a nearly identical conversation, but she comes around the same way that Eyal did, and sets her sights on putting together the second team to get supplies. There's a reason they're my closest confidants on the *Audacity*. Poet is the voice of the crew themselves, and while occasionally we butt heads, we're in agreement that the goal is keeping everyone safe.

It's a testament to Bastian's exhaustion that I don't see either him or Siobhan in the hours it takes us to circle widely around the islands. A flicker of guilt inside me says that I should go explain the plan to them before leaving, but after that last conversation, I'll admit that cowardice is winning. There are too many messy emotions inside me, and they run the risk of distracting me when I need my focus the most.

Or that's what I tell myself. The truth is significantly uglier. Bastian didn't have much to say after my proclamation, and Siobhan hustled out of the room rather quickly. I'm afraid that, while they both independently showed interest, their intentions never went beyond *interest* and into action. Someday, when this is all over, they'll resume their relationship, I'll retreat back to the safe embrace of my crew, and we'll never see each other again. Better to start that retreat now, before my heart becomes any more entangled.

The crew is looking particularly haggard as we find a spot just past the wave break on the north side of First Sister to throw down anchor. It's several hundred yards to shore, and even with my magic, it's going to be a rough ride, but at least the *Audacity* will get to rest for a short while.

I glance at Poet as the pair of boats are lowered toward the surface of the water. "If there's trouble, cut anchor and go. Don't try to come for us, and certainly don't wait. We'll catch up with you when we can."

Poet's lips thin, but she finally nods. No one likes giving that order, but it's the smart one to follow. It makes no sense for them to die trying to save us when we are more than capable of stealing a sloop and following. Assuming we're alive to do it.

Bowen and Evelyn appear, both their cheeks rosy enough

that I suspect they were having one last hurrah before heading into even more direct danger. I don't tease them. I'm too busy weighing exactly how empty my magical reserves are. I've recovered from the fog, more or less, but when I get this low, my well refills slower than it usually does. Normally, I find that spending hours in the midst of the elements themselves, swimming or other things, helps, but there hasn't been time for that.

I prod at my magic, frowning. Is my well shallower than it was before? Surely not. I barely passed out after using the amplification circle. I wasn't even unconscious for an hour, let alone long enough to require Orchid's help. Even so, my skin prickles in warning. I'll have to be careful going forward—or at least attempt to be.

I turn to the four crew members doing the supply run. "Take the ship around the west side of the island, closer to the city. It's best that you aren't seen with me." They nod and climb down into their boat. My magic aches as I pull it forth and use the waves to send them rushing west. They'll have to start rowing before too long, but the boost is helpful all the same.

Then I turn to Evelyn and Bowen. "We'll only take Dia if she wants to come," I say quietly. "This isn't a kidnapping. We'll ask our questions, and that'll be the end of it."

"That's good, because I wouldn't allow you to kidnap her. That woman is like a mother to me, and if she's managed to avoid joining another crew, there's a reason for it."

"It will be nice to see her again." Evelyn's pretty face goes a little wistful. "She reminds me of my grandmother."

The waves are too choppy to safely exit the ship for the boat, so Bowen lowers us one by one into the waiting boat and then follows us down. We have enough magic between the three of us that we'd manage just fine, but this is simpler.

As soon as we're settled, I send us moving forward. My magic ensures we have no need for oars. "The reef makes the route to shore damn near impassable in places, but we should be okay."

"As long as we aren't foolish," Bowen says mildly. He's got a fistful of Evelyn's shirt, his hold actively keeping her from spilling into the sea as she leans over the edge of the boat to peer into the depths.

"I forgot how clear the water is here." Evelyn is nothing if not an opportunist when it comes to new experiences. She and Bowen spent some time on First Sister before coming aboard my ship and helping me rid the world of Hedd. They don't talk much about what happened here, but it seemed to change everything when it comes to Bowen's perception of the Cŵn Annwn. After leaving First Sister, he was firmly on the side of the rebellion.

"Careful there." I don't reach out and add my hand to Bowen's to keep her aboard. All my concentration is required to navigate the reef that seemed to rise up out of nowhere. The good news is that this small bay is dangerous enough that not even the most foolhardy local would attempt to swim or fish here. As a result, we have no witnesses to our journey.

Evelyn grins as if she wants to push us, but manages to sit back firmly in her seat once more. I can't quite tell if Bowen breathes a sigh of relief, but I surely do. She tilts her head back and closes her eyes, her blond hair ruffling in the wind. "You know, it would have been so much faster if Bowen just lifted the entire boat and brought us to shore."

"I'm aware of Bowen's power, which is why I'd like to keep it saved for a moment when we truly need it. There's no reason to exhaust him with this sort of thing." I shoot him a look. "And if we have to make a quick exit, we're going to *need* it."

CHAPTER 20

Siobhan

I STARE AT POET, SURE THAT I AM MISUNDERSTANDING what the fuck she's saying to me right now. "Nox . . . left?"

Unlike her wayward captain, Poet has the grace to look guilty. Her face flushes and she can't quite meet my gaze. "A bare hour ago."

I turn without entirely meaning to and stare hard at the coastline. There are plenty of nooks and crannies on most of the islands in Threshold, and I know the best places to approach if I don't want to be seen. That kind of secrecy isn't possible on the *Audacity*; it's too large. It makes sense for Nox to lay anchor out here and then ride in. What *doesn't* make sense is leaving me behind.

"Unacceptable."

Poet's mouth thins. "They took Bowen and Evelyn, and even if they hadn't, Nox can handle whatever Kanghri can throw at them."

I'm not convinced. My sister is on the hunt. No matter what experience Nox has with Morrigan, they still don't fully understand what she's capable of. They can't.

I glance over as Bastian walks up. His skin still appears waxy and the deep circles under his eyes haven't fully faded, but he's looking significantly better than he did even a few days ago. I quickly bring him up to speed.

Unsurprisingly, he's just as thrilled as I am by this new development. "They didn't even tell us that they were going to shore."

"I know." I once again study the shoreline. "They're running."

It's a testament to Bastian's long history with me that I don't have to elaborate for him to understand what I'm saying. "It's understandable that they'd be spooked. From what I've gathered from the people who have sailed with them the longest, Nox has had plenty of romantic entanglements over the years, but they've never had . . ." He shifts uncomfortably. "I hurt them badly, Siobhan."

I may understand Nox's reasoning, but they have flirted with magical burnout twice in the relatively short time since I came aboard. If they're fleeing an emotional entanglement with us, they're more likely to take dangerous risks. I shrug out of my jacket and pass it to him. "I'm going after them."

Bastian looks at my jacket as if it might bite him. "I'm going, too."

"Absolutely not."

"Neither of you can go." Poet clears her throat. "We can't spare another boat, and even if we could, you won't make it safely to shore."

"I can." After a short debate with myself, I remove my boots and tie them together with enough slack that they can loop around my shoulders. "I will."

"But—"

"And I won't need a boat."

"Siobhan." Bastian stops me with a hand on my shoulder. "If you mean to shift, then you need me. I can use my magic to keep you invisible, but only when you're within eyesight. It will be significantly less effort if I'm with you."

I want to shut him down, but he has a point. A gigantic hound being sighted will cause a panic and ensure that the Cŵn Anwnn show up even faster. I step closer to Bastian and lower my voice. "Can you do it safely? Don't lie to me."

"Yes." He answers with no hesitation. "It's a lot easier to hide something than it is to create a new image from nothing. I won't be a burden, Siobhan. I swear it."

"So be it." I can't help the fierce smile that plasters itself across my face. It's been so long since we've done something like this. Even though I have taken more and more risks in some ways, the end result is that I'm not needed directly as often as I used to be. Our network is vast and varied, and that's a blessing in every way. But there's a part of me that misses it. That misses this.

"Let's go." I walk to the railing and step up onto it. Some of the crew members are whispering among themselves, but no one tries to stop me as I dive deep beneath the waves. Seconds later, Bastian joins me, a rope looped around his chest.

"Here." He tosses the other end to me, and I waste no time slipping it around me. We've only done this a few times, and never in circumstances as dangerous as this, but I'm more than strong enough to see us through.

Without another word, I cut through the waves, towing him behind me. The currents are particularly nasty in this area, but I'm far stronger than any human and most monsters. I drag us beneath the surf to avoid the break. The reef is a bit trickier to navigate. It's home to small sharks, and although they are shy and tend to keep to themselves, they are fiercely territorial when breeding season is upon them. Thankfully, that's still months out from now. We're able to pass by without issue.

Even with all my strength, I'm shaking by the time I stumble up on the rocky beach and help Bastian to his feet. "You okay?"

"I'm good." He's as out of breath as I am, but there's a small smile pulling at his lips. "Just like old times, eh?"

"Yeah." I can't help returning his smile. It really is nice to be moving again. I give myself a rough shake. Walking to Kanghri in wet clothing is not ideal, but there's a safe house not too far from here.

I turn around and cast one last glance at the ship. It seems shockingly small in the distance. I can't help but search the relatively calm waters that stretch to the horizon, half-certain that the moment I turn my back, my sister will appear and lay waste to the innocent people aboard. But the horizon is empty. They're safe enough for now.

"Straight to Kanghri or stop at the safe house first to change?"

We're about an hour behind Nox and the others, which would be enough to ensure they'll reach the city before we do. That is doubly true if we stop at one of the safe houses on the island to change our clothes. Or at least it would be true if I stay in this form. "Safe house first."

I clamber over the rocks and out of sight of the ship, Bastian on my heels. He keeps quiet as I pause and slowly strip out of my clothing, knowing how hard this is for me. My hands are shaking. How strange and odd and silly. I've only shape-shifted fully a handful of times since fleeing Lyari all those years ago.

To do so now feels like the height of recklessness, even with Bastian's glamour hiding us, but there's no damned time. With an hour lead, Nox and the others will reach Kanghri before nightfall. I can get to the safe house and back in my second form well before then. This is logical and a good choice.

Fear still curls through my stomach as I close my eyes and exhale slowly. From what I understand, normal shifters have to summon their other selves. It's an effort, a fight, a bloody battle that leaves them shaking and weak for a few moments afterward while they become accustomed to their second form. It's not like that with me.

Instead, it's an unclenching. I allow a part of myself to relax that I normally keep twisted up tightly. Between one breath and the next, my center of gravity changes and I hit the ground on four paws. There's no pain, only a slight tingling that courses over my body as skin changes to fur and my eyes shift red and become capable of seeing a great distance and even better in the dark.

I am . . . home.

"Siobhan," Bastian breathes. "Gods, but I forget how stunning you are in this form." I lower myself so he can clamber up onto my back and wait until he's settled into place. His weight is barely noticeable. He strokes my back as the air around us wavers slightly. "We're covered. Go."

I take off running. This is what freedom feels like, and I've denied myself for so long. When I was young back on Lyari, I used to sneak out of the house and then out of the city and run through the forest for hours in the night. At least until my parents found out and punished me so severely that I never dared do it again. At the time, it felt unnecessarily cruel. Now, looking back, I recognize how terrified they were when they learned of my recklessness. If a single person had seen me, had recognized what my white fur and red eyes meant, had thought to report their strange sighting to the Council, it would have spelled ruin for all of us.

Not even the Cŵn Annwn can cry in this form, but emotion still wells in my throat as the ground flies beneath my paws. Sharp rocks and tangled undergrowth would have kept my human form occupied for some time, but I slide easily over and under and through, slowing down slightly to avoid tossing Bastian in the process. I'm moving so quickly that I almost feel more liquid than solid. I feel *elemental*.

I'm so caught up in the process of running that I almost miss the safe house entirely. Bastian has to smack my shoulder to gain my attention. I circle back along the pebbled beach and cut into the narrow crevice that leads back to the house built partially into the cliffs. If I remember correctly, this is the same safe house that Nox sent Bowen and Evelyn to after they were cast ashore. We have people in Kanghri who ensure that it stays stocked for anyone who may need it, and I'm not surprised in the least to find nondescript clothing in a variety of sizes.

While Bastian changes, I pack a small bag with pants, a shirt, and boots, and loop it around my neck. He comes back into the room, his hair still windswept and cheeks still flushed.

"There were a couple times back there that I thought you forgot I was on your back."

I clear my throat. "I sort of did."

He laughs a little. "It's good to see you like this, Siobhan." He moves closer and cups my face, urging me down until our breathing mingles. "Wild and reckless and *free*."

"It feels good," I whisper. I kiss him hard, desire punching me in the stomach. It would be so easy to . . . Except, no. We don't have the freedom of time. I exhale shakily. "I missed you, Bastian."

"I missed you, too." He tugs my hair until I move back. "We have to go."

"I know." I brush one last kiss to his lips and retreat. "Let's go get our wayward captain." This time, it's even easier to shift. As easy as breathing. I race along the beach and then cut inward toward the city. Even at this distance, I can smell it. All cities have a particularly rancid scent of human waste, garbage, and all the smells that come with a populace living in close quarters. Kanghri is no different, for all that it's a relatively small city: larger than a village, but perpetually striving to match the expanding pace of Mairi—and perpetually coming up short.

Night has only just fallen when I stop outside the city and change back to my human form so I can dress. Bastian stumbles over to sit on a rock while I do. "I'm out of shape. I haven't ridden since Lyari and . . ."

The thrill of the run still has me giddy. "You've ridden me plenty of times over the last year."

"Well, uh, I, yes." He clears his throat. "That's not what I meant and you know it."

"I do." I pull on boots and straighten to pull my hood up

over my head to conceal my features. "You know, it strikes me that part of the reason joy has shadowed my steps since leaving the *Audacity* is that I'm finally able to *move*. Even though we'll be returning to the ship shortly, even though my presence here will be helpful but not fully necessary, it still feels good to take action. I'm not built for sitting back and letting others make decisions and take risks."

"I know." He moves to stand next to me. "I feel the same way."

"Let's go." I don't bother trying to track Nox and the others. My nose is nowhere near as good in this form, and even if it was, the city shields all when it comes to that particular sensory experience. I don't need to anyway. I know where they're going. Even if they don't yet.

My most recent information on Dia places her with Cato, one of the few healers doing good work in Kanghri, despite it being a mostly thankless task. Ze also somehow manages to straddle the line of providing services for both the rebellion *and* the Cŵn Annwn. It means the latter overlooks a whole host of sins—and the prices ze charges them funds services for those who can't afford it.

Hopefully Dia hasn't moved on since my last update.

To my relief, when I knock on the door with a series of raps to indicate that I'm friend, not foe, it's Dia herself who opens it to allow me in. She's a short, wizened old woman with medium-brown skin and twinkling eyes. She grins up at me. "I wondered when you'd come around."

"Hello, Dia." I don't point out that there is absolutely no possibility she could be expecting me. Dia is a weather mage, which is distinctly different from elemental users. She has no ability to control the weather itself, but she has an almost unprecedented foresight when it comes to weather patterns. It made her a navigator of unparalleled success when she was among the crew of the *Crimson Hag*. "There are others following behind us. Once they arrive, we'd like to ask you some questions."

"By all means." She opens the door wider to allow me and Bastian inside. "It was getting time to move on anyway. Cato is getting cranky about having to share zir space."

There's nothing else to do but step inside . . . and wait.

CHAPTER 21

Nox

IT TAKES FAR LESS EFFORT THAN I EXPECTED TO SNEAK into the city. It's been a few months since we've sailed this way, and that time hasn't been kind to Kanghri. Trash is piled high on the edges of the road, and everyone moves around with shadows in their eyes and furtive looks over their shoulders.

At my side Bowen makes a rumbling sound of displeasure. "What happened here?"

I shake my head. "I don't know." There are no signs of an attack. If someone had come for the city, I would have heard about it. All of the Cŵn Annwn would have turned out to defend it. Or at least that's the theory. They're supposed to protect the civilians in Threshold, but how many times have I seen the Cŵn Annwn themselves be the perpetrators of harm? Even so, surely the Council wouldn't allow this . . .

I fall back and let Bowen lead the way. We agreed the best route to find Dia's current residence is to talk to one of Bowen's contacts in the city. I've never personally dealt with zir, but the healer Cato has a reputation for being a pain in the ass.

Our route takes us from the outskirts of the city down toward the docks. Every step has tension riding higher in my body. I'm not dressed in my customary crimson—I haven't been since we switched over the sails—but I still feel too exposed out here. Even with the buildings pressing close on either side of the narrow street we move along. Both Lyari and Mairi have neighborhoods around their respective docks that are run-down and dangerous to travel through after dark. Kanghri's has always been more dangerous than both of them combined. Even so, I watch four different people be pickpocketed in the space of ten minutes. "That's new."

Next to me, Evelyn shivers. "It wasn't like this even a few months ago."

In response, Bowen puts an arm around her shoulders and tucks her in against his much larger body. If he was anyone else, the move would leave him open to attack, but when your mind is the weapon, I suppose you don't need your arms as much. Or at least a normal person would view it that way. Even though he's one of the most powerful people in Threshold—at least to my knowledge—he's achingly aware that if something happened to his power, he would still need to be able to defend himself, so he's nearly as fearsome with a sword as he is with his magic.

We finally stop before a door that looks identical to the others around us. Bowen doesn't release Evelyn, but he shifts her slightly behind him so if something happens when he opens the door, he'll take the brunt of the hit. Then he knocks in a series that I instantly memorize.

It isn't the healer who opens the door to allow us entry. It's

Siobhan. And she doesn't look happy to see me. Over her shoulder, I catch sight of an equally furious Bastian. "How?" I actually take a step back before I catch myself. I have no reason for the guilt that flowers in my throat, but no amount of logic can curtail the emotion . . . or the sudden desire to apologize.

"Yes, yes, you're surprised to see us. Now get off the street and get in here." She waves us into the shadowed interior of the house. Things are piled high across almost every available space, with the exception of a pathway someone made through the middle of it all.

I ignore my sudden urge to put as much distance between us as absolutely possible and instead follow Bowen and Evelyn into the darkness.

There's one additional person waiting for us inside. Dia hasn't changed much since I saw her last; she's still a small old woman with arresting energy.

Bowen pulls her into a thorough but gentle hug. She returns it with no small amount of strength. "Bowen, my boy, it's good to see you." She reaches up to take him by the shoulders—he has to bend down to allow it—and holds him back so she can search his face. "You look well. The rebellion sits nicely upon your shoulders."

Bowen, bless his heart, actually seems surprised. Even in the dim light, I can see his sudden blush. "You know about that?"

"The weeks since we last spoke have been incredibly . . . enlightening." Her wrinkled face goes sober, the smile fading away. "It was a different time, sailing under Ezra. Even if we couldn't control what the rest of the Cŵn Annwn did, at least on our ship there was a code of honor. I'd like to think we did more good than harm." She glances at Siobhan and lets her hands drop from his shoulders. "But less harm is not no harm. There's penance to be paid."

Oh gods, not another one.

Bowen isn't a bad man, but he was thoroughly consumed with the mission of the Cŵn Annwn up until only a few months ago. Evelyn was the one to snap him out of it, to make him question things that he'd always taken as truth, and who finally enlightened him on exactly what the Cŵn Annwn are. Since then, he's been intent on rectifying the harm that he unwittingly committed. Obviously it's not as simple as bringing the murdered monsters back to life, and his code of honor has become something he speaks about periodically, and it makes me roll my eyes so hard it's a wonder I don't pass out.

Honor is a fallacy. I recognize that having a code is valuable—I have one myself. But the idea that there may be a single unifying set of rules on what honor is and isn't? It's foolish. Naive, even. There are more cultures in this realm and all the others than I could possibly begin to count. Cultures with different values and systems and people. The idea of "honor" allowed the Cŵn Annwn to use their help to enable a massive overreach of power. They kill monsters and save the people of Threshold from harm. What is that if not *honorable*?

The answer to that question depends heavily on whether or not they consider you a monster.

But Bowen will never be someone who embraces shades of gray when it comes to morality. Apparently Dia won't, either. That shouldn't have surprised me; he views her as a stand-in mother. Or grandmother, considering her age. Of course he picked up his viewpoints from somewhere. She and the last captain of the *Crimson Hag* raised him from his early teen years when they found him floating in the waters of Threshold. Naturally, he imprinted on them.

Bowen takes her hands in his larger ones and stares down at her intently. "You're more than welcome on the *Audacity*." I don't correct him, but I do grit my teeth as he continues. "But we didn't just come for that. We have some questions for you. You're the only person I could think of who might have the answers."

"If I have the answers, they're yours." She squeezes his hands and takes a step back, nearly knocking over a stack of what appear to be hats. I watch with bemusement as she picks up a pile of clothing and dumps it on the floor, sinks down onto the revealed rickety chair, and proceeds to start the process of rolling a blunt.

Bowen looks at me, and I'm only too happy to take the lead. I open my mouth, but Siobhan gets there first. Of course she does. The fact that she's held her silence for this long is no small miracle. She glares at me and steps forward. "We have a question about an item held in Lyari."

Bastian picks up the conversational thread without missing a beat, excitement lacing his voice. "There's a massive horn in Lyari. It's kept beneath the meeting chambers of the Council, locked up with the other specialized texts in the library. We think it has some connection to the originals."

Dia's silver brows rise. "You came all this way to ask me about a horn in Lyari?"

"How does one summon the Cŵn Annwn?"

Dia turns her attention to me, and while I expect there to be some kind of surprise or confusion in her dark eyes, instead they are narrowed and intent. "Why would you want to summon them? Best I can tell, you're fleeing them currently. A whole fleet is quite the enemy to face." She finishes her task and snaps her fingers at me. "Give me a light, dearie?"

I swallow down my sigh and lean forward to summon a tiny flame to light the end of her blunt. "I think you know we're not talking about the faction who stole that title and used it to hurt the people of Threshold."

She inhales deeply, gaze going distant, and then exhales a perfect circle. "I suppose I do know that. Regardless, that horn is dangerous."

"That horn is marked with a language I've never seen before," Bastian says slowly. "We have every reason to believe it links back to the originals."

"It does," Dia says simply.

Siobhan has the perfect stillness of a predator about to pounce. "How do you know where it came from?"

Dia smiles thinly. "My family has always kept particularly detailed records." She taps her temple lightly with a single finger. "I'm old, and some of the records are faded, but give me a little while to think and I'll come up with an answer—if I have one."

I exchange looks with the others. Surely this old woman isn't going to sit here and . . . Oh, apparently she is. She closes her eyes and continues to smoke, humming softly under her breath. Evelyn lets out a surprised laugh that she quickly stifles. "Oh gods, she's going to her mind palace."

Bowen frowns. "Her what?"

"Silence would allow this to go significantly faster," Dia says without opening her eyes. She takes another puff and exhales the sweet-smelling smoke. Without turning, she offers it to me. "You look like you could use a little relaxing."

Bastian makes a choked noise, but I don't hesitate to take the blunt and inhale. I don't smoke much, first because being a member of Hedd's ship meant you had to sleep with one eye open. I might find the concept of honor laughable, but Hedd had none. He allowed his people to do whatever they pleased. The only rule was that if you had the strength, then you had the right.

I may be powerful, but I don't look it. As a result, a lot of his people lost their lives at my hands. They thought they could abuse me, and I *disabused* them of the notion. Permanently. But that meant I couldn't allow myself to let my guard down, certainly not with drugs or alcohol.

Since becoming captain, there's been no space to relax. I'm at the top of the ladder, but that means everyone relies on me to keep them safe. Being a sloppy captain who engages in mind-altering substances is a good way to ensure I don't deliver on the promise of my position. And *that* is a good way to end up voted out.

Almost immediately, a pleasant fuzziness gathers around my racing mind. I close my eyes and inhale one last time before taking Dia's wrist and placing the blunt in her hand so she doesn't have to open her eyes.

I barely register that Siobhan is moving before she takes my elbow and tugs me away from the others, to a remarkably clear corner where Bastian waits. Not quite out of earshot, but close enough that the others can pretend they don't witness their hissing words in my ear. "What the fuck do you think you were doing, leaving us behind?"

I might not be able to summon my charismatic mask with my current stress level, but the drugs unwind me deliciously. I shrug easily and smile. "I would think that that was apparent. And yet neither of you follow orders all that well, do you?"

"Not particularly," Bastian murmurs. "It's one of my many charms."

"How could I follow orders when you're avoiding me and so have given none?" Siobhan looks like she wants to shake me, but thankfully manages to resist the impulse. "This won't work if you keep going around me—around us—and taking unnecessary risks. We have to work together, Nox. All three of us."

We.

With the whole of the Cŵn Annwn's fleet on our heels, I have so much to worry about, so much to fear. And yet that single word, those two little letters, strikes terror into the very heart of me.

CHAPTER 22

Siobhan

THERE IS NO 'US,'" NOX SNAPS.

"There could be," Bastian counters. "If you'd stop running."

All it takes is one look at Nox's expression to know that Bastian was right. They *are* running from us. I even understand why. I've avoided taking steps past the point of no return with the rebellion for longer than I want to admit. Stepping into the light and revealing myself to be alive, facing down my sister, watching the people I've come to care about die in a fight that might not be victorious? It's terrifying . . . but no less terrifying than the more personal battles for the heart of someone I care about.

Nox knows the stakes better than anyone, both for their heart and their life. Of course they'd try to put enough distance between themself and that potential pain.

I don't have the words to reassure them. There are no guarantees in life, but especially in this situation. I think experiencing love is worth the potential pain of losing it, but I can't make that choice for Nox.

Dia saves me from potentially saying the wrong thing and ending this before it's had a chance to begin. The old woman exhales another circle of smoke. "Ah, yes. The horn."

Instantly, every one of us goes still, Bowen and Evelyn ceasing their quiet conversation in the corner. We all turn to Dia. Bastian cautiously says, "We need to know about the horn."

"My great-grandmother, several times removed, was the one who created the case that it now resides in." She speaks in a low, even tone that almost sounds like she's in a trance. She still hasn't opened her eyes, but she continues to smoke regularly between sentences. "She didn't know where they found it, only that it was of the utmost importance to ward it as quickly and as thoroughly as they could. She wasn't the kind of woman to allow sloppy work under her command, so it was something of a fight with her and the Council of her time."

I lean forward. We are so close to an answer, and the slowness of her speech makes me want to do something to cause her to pick up her pace. I don't realize that I'm actually moving closer to the old woman until Nox grabs my arm in a gentle grip and shakes their head.

From her seat, Dia continues. "My ancestor didn't like being pressured, and so she took it upon herself to find out exactly what was so dangerous about this horn as to get the Council into a tizzy."

"What did she find?" Bowen asks softly. I don't think I've ever heard him speak so quietly, and it's an indication that Dia has used this method to retrieve information before.

"Inconclusive," Dia says slowly. "There was a lot of whispering, but no definitive answers. All she could discover was that the Council feared the horn enough that they wanted it close instead of hiding it away where no one would ever see it. There was something about the noble families fighting them on this choice, which is why it ended up in the section of the library where only the nobles can pass freely. But still warded, still kept away from curious hands and minds." She exhales in a shuddering breath and opens her eyes. "I'm sorry. That's all I have."

"It's perfect, Dia." Bowen goes to her and offers a hand so that she can rise, even though she seems spry enough not to need it. "It helped immensely."

It didn't help at all. I barely manage to keep the words trapped behind my teeth. We came all this way, risked so much, and for what? Rumors passed down from an ancient ancestor? The Council are afraid of a lot of things. Just because they seemed particularly worried about this one doesn't mean it can actually be wielded against them. It might blow all of Lyari off the map. That outcome is just as likely as summoning my legendary ancestors.

I glance at Bastian to see my frustration mirrored in his face. This wasn't enough. We needed a guarantee in order to make the trip to Lyari. If the horn was a weapon that could take on the whole of the Cŵn Annwn, then it would have been a neat side step to avoid war. It still might be, but sailing into certain danger on the strength of rumors and assumptions is a large ask.

Nox pulls their frustration together quickly. They give a short bow to Dia. "You are always welcome on my ship, though it's bound to be more dangerous than normal in the near future."

"Life is dangerous. I'll still take that offer." Dia snuffs out her blunt and tucks the remainder into an interior pocket in her jacket. "Let me grab my bag and we'll go."

Nox barely waits for her to exit the room before they turn back to me and Bastian. "I know what you're thinking and the answer is *absolutely not*."

"We still don't have a better option," Bastian cuts in. "Even without a guarantee, we have to try."

"On the contrary, we have thousands of better options than certain death. Because that's exactly what will happen if we sail to Lyari. Even if they don't know we're coming—and they will because they have such an intricate system of information networks—you want me to take my crew into an openly hostile harbor. And *then*, if we somehow survive that, get close enough to the damned Council to be one room below their meeting chambers to break the wards around this thing that have been in place for generations, and then blow a damn horn and hope it doesn't bring about the end of the fucking world. Because right now, that's as likely as anything else."

They're right. I know they're right. "The Cŵn Annwn used to do good."

Nox blinks. "Oh, so now we're trading in fairy tales."

"It's not a fairy tale. My grandfather passed the same stories to me that his grandfather passed to him and so on back to the beginning of Threshold. The Cŵn Annwn protected our realm. It's only in the intervening time that that purpose has become perverted and used to abuse power."

"Sure, and why don't you spin a tale on turning straw to gold while you're at it. *If* the Cŵn Annwn ever existed, which, I'll grant you, your presence seems to suggest, then no doubt they were just as corrupt and selfish as those who currently call themselves by the same name. I've seen what power does to people. You've seen it, too—both of you. Just because they were here first doesn't mean they're immune to that. Even if this damn horn does summon them, it's entirely likely that they will be a worse problem than what we're currently dealing with."

There's no reason to feel betrayed by their words. This has been a long shot from the beginning, from the moment that I took the first steps to create a rebellion that would help people. In my heart of hearts, didn't I know it was a losing battle?

"The Council is scared of the horn," Bastian says. "That means something."

"It means it's a threat. There's no telling the size or shape of that threat," Nox snaps.

"The legends in my realm are varied," Evelyn says slowly, almost apologetically. "Sometimes they hunt those who deserve it, but almost as often, it's a proximity thing. If you are in the wrong place on the wrong night, the Wild Hunt will take you, too." She frowns a little. "Though in this scenario, 'taking' could qualify as everything from killing to kidnapping to just dragging along for the ride, only to be deposited somewhere far from where you originally joined up."

"See." Nox motions at Evelyn. "Even if we had endless amounts of time for research and were able to travel to the other realms where the Cŵn Annwn hunted, we would find the same conflicting stories and legends. There is no such thing as uniformly good or uniformly evil. Siobhan and Morrigan are more than proof of that. She's descended from the Cŵn Annwn, too, and she's vicious, violent, and cruel."

As much as I hate to admit it, that is one angle I can't argue. There may be no such thing as uniformly good or evil, but my sister is damn close to the latter. I don't know if she was just born a particular way, or if something in our upbringing went wrong with her. All I know is that her ambition burns inside her with a heat that incinerates anything standing in her way.

Including our parents. And me.

"Nox," I start. "If you have a better plan, I'd love to hear it."

"We run. We hide. We fight. All of those are better plans than sailing to the heart of the Cŵn Annwn on rumors that don't even prove your thesis." Nox turns away and drags a hand through their short hair. "It doesn't matter. We can fight about this back on the *Audacity*. We need to move. The longer we stay in one place, the greater the target upon us is."

At least on that we're in agreement. There's an itching under my skin that seems to be growing with every minute that ticks past. There's no reason to think we were followed here, and we intentionally avoided the busy docks where secrecy is impossible.

And yet . . .

Dia walks back into the room with a bag nearly the size she is. Bowen promptly takes it from her and slings it over his own shoulder. There's nothing left to do but leave. He's the first one out the door, Evelyn and Dia close behind. After a short, silent battle, Bastian follows, then Nox, and then me. I softly close the door behind me and look around.

Where the streets weren't particularly busy before, now there isn't a single soul visible. The itching beneath my skin reaches a frenzied threshold. I shiver. "Something's wrong."

Dia shudders and almost goes to her knees. Only Evelyn's quick thinking is enough to catch her before her old knees hit the cobblestones. She gasps out a harsh breath. "Storm. Magical. Acid."

Even as she speaks, realization rolls over me. Bull, Morrigan's quartermaster. I'd heard rumors about his powers, but even in Threshold it seemed exaggerated to a laughable degree. Summoning a magical storm that drops acid instead of rain? Even as my disbelief tries to take hold, clouds gather above us, a deep and worrisome green.

Bastian follows my gaze and makes a sound of rage. "It will eat through the roofs, will kill people. How is Morrigan justifying this to the Council?"

"This is Kanghri," I say quietly. "As long as she keeps the damage far from Mairi, it's likely they'll look the other way. What's a little more damage to this place?" I motion around us.

"It's wrong," he snaps.

"This is Threshold. You know better." Nox rolls their shoulders, and I already know I'm not going to like their next words as soon as I see the determination in their pale gray eyes. "I can stop him."

Bastian and I speak at the same time. "Absolutely not."

Bowen cuts between us, breaking our line of sight with each other. "Now isn't the time to argue. We have to move. If Nox can help, then let them do it." He turns to Dia. "I'm going to have to carry you."

She grumbles a little but allows him to carefully lift her into his arms. He glances at Evelyn, but she's already shaking her head. "I can keep up."

I turn back to Nox, only to find their eyes distant. Around us, the wind begins to pick up. "Damn it, Nox. We don't have—" There's no time to argue.

"I've got Dia's bag." Bastian takes it from Bowen. "You carry Nox. The faster we get out of here, the less magic they have to use."

"As if that's going to stop them." I sweep Nox into my arms and we rush after Bowen and Evelyn, cutting through the streets at twice the pace that I came in. What's the point in stealth when there's no one around to see? Morrigan won't be here. She won't risk any of her people being harmed by Bull's attack. The bitch.

In the fifteen minutes it takes to reach the edges of the city, the wind has increased in strength until it's a fight for every step. I lean down to murmur in Nox's ear. "It would be helpful if you didn't make it more challenging for us to flee. Direct the wind overhead and into the storm." I hate asking them for more effort when I know the cost, but there are thousands of people who live in Kanghri. If I don't let Nox fight Bull, then the death toll will be astronomical.

"I know what I'm doing." But the wind shifts around us, no longer a wall to be burst through. Bowen is moving so fast that I have to sprint to keep up with him, and though Bastian is breathing hard enough to make me worry, he keeps pace. Evelyn, on the other hand, is having a difficult time despite her confident words. With a soft curse, I dodge in front of her and go down on one knee. "My back. Hang on."

"This is so fucked." She gives a soft *oof* as she wraps her legs around my waist and her arms around my neck. Even though she tries not to choke me, it's all but impossible.

We are so fucked.

CHAPTER 23

Nox

DESPITE MY ASSURANCES TO THE OTHERS THAT I CAN fight Bull, dismantling a storm is damn near impossible when it's natural. When it's magical? It's a feat that only the most skilled and powerful could pull off. Maybe on my best day I'd have a decent shot at it despite the danger of burnout. This is not my best day.

Being jostled in Siobhan's arms doesn't help my concentration, but I know better than to ask her to stop or, gods forbid, to put me down. More importantly, my magic well hasn't refilled from the last fight. I dip down into it, pulling what I can to me, and can't stop a sliver of fear at how little there is to gather.

It doesn't matter. If I don't fight, then more people will die. People just trying to live their lives. People who didn't choose to settle in a city that the Cŵn Annwn have apparently decided is disposable.

I close my eyes and devote all my magic to picking apart the gathering wind above us. I'll make do with what I have. I can't siphon off the power of the storm with my elemental magic, but I can direct the wind in increasingly chaotic waves that will fight Bull's hold on it. And if he loses hold, then we'll be dealing with a normal storm instead of an acid rain. I hope.

"Bowen," Evelyn calls, "the moment it starts raining, create a shield above us." She mutters under her breath, and Siobhan's steps stutter as she shifts on her back. "Sorry. I'm trying to figure out a spell to help."

"If you want to help, stop fucking moving." Siobhan tightens her hold on me. "And *you*. Don't you dare fucking die."

I have no plans to. But I can't speak without losing my hold on the air currents. Damn, this fucker's strong. Bull must have built up the storm out over the sea and then directed it here. It's fully formed and fearsome.

A fiery dollop of pain splats my forehead and my eyes fly open, my concentration faltering. "Damn it!" Overhead, the sky is even uglier than it was earlier, orange and purple having blossomed in the midst of the green. I curse hard. "I can't stop it. I didn't do anything but let him know that we're here." I fucked up. Truly fucked up.

And now the people of Kanghri and all of First Sister will pay the price.

Except Bowen is slowing and turning back. He deposits Dia in front of us. "Bastian will take you if you need to run."

Bastian looks a little green. "I will."

Bowen pivots to face the way we came. "I can hold it off."

Siobhan tenses, but I'm already speaking. "Absolutely fucking not. If I can't pull it apart, there's no way you can."

He shakes his head, expression distant. "I'm not going to dispel the storm. I'm going to shield the city."

My eyes go wide as shock grips me. What he's suggesting . . . The sheer amount of power that kind of feat would require . . . "Impossible." I struggle to get out of Siobhan's arms, failing spectacularly. "Even if you could manage it for a beat, the burnout will kill you. I won't allow it."

"You don't have a choice. And it's not impossible—not with an amplification circle." He looks over me into Evelyn's eyes. "I know this is dangerous, but you understand that I have to do it."

She appears absolutely miserable, but she slides off Siobhan's back and nods. "You have to try to save them." She swallows hard. "Don't you dare die."

"I would never leave you willingly."

She pulls a piece of chalk from an inside pocket. "I need a flat surface to work with."

The words are barely out of her mouth before the rocks beneath our feet disintegrate and are swept away, revealing a mostly flat dirt surface. And he did it with a simple thought, faster than I could fully come up with a plan to give her that flat surface.

I wriggle in Siobhan's arms. "Put me down."

Instead of obeying, Siobhan gives me a severe look. "I'll put you down the moment you promise me that you aren't going to do anything foolish like try to fight Bull with wind when he's drawing forth a storm that's not even elemental."

"We're heroes, Siobhan. Noble sacrifice is what heroes do." I use her huff of outrage to slide free and come to my feet next to Evelyn. She's already got half the circle drawn, Bowen's shield above us, keeping the increasing acid rain from peppering us with holes. She glances at me. "I'll need an extra second to create a shield for us and Bowen so he can concentrate on the city. Don't let him start until I'm ready."

Impossible words, an impossible promise. The only person who can stop Bowen is Evelyn, and even then, she's not always successful. It's that damn fucking honor again. It makes even the smartest people into fools. "I'll try."

I move to Bowen, only pausing long enough to ensure that Siobhan is keeping an eye on Dia and Bastian. "This will be a battle of stamina. Can you hold him? Because if you can't, we're better off running now and getting ourselves far from here while he unloads his fury."

"Unloads his fury on the unsuspecting and innocent people of Kanghri." His dark eyes are steely. His jaw set. "You would know that's unacceptable if you weren't so distracted."

I rear back as if he reached out and slapped me. "Forgive the fuck out of me if I prioritize the people I care about over strangers."

Bowen shakes his head. "That might be what you tell yourself, but it's not the truth. You help strangers all the damn time, Nox. That's what the rebellion is, and you realized it long before I did. That's why you just risked killing yourself to save Kanghri. I can do no less."

It feels like he just stripped away all my defenses in a few sentences. Damn him for seeing me so clearly. Damn him for being a good man who is part of my crew. "You should know better than to fight against impossible odds."

He gives a thin smile. "I learned it from my captain."

Gods, I hope he can pull this off. Fear is a live thing inside me, but this big bastard is right. We have to try, to keep trying, even if it means we burn ourselves to ash in the process. I find myself grinning back at Bowen, just as fiercely. "This captain of yours must be brilliant and inspiring."

"They certainly think so."

"Done." Evelyn turns fully around and, without hesitation, creates a secondary circle next to the amplification one. In less stressful times, I enjoy watching her put these together. Her chalk becomes an extension of her arm, her wrist fluid as she draws out the symbols that will wrestle the magic into following her will. Right now, though, it's everything I can do not to tell her to hurry. She knows. She is. And yet we're still running out of time.

It's probably a bare three minutes after she starts the second circle that she finishes, but it feels like eternity. Evelyn pulls out a small knife and pricks her finger. She looks at Bowen. "My shield can't cover you fully—otherwise it'll block you in. You're going to take some damage, but the moment you look like you're in actual danger, I'm extending my shield to cover you and to hell with anyone else."

"No, you're not." He withdraws his own knife and creates a shallow slash over his forearm as he steps into the amplification circle. I know what it feels like to use one, a dizzying descent and even stronger vertigo as you rise back up, with all your power trailing behind you. There's a reason they're dangerous. There's a reason they aren't used often, even by those who rely on rituals to cast. They can drain you faster than you can drain yourself naturally. Even with Bowen's deep reserves.

I knew that when I stepped into the amplification circle on the ship, but it's one thing to risk myself. It's entirely another to watch one of my people knowingly put themselves into danger.

"All right. Everyone in the circle."

Bastian lends his arm to Dia, guiding her to the circle despite the fact that she looks spryer than he does currently. I stand behind Evelyn and slightly to the side, the better to keep my attention on Bowen and, in the distance, Kanghri. "We're ready."

Evelyn plants her hands on the circle and there's a strange sensation as if something just tugged on my stomach. Her shield pops up around us, holding off the acid rain. At the same time, Bowen's blood hits the amplification circle and everything . . . stops.

Sound. Movement. Everything.

I'm crouched on the ground with no memory of moving. I slowly lower my arms, staring up at thousands upon thousands of acid raindrops held in place. Above us, the storm clouds still circle, obviously outside of even Bowen's impressive range, but closer to the ground, not a single drop makes contact. Not as far as I can see. It's terrifying. It's exhilarating.

I should have told him to blow Morgan's ship out of the water after we rescued Bastian. With her wards and crew, maybe it wouldn't have been possible, but Bowen's magic runs so deep. It might have killed him, but then we would have one less enemy.

But that's not an equation I'll ever accept. Bowen is a member of my crew, valuable and human and loved, a vital part of my community. We don't throw away lives. That's the thing we're fighting against.

I recognize I can't save everyone, but it's not going to stop me from trying.

I hate that he's in this fight on his own, but he's winning. He's doing it. Hope flourishes in my chest, but before it can take root . . . the drops quiver.

At first, I think it's a trick of my eyesight, my gaze trying to correct something that absolutely cannot be natural. But then it happens again, the drops shifting downward. More come, and more yet, until the sky is filled with deadly liquid, a veritable sea above our heads.

"Fuck," I breathe. Stopping the storm is one thing, but at some point that acid has to go somewhere. There's no safe place to deposit it. Not the land, not the city, certainly not the ocean. The loss of life would be catastrophic.

How the fuck is Morrigan explaining this to the Council? This is no targeted attack; this is wholesale slaughter. Even if we spare the people now, we're going to decimate their fishing waters, their main source of food. They will become reliant on trade that they have no resources to accommodate. And if we hadn't saved them, the runoff would accomplish the same fucking thing, in addition to all the human lives lost.

The devastation we're looking at boggles my mind. Siobhan is following my same train of thought. She grabs my shoulder, but her words are for Bowen. "There's a rock canyon about a mile west of us. It's north of the city, entirely encased. There's no runoff to drinking water or the sea. Send it there."

"How the fuck do you know that?" I say under my breath.

"I'm the leader of the rebellion, and I've spent nearly half my life in various forms of hiding. You don't run an organization like this without having all the information you can possibly have at your disposal."

I can't imagine a scenario where an enclosed rock canyon would become useful, but then I never would've imagined a scenario where we'd be looking at a sea of acid over our heads, held in shivering place by a single man's power. I look to Bowen. Every muscle stands out in sharp relief. He shakes, fighting against the force of gravity and Bull's power. He has to release his magic soon. It's draining too quickly.

"Bowen! The canyon!"

"I heard," he grits out. "But he's still sending rain."

"Oh, you bloody fool." Evelyn makes a sound impressively like a snarl. "Don't you dare die out of pure stubbornness. Send what you can. He's not going to be able to maintain this level of attack forever—and neither are you."

Bowen makes a pained sound and weaves in place. At first, I think he's going down, and I tense, ready to grab him and pull him to the relative safety of our shield, but then I realize he's moving the liquid overhead in the direction that Siobhan indicated.

It courses northwest, faster and faster. Siobhan watches the movement with narrowed eyes. "You're almost there. A little farther and then you can release it."

I don't ask her how she can possibly see that far. Her eyesight is better than anyone else's I've ever met, courtesy of her heritage. I trust her word. Apparently Bowen does, too, because when she says, "Now!" the acid falls from the sky in a waterfall of death.

I don't know if I believe in gods, ancient or dead or otherwise, but I almost pray right then and there that no one is in the location Siobhan has directed Bowen to deposit the acid. If they are, they're not long for this world or any other. The thought makes me sick.

But not as much as the realization that washes over me when I look up. Because, although Bowen has deposited a large lake's worth of acid away from us, it's not over.

It's still raining.

CHAPTER 24

Siobhan

ACID RAIN. ON AN ENTIRE FUCKING CITY. I STARE INTO the sky through Evelyn's shield and wonder where it all went so wrong. My sister isn't a fool; she wouldn't have successfully joined the Council if she was. This kind of attack would never be sanctioned. How can you pretend you're hunting monsters and protecting people when you send out a damn storm that will kill anyone caught in it?

"We have to stop her." Even as I say the words, the realization of what Morrigan is attempting to accomplish with this reckless move rolls over me. Of course we have to stop her. Of course she's using extreme violence to draw me out. She's tired of chasing me and wants me to come to her. "That bitch," I breathe.

Bowen is on his knees, all color bleached from his face. The fact that he's still conscious after that display of power boggles the mind. I knew he was powerful, but I had no idea the depth of it. "It's still raining," he rasps.

"Yes, but not as hard." Evelyn doesn't look too good, either.

Her hands shake where they dig into the earth at our feet. Her spells truly are something to be coveted. It's a good thing the Council isn't aware of her, or they would have sent someone to haul her to Lyari to work directly for them.

Bastian squints at the sky. "I think it's stopping."

"It is." Dia has her head tilted back and is fully relaxed, trusting us to ensure she makes it out of this. Or at least trusting Bowen. "If you send some of that wind now, Nox, it will disperse the remainder of it. He's not feeding energy into the storm any longer." She huffs out a breath that's almost a laugh. "No stamina, that boy."

I haven't spent much time among the elderly. Life on the streets of Lyari is hard, and the privilege of growing old isn't given to many. Even after leaving Lyari, my experience has been limited. The sea isn't the kindest mistress. If sailors and fishermen live long enough to reach old age, they shift to a life spent with their feet planted firmly on the ground, rather than at the whim of the waves.

Even so, surely Dia is . . . different . . . from other people her age—and not simply because she's still sailing.

Bowen staggers to his feet. "I can—"

"I've got it." Nox sounds more tired than I've ever heard them. I want to tell them not to do this, not to drain any more magic from their depleted reserves, but I already know they won't listen. And the people of Kanghri don't deserve to suffer because my sister wants me dead.

I exchange an agonized look with Bastian, understanding blooming between us. It will always be like this. If not Nox, then it will be one of us, putting ourselves in danger in service of the greater good. "Be quick," I finally say.

I go and stand behind them, bracing them with my body and my strength as they send their magic out in the form of air streams. Within moments, the clouds overhead break apart as if a giant reached up and swiped them away. The acid rain eases and then stops altogether.

Nox slumps back against me. "I'm tapped." Their words slur a little. "Well isn't as deep as it used to be."

Fear slashes me, but I work to keep it out of my voice. We don't have time for me to have an emotional reaction. "I know."

"They did so much damage," they murmur. "Any crops they managed to drag from the earth here will be destroyed. Fishing might be a problem, too."

"Not to mention they have a brand-new acid lake." Bastian scrubs a hand over his face. "How many people will die there before they realize what it is? How many kids will die after, ignoring the warnings of their elders about the danger?"

Evelyn frowns. "With a few earth-users, maybe they could cover it up and bury it away."

"And have it resurface later, even worse than before?" Nox shakes their head. "I'll send word—"

"How?" I guide them down to sit on the ground. "Your communication with the Council has been destroyed."

They set their jaw. "There are other ways."

"Those ways are going to have to wait." Bowen stumbles a little as he makes his way to us. "I think we're about to have company."

I look over his shoulder and, sure enough, a small group of people are following the same path we took out of Kanghri. The distance is too great to pick out their features, even for me, but their movement is intent enough that I have no doubt they're tracking us. "We need to move."

Which is a damned problem because most of our party is dead on their feet. Nox can barely stand up on their own. Bowen is leaning heavily on Evelyn, Bastian has deep circles beneath his eyes, and Dia, while spry enough, is as old as dirt. With how fast the other group is moving, they'll be on us well before we reach the beach, let alone manage to row out to the ship.

"We'll never make it." Bowen rolls his shoulders. "Better prepare for a fight when we can choose the location."

A fight where all of our magic users are tapped. Best case, they remove the threat and go under from magical burnout. Worst case, we all die.

No. Not today. Sure as fuck not *here*.

"I'm going to shift." I speak the words numbly. It was one thing to shift with only myself and Bastian as witness, but doing it in front of other people—especially when one of them is a person I care about deeply—feels vulnerable in a way I'd normally do anything to avoid. "I'll carry you."

"You're a shifter." Evelyn blinks. "Right. That explains a few things. What is your other form?"

"A hound."

Nox plants their hands on their thighs and seems to focus on breathing. "Even though shifters are larger than normal animals, at best you can carry one other person."

Bastian shakes his head. "You're talking about normal shifters. Siobhan isn't a normal shifter."

"I can carry all of you."

Nox is already shaking their head. "Not if you want to actually make it. Take Dia. Figure out the horn business. We'll hold them off."

Of all the— I can't decide if I want to declare aloud that I love them or if I want to knock them over the head so they'll stop being so damned dramatic. "No one is dying today." The longer we stand here arguing, the more time we give our enemies to reach us. So I do the only thing I can think of to get us moving. I start pulling off my clothes. "Bastian, get ready with the glamour."

Bowen spins around so fast, he almost topples over. "A little warning would be nice."

"You're so cute." Evelyn gives him an indulgent look that's only partially dampened by her clear exhaustion. "It's just a little nudity. Shifters don't tend to put emphasis on it the same way some cultures do."

"All the same. The only person I'm interested in seeing nude is *you*."

I do my best to ignore them and kick off my boots. I pass the bag I carried my clothes in to Bastian. "Hang on to this, please."

Nox stares at him, the bag, and then at my half-naked body. "You certainly know how to make a statement, don't you?"

Bastian laughs a little. "Siobhan is a true showwoman."

I flush hot and then curse myself for reacting at all when there's so much at stake. "There's no more time for arguing." I skim off my pants and shove them into Bastian's hands. The cool air kisses my bare skin. Evelyn is right that shifters don't worry overmuch about nudity the way some folks do, but I'm not a normal shifter. I don't have a community like the solitary shifters do. Even before my parents died, they drilled into my head that no one must ever know our secret. In the rare times when we shifted, it was always alone and never as a pack; the better to avoid drawing attention to ourselves.

I allow the magic to unclench inside me. Between one heartbeat and the next, I shift into my other form. My eyesight becomes even better, my sense of smell incomparably superior to a human's. My body stretches, and I land on four paws before the others.

A second later, the faint feeling of Bastian's magic settles against my skin. He exhales shakily. "We'd better get moving. I can hold it for some time still, but the more people who are covered, the greater the strain."

Evelyn's eyes go wide as she takes me in. "That's . . . I was under the impression that the laws of matter apply even to shifters. Usually they're larger than their mundane counterparts, because humans are larger than most animals, but even if they grow a bit in half form, they don't, like"—she motions at me—"quadruple in size."

"Silly girl." Dia says it fondly as she approaches me. "The Cŵn Annwn aren't shifters. They're gods. Your human rules don't apply." She bows a little to me, which makes me shift my feet restlessly. "If you'll lower yourself a little, I'll climb onto your back. Thank you for the privilege."

I have no words to tell her that I'm not a god, merely the distant descendant of one, so I lower myself to my belly. My shoulder still reaches the top of Dia's head, but Bowen finally manages to shake himself out of his shock and moves to lift the old woman up onto my back. I barely register her weight.

Bastian shoves my clothing and boots into the bag and nudges Evelyn. "You next."

Bowen hoists Evelyn onto my back, and then Nox, ignoring

their muttered curse. He pauses as if he might argue I can't hold his weight as well, but then gives a curse of his own and climbs up.

Bastian pats my shoulder as he settles near my neck. "No one else will see, Siobhan. I promise."

I *do* register the weight of five adults, but it's nowhere near enough to keep me from rising easily to my feet, giving them a moment to adjust, and then taking off toward the north shore. Through it all, Bastian keeps us hidden with his magic, giving me the freedom to run. Even so, I'm slightly slower than normal; it takes a little over an hour to reach the shore.

"Let us down here," Nox calls. "I can— *Damn it, Siobhan.*"

I ignore them and plunge into the water. If recent experience has taught me anything, it's that Nox will drive themself straight into magical burnout if I give them half a chance. Bowen could probably levitate the boat, but he's tapped, too. So are Evelyn and Bastian, for that matter. I'm only marginally winded, and a short rest will be all it takes to get me back to full stamina and health. I can make the swim easier than they can.

"Hang on!" Bowen roars as the first wave hits.

My powerful strokes bring us through the wave break in seconds. There are still the currents to contend with, of course, but I've been swimming since I could walk; I know how to navigate tricky currents.

I take an angle almost parallel to the shore until the pressure against my body guides us in the direction I actually want to go. My fur is soaked, my legs churning, and I am finally starting to register the drag of my passengers, but I haven't come this far to stop now. The *Audacity* bobs gently in the distance, less than a mile out. I can do this. I *must* do this.

Between one stroke and the next, the currents suddenly shift again, this time to propel me forward. Magic tickles my nose, and if I had a mouth made for words, I would curse Nox for using their magic when they're already so drained. Since I don't, I put all my remaining strength into paddling as quickly as possible.

With Nox's water magic propelling me, we make it to the ship faster than I could have dreamed. Bastian clings to my neck. "Do you want me to drop the glamour now, or wait until you shift back?" His voice is ragged with strain.

Nox rolls off my back and treads water a short distance away. "Take the glamour off me."

Bastian hesitates, but I can tell the exact moment he obeys, because a surprised shout goes up from the deck overhead. "It's the captain!"

Someone unrolls a ladder, and Nox waves. "Thank you, darling! I'll be up shortly." They twist to face us, their eyes narrowed. "I can't see any of you, but get moving. We didn't come this far to drown now."

I swim closer to the ladder, treading water as Dia, Evelyn, and Bowen scramble up the side of the ship. Then it's only me, Bastian, and Nox.

Bastian eases off me, but doesn't move far. "Change back so you can climb."

Of course. I must be more tired than I realized, because that's the obvious next step. I draw my magic into myself, tucking it down deep as my body shifts back into its human form. I go under for a brief moment while I rework how to swim with human arms and legs instead of a hound's. When I surface again, Nox is directly in front of me, their gray eyes wide.

"Worried about me?" I rasp.

"Every damn day." They finally manage a smile, though it's strained around the edges. They glance at Bastian. "We have another flight before us."

"I know." We expected Morrigan to be far enough behind us that we could recharge the crew with a slower pace. That's obviously not happening now. Even if the group following us turned back, it won't take long for the *Bone Heart* to sail around Three Sisters to our position.

Bastian goes under and surfaces near the ladder. He grabs the closest rung. "We have to get moving."

"Go."

For a moment, it looks like he wants to argue, but *someone* among the three of us has to go first, so he sighs and hauls himself up the ladder. "Don't linger."

"Nox is right behind you."

Nox shakes their head. "You first, darling."

Despite everything, I find the capacity to grin. "So you can stare at all my unmentionables while climbing up behind me? I think not."

Nox rolls their eyes. "I've been staring at your *unmentionables* since you came aboard my ship. You're just giving me fodder for fantasies. It's charity work, honestly."

I should be focusing on the imminent danger we're in, but flirting with Nox is so fun that my exhausted brain doesn't want to do anything to break this moment. "It doesn't have to be fantasy."

Nox opens their mouth, pauses, and starts for the ladder. "Very well. *You* can stare at *my* unmentionables while we both climb."

They're running. Again. I make an effort to shrug off my disappointment and follow them. The wet fabric of their pants clings to their backside, showing every flex of muscle as they climb. I want to sink my teeth into them in a way that would truly worry me if I could dredge up the energy for it. Each foot I climb drains away the joy I found in the flirting, driving home the dire situation we're currently in.

No guarantees that the horn will do anything. The only way to find out is to test it, and breaking into the Council's seat of power is a good way to end up dead. There are no good choices.

Guess it's time to make a bad one.

CHAPTER 25

Bastian

SEEING SIOBHAN IN HER HOUND FORM NEVER FAILS TO
feel like I'm witnessing a miracle. She's gorgeous, a massive
white hound, long and lean, with crimson ears and eyes. Her
strength humbles me. Any other shifter trying to carry five
adults through dangerous currents would drown and take the
lot with them. Not Siobhan.

Eyal and Poet haul me over the railing and then reach down
to do the same to Nox and then Siobhan. Our little group looks
terrible, soaked and shaking on the deck. Of us all, Dia appears
the least bothered by the harrowing experience. The fact that
Bowen and Nox are still on their feet remains shocking. We're a
mess.

Nox gives themself a shake and straightens. They lift their
voice. "I'm sorry, friends, but we have to run again. Did the
other team get back?"

"Just before you did." Poet nods at the hatch. "They are un-
loading the supplies now."

"We're running again." Eyal's shoulders drop. "They found us so quickly?"

"Found us and aren't interested in playing subtle." Nox quickly recounts what occurred. I barely had time to process what I was witnessing while experiencing it, but the sharing of the events drives home how powerful Bowen and Evelyn truly are. I don't know who else could have accomplished what their shared magic did, saving so many lives.

In Lyari, the noble families all have inherent magic, and the Council is formed of the most powerful of those, but they hoard their power and are secretive to the point of being paranoid. It made sense with Siobhan's family, hiding their history. Or with mine, concealing forbidden magic. But the others tend to have significantly more mundane skills, if on a scale that supposedly would boggle the mind—if they ever demonstrated it. Instead, they deal in rumors and reputation, ensuring they never actually show their full hand.

If they're all hiding people with power like Bowen's, it's a wonder they haven't razed Lyari to the ground in the small wars that crop up between houses every few generations.

I shrug out of my cloak, wet as it is, and pass it to Siobhan. She wraps it around herself, but seems faintly amused when it barely conceals her nakedness. She clears her throat. "I'm going to get washed up and change."

Nox snaps their fingers. "Hold, please." They glance at Poet. "Get everyone on deck. We need a vote before we go any further."

She nods. "Give me five."

"Nox, what are you doing?" I say.

They don't look at me. "I made the call to save you because

Siobhan asked me to, and we've been fighting to survive ever since. What we aim to do next is nothing short of suicide, and I won't even attempt it if the crew isn't in agreement."

In what world will the crew be in agreement? Especially if they talk like *that*. I lean forward. "Then let me talk to them. Let me explain—"

"And use your glamour to get their agreement." They shake their head sharply. "Absolutely not."

I jerk back, stung. "You truly think so little of me?"

"Not under normal circumstances." Their jaw is set and they're still not looking at me. "You're not a bad man, Bastian, but right now you're desperate—and desperate people cross moral lines they never would have imagined crossing in other times."

I can't even argue with that. I *would* glamour the crew if I thought I didn't have any other choice. Not to sail directly into Lyari—not even I am that cruel—but to drop us on the other side of the island so we can make our own way into the city. That's honestly the preferable course of action, for all that time is of the essence. The officials in Lyari tend to focus almost entirely on the bay, instead of on any foot traffic into the city. There isn't much of it, so it would be a waste of resources.

"I will—"

Nox cuts Siobhan off. "No. They're *my* crew. They'll get their vote and we will abide by it." They rub the back of their hand over their forehead. "No matter what the vote is, I'll see it through. But I won't let them continue this fight without understanding the full stakes."

True to Poet's word, within five minutes the crew is gathered on the deck. I search their faces, trying to divine the mood. Exhaustion seems to be the overarching theme, but beneath that, it's hard to tell what they're thinking.

Nox steps easily onto the railing, putting themself head and shoulders above even Bowen, the tallest here. "You all know we came to Kanghri for information. Well, we have it." They motion at Dia. "There is a horn in Lyari that may summon the ancients that the Cŵn Annwn take their name and reputation from. We don't know what will happen when we blow it, but it's still a chance to avoid a full-out battle."

Siobhan growls. "That's not all of it." She turns to the people gathered, every inch a leader despite her relative nakedness. "There are a lot of stories about the originals, and some of them come from my family, who can trace their lineage back to those very originals."

A shocked murmur goes up among the crew. They knew she was powerful, of course; she's displayed prowess in a number of ways since coming aboard, let alone before. But my glamour did its job and concealed the sight of her from enemy and ally alike. They haven't witnessed her in her true glory, and even without that, I can see the effect she's having on them.

She seems to meet every gaze individually. "The theory is that whoever blows it will be able to ask one favor of the originals. In this case, that favor would be to purge the rot from Threshold. Nox is right: we have no guarantee that it will work—or that it will result in the outcome we want. It's entirely likely that nothing will happen if we blow it. Or that if the ancients *do* show up, they'll simply kill us all."

Lizzie snorts. "What a rousing speech."

Nox gives her a long look and cuts in. "I won't lie to you or anyone else on the crew. Siobhan has been searching for a way to bring the Cŵn Annwn down for years. This is the only plan that has even a chance of succeeding without a massive loss of life." They take a breath. "I want you with me. I won't pretend that any other outcome is preferable. But I value you and I won't hold it against you if you want nothing more to do with this."

Poet steps forward, drawing attention to herself. "We're calling a vote. Yay to continue on this course. Nay to drop Nox and the others at the nearest safe port and sail through the portal in Skoiya to wait out this trouble in that realm."

From the way Nox's eyes widen briefly, they had no idea Poet was going to offer another option like that. It's a good option, as such things go. The Cŵn Annwn aren't above traveling to other realms when the situation calls for it, but it's likely that with the right sleight of hand, Poet would be able to make a good showing of the *Audacity* going down, freeing the crew to disperse and start new lives.

It won't do a damn thing to help the people stuck in Threshold, though.

The crew murmurs among themselves. Even as I try to make out the individual words, it's impossible to know which way they're leaning. I had foolishly thought they would take us to Lyari's island, which shares the same name as the city. If they drop us somewhere else, we're going to be starting from less than zero. We'd have to find a ship, and then contend with the fact that no ship can match the *Audacity* in speed.

There's every chance we won't make it to Lyari before the Cŵn Annwn find us.

Poet goes through the crew, quietly collecting yays and nays. Most people speak so softly, I have no idea what they're saying. I glance at Siobhan. "Can you hear their answers?"

"Shhh. I'm counting." She narrows her eyes, her lips moving silently.

I shift to Nox's other shoulder. They're holding themself perfectly still as if bracing for bad news. I honestly don't know which way the vote will go. The crew seems to all but worship their charming captain, but if it's a choice between love and survival? I honestly don't know. They were happy enough to work for the rebellion, which is dangerous, but this is on another level entirely.

Poet steps forward. "I'm finished. We have three nays...and fifty-five yays. We're with you, Nox."

Nox's knees buckle. I slip under their arm and grab their waist, keeping them on their feet. Their voice is only a little thick as they say, "Set sail for Lyari. Swing southwest, skirting the storms as best you can. They shouldn't expect us to choose this destination."

I hope they're right. In any event, everyone from our party looks dead on their feet—except the old woman, Dia. Bowen leans heavily on Evelyn, or maybe she's leaning on him; I can't be sure. Siobhan is still standing strong, holding my cloak to her naked body, but she's paler than normal. And Nox...well, Nox is shivering in my arms.

I'm not doing too well myself. Despite my claims to Siobhan that I could hold the glamour to hide her—hide us—it took a toll. I'm exhausted and weaving on my feet.

I start toward their cabin, half carrying Nox. "You can't keep being so reckless. We need you." *I need you.* Words I don't have any right to say, but that doesn't change the way they linger on my tongue.

It's a testament to Nox's exhaustion that they don't try to

shrug off my touch. Instead, they lean a little deeper into me. "You know me. I do nothing halfway."

I feel Siobhan at our back, which is a small relief because I was going to have to track her down after dealing with Nox. This way, I can deal with them both at the same time. I push the cabin door open. "It seems like we're in a constant state of patching each other up and we haven't had a true battle yet."

"It feels like a battle," Nox murmurs.

"I still can't believe they were willing to sacrifice the entire city. I know it's not as large as Mairi on Second Sister, but that's still tens of thousands of people. They don't have magically re-inforced buildings; acid would eat through the roofs in short order and harm or kill the people inside."

"Yes." Nox slumps against the doorframe. "She has to have Council approval."

Siobhan's eyes go wide. "Surely not. The Council might favor Lyari in all ways, but this is too far, even for them."

"I wish that were the case." Nox pinches the bridge of their nose. "No matter how powerful Morrigan and her crew are, they wouldn't have dared try something like this in full view of half the nobles summering in Mairi if she thought it would blow back on her."

Obviously the Council is aware that something is amiss. They were the moment the *Crimson Hag* took me. Shame weighs down my shoulders. "I'm sorry. If I hadn't fought with Siobhan. If I hadn't tried to save that woman . . ."

"It would have happened anyway." Siobhan tugs at her wet hair. "It was only a matter of time before the Council and the Cŵn Annwn became aware of the rebellion."

"Yes, but . . ." My throat feels so tight. I was so fucking *foolish*.

I don't know how else to describe it. "When I told you we needed to take the rebellion into the light, I didn't think the Council would be so comfortable with sacrificing civilians."

Nox smiles, the expression more cutting than warm. "It's a rebellion, Bastian. One that has operated under their nose for years. There are no civilians—at least not in their eyes. No one is safe until they're satisfied that they've put us down."

It's so grossly unfair and ugly . . . which is how the Cŵn Annwn operates. Despair threatens, and I only hold it off with sheer determination. "Well, at least your crew hasn't abandoned us."

"No, my crew hasn't abandoned us. But maybe they should have." Nox pushes forward, wearing every single one of their years. "I can't stand the thought of them dying. Better they sail off to safety."

"Nox," I say quietly. "There is nowhere safe. Not if we don't stop them. You just said as much, and you're right. It's sheer luck that the Cŵn Annwn have restrained themselves to Threshold for this long, but that won't be true in a generation or two. The nobles are too greedy, the Council too willing to expand at the expense of everything they're supposed to protect. Now that they've secured their base here, it's only a matter of time before they turn gluttonous eyes elsewhere."

Siobhan sighs. "We don't know that." It's part of what we've fought about so fiercely in recent months. I can see the path forward, and Siobhan refuses to. "It would be a huge risk to expand their power to other realms."

"Not if they start with ones where magic is less common. The people there will have no way to defend themselves."

"Damn it." Nox curses. "I hate that it doesn't sound far outside the realm of possibility."

"Because it's not." I hold their gaze. "We've been saving people from the beginning, but now it's time to save, well, everything."

Nox's smile loses some of its edge, becoming almost fond. "You're making me feel all heroic."

"You *are* heroic." Siobhan's gaze flicks to me. "You both are the most heroic people I know. It makes me ashamed that I've hidden in the shadows for so long."

Nox tilts their head back and stares at the ceiling. "When you say things like that, it's hard to fight against the pull of you—of both of you."

"Then don't fight it." I don't mean to say it. I'm trying to respect the distance Nox has put between us, respect the fact that they continue to evade any entanglement despite the unresolved feelings both Siobhan and I obviously hold. I've already caused them more than enough harm because of our past, and I won't let my selfishness add to that.

"As if it's that easy." Nox inhales sharply. "I'm not proud of the fact that you broke my heart and it still hurts fourteen years later."

"I'm sorry." I've said it before, but I'll say it again and again, backing it up with actions. "I should have listened to you. You were right."

They smile a little. "That's the thing. I can't hate you anymore, Bastian. Not when it's clear that you *have* changed." They transfer their attention to Siobhan. "As for you, I . . . I'm afraid. You're the leader of the fucking rebellion, Siobhan. You're in danger more than anyone else I know, and the thought of giving my heart to you, only to lose you, scares the shit out of me."

"I understand, but we all very well may die."

I can't stop the laugh that bursts from me. "Very rousing, Siobhan."

Nox inhales slowly and exhales just as slowly. "No, she's right. We're sailing toward nearly certain death. What's the point in fearing a broken heart when we might not survive to experience it?"

The energy in the room shifts, somehow both losing and gaining teeth at the same time. Nox tilts their head down and takes in Siobhan where she holds perfectly still in the center of the room, the cloak still clutched to her chest and concealing very little of her strong body. The long lines of her legs are bare, and Nox takes their time dragging their gaze north to Siobhan's eyes. "Drop the cloak," they finally say. The three words have none of their normal playful tone.

It's a command, plain and simple.

Siobhan doesn't hesitate. She unclenches her fist and the fabric falls to the floor, leaving her gloriously naked. No matter how many times I've seen her this way before, the sight still steals my breath. She wears cloaks so often, slouching carefully to never reveal the breadth of her shoulders, the true stretch of her height. There's none of that facade now. Just Siobhan, body carved with muscle, small breasts peaked with dark berry nipples, golden skin still faintly damp from her swim.

I've wanted Siobhan from the moment I met her. She exhibits a magnetic draw that I never tried to resist. That draw isn't directed at me right now, though. It's all for Nox.

I'm . . . not invited.

Sorrow hits me in a wave that I swallow down in large gulps. I'm not entitled to the intimacy, for all that I love her and she loves me, for all that I never really stopped loving Nox. The act of loving is meant to be selfless, independent of circumstance. To do anything else, to demand something in return, is to poison the very emotion.

I take a staggering step back, and then another. Neither Nox nor Siobhan looks at me, their eyes only for each other. Even as it feels like my heart is being carved out with a rusted knife, there's a part of me that's glad they found each other properly. Nox deserves to be loved with all the ferocity Siobhan is capable of.

My hand closes around the doorknob. One more step and I'll be gone from this place. I don't know what I'll do. They don't need me. My glamour is useful, but Threshold has operated under the assumption that glamour has been extinct for generations. Me being here doesn't change that. Not really. Maybe the *Audacity* can drop me somewhere and I'll head in the opposite direction, determined to lead Morrigan away from their path. It will mean my death—I can't be taken alive again—but one life is a small price to pay if it means Threshold is finally free of the iron boot on our necks.

"Bastian." Nox says my name on a sigh. "If you don't want this, you're free to go, but . . ." They hold out a hand without looking at me. "I'd like you to stay."

"*We'd* like you to stay," Siobhan says.

I don't know if it's possible to get whiplash from swinging from heartbreak to overwhelming joy in a single instant. I don't care. I release the doorknob and start for them.

CHAPTER 26

Nox

I DON'T SIGH WITH RELIEF WHEN BASTIAN TURNS FROM the door to face us; there's not enough air in the room for that. I feel strange and boneless, dizzy with fear and joy in a way I didn't know I could experience. I've been so damn afraid of being hurt again that I've put up walls between myself and my lovers, but there are no walls to be found when it comes to Siobhan and Bastian. They both see me too clearly in their own way. That seeing terrifies me, but when your life is numbered in days, hours, minutes, a broken heart is barely worth mentioning. If I experience it, then at least the pain has an end point this time.

No matter what they think, no matter the confidence I've portrayed to my crew, there's a part of me that doesn't believe the horn will do anything.

That's a worry for another day, another me. Right now, Bastian is crossing to stand before me, Siobhan on my other side, her perfect body on full display. Even as Bastian takes my hand, I drink in the sight of her, doing my best to memorize every line, every curve. She's every inch a warrior, strong and solid and fierce.

And she's looking at me like she wants to take a bite out of me, her honeyed eyes shining in the low light of my cabin.

"I—"

"What terms would you like me to use?" she asks softly. When I don't immediately answer, she motions to my body. "Do you have preferences?"

Shock makes my knees buckle. I manage to stay on my feet through sheer habit, grounded by Bastian's hand in mine. I usually take the lead when it comes to sexual encounters. It's easier that way, to tell my lovers what I need from them before they have a chance to disappoint me. For Siobhan to ask this now shows a level of care that I don't know how to deal with.

Bastian squeezes my hand, but is otherwise silent. I appreciate that. I was still feeling out my identity when he and I were together, and what I wanted from him then is not the same thing I need from lovers now.

I clear my throat. "Uh, chest." I press my hand to my chest and then slide it down my stomach. "Sex."

"Good." Siobhan makes a rumbling sound somewhere between a growl and a purr. She takes the single step that brings her close. She surveys us for a beat. "Let's get cleaned up before we begin."

I've never been at a loss for words in my life, but I can't seem to draw forth the breath required to speak. Bastian presses a kiss to the sensitive spot on my neck, right behind my ear, and chuckles against my skin. "Best not argue. Siobhan always gets her way."

Argue? I can't even *think* properly as she leads us into the bathroom. The sensation only gets worse—better—as she catches the hem of my shirt and pulls it slowly up, her knuckles coasting over my stomach and chest, sending little zings in their wake. I'm so distracted, I almost miss Bastian's hands on my belt, effortlessly tugging it free and sliding my pants down my legs. He gets tangled up in my boots. "Well, fuck."

Siobhan makes that delicious rumbling sound again. "I have a solution." She bands her forearm under my ass and lifts me, pressing me tightly to her naked body.

Distantly, I can feel Bastian freeing me of my boots and pants, but all I can focus on are her honey eyes and the fact that her mouth is . . . right . . . there. Just like that, I'm not frozen any longer. I wrap my legs around her waist and dig my hands into her hair. Then I kiss her the way I've wanted to for years, a slow savoring of the simple press of her lips to mine before I nip her full bottom lip and tease her mouth open.

Gods, her *taste*. It's as wild and heady as faerie wine—and just as quick to sweep me away.

My back hits the cold tile wall, and not even that is enough to shock me out of the need for more. I lock my heels against the small of her back, grinding against her mindlessly as she kisses me back like she wants to consume me, bite by bite.

The sound of water running is a distant thing, even as steam fills the room. And then there are more hands on my body—*Bastian's* hands—soft palms and clever fingers running up my legs to cup my ass, squeezing and parting me even as Siobhan keeps kissing me like her life depends on the stroke of her tongue against mine.

Bastian's touch changes, becomes less exploration and more guidance as he tugs us back into the shower and beneath the hot spray. It feels so good, I have to break the kiss just to moan a little. "Nothing better than a hot shower after a long day."

"*Nothing* better?" Siobhan laughs roughly. She shifts her grip on me so she can palm my sex. "Are you sure, Nox?"

I moan again, grinding against her touch. It's been *so long* since I had a lover, and never like this; never in *my* space, my cabin, my shower. Sex was strictly for our times ashore, in rooms in inns or brothels. Allowing someone so close to where I spend my days and nights was an intimacy that I shied away from.

There's no shying away from this. From *them*.

Siobhan turns us and then Bastian is at my back, his naked chest pressed to my skin. He's not quite as tall as Siobhan, but all that means is that his cock lines up quite nicely where I'd like it, and he has easy reach to press open-mouthed kisses along my neck. He slides his hands between my and Siobhan's bodies, cupping my sex over her touch and, from the way she shivers and moans, stroking her pussy with the other.

We're a mess of questing hands and writhing bodies. It's fucking divine. For all the desperation that pulses between us, no one is rushing.

At least not until the hot water abruptly goes cold.

"Fuck!" Bastian slips around us to scramble at the knobs. "Holy shit. That's freezing."

Siobhan loosens her grip, allowing me to slide down her body, until I'm standing on shaky feet. Her lips are swollen from my kisses, her eyes both sharp and hazy with desire. She hesitates. "Second thoughts?"

"No." It's the truth. It's not just because of the lust throbbing through my body in time with my racing heart. Lust is simple.

This feels like fate. "I want you in my bed." I look past her to where Bastian has pulled down a few towels. "Both of you."

He looks . . . I don't know if I have the words. Bastian is always gorgeous to the point of being pretty. But wet, with his longish hair slicked back, water droplets making their slow way over his warm, light brown skin? I shiver. I want to follow those rivulets with my tongue. I want to see if Siobhan tastes as wild and free everywhere. I *want*.

We towel off quickly and there's another moment of awkward transition from the bathroom to the cabin. I pause long enough to lock my door. When I turn around, Siobhan is stretched out across my bed and Bastian is standing a nearly polite distance away. He looks like he's about to try to be honorable again. This is something that hasn't changed in the years since I loved him with my whole—if bruised—heart. Bastian has always been aware of the power he wields as a Dacre; even a second son holds more value in the eyes of the Council and the rest of Lyari than a street kid. He could do anything he wanted to to those less powerful than he is.

And he never has.

I close the distance between us in a single step and press my fingertips to his lips. "Do you want to stop?"

His dark eyes go hot enough to chase away what little fear remains. Bastian holds my gaze and shakes his head slowly. "No," he says against my touch. "I don't want to stop."

"Me, either."

Kissing Siobhan was as inevitable as the tide. Kissing Bastian feels like the best kind of recklessness. There's no exploration here; we don't need it. The years fall away as if they never happened. Somewhere deep inside me, I can admit that a part of me will always know this man, will always recognize him as holding a part of my heart.

He backs me toward the bed and then Siobhan is there, tugging us both down. Being between them is like being caught in a violent storm. I lose all track of myself, of time, of everything. There's only her and him and me. Today, yesterday, tomorrow? It all ceases to exist.

Bastian kisses his way down my body, pausing to nip along my chest, to lavish my nipples with his tongue until I squirm and moan. Touching him again is . . . like coming home. He has new scars and his body has shifted over the years, the softness of young adulthood and a life lived easy have been burned away, leaving carved muscles and a strength that makes my mouth water.

And Siobhan? She's a force of nature. Her strength makes me quiver. Her touch is sure and skillful, moving in perfect harmony with both mine and Bastian's. She grips his cock and runs one careful nail down his length. "Have you missed this, Bastian? Missed *us*?"

There it is again. That terrifying, exhilarating word. "Us."

"Yes," he grinds out, his head thrown back, the long line of his throat exposed.

It's the most natural thing in the world to kiss that throat. To push him down onto the bed next to Siobhan and continue exploring his body with my lips and tongue as Siobhan lazily pumps his cock, a satisfied smile on her face.

Having them this close together is a fantasy I've been too afraid to even entertain. Now that it's truly happening, I can't stop touching, tasting. I cup Bastian's balls with careful fingers. I shift over to rub my face against Siobhan's strong thigh and bite her just hard enough to make her gasp. Her pussy is *right there*, and even as I keep fondling Bastian, I dip down and drag my tongue through her folds.

I was right. She tastes just as wild here as her kiss did. Wilder, even. Especially when her thighs quiver on either side of my head. Siobhan is as unshakable as a mountain, but she's shivering for *me*? That's an addiction I could spend the rest of my life in service to.

Bastian jerks and hisses out a breath. "Gods, I've missed you."

I tell myself not to look up, not to witness the fact that I'll be forever on the outside of their relationship—no matter how short my *forever* is meant to be—but Bastian doesn't appear consumed with Siobhan alone. He has one hand fisted in her hair, tugging her head back so he has full access to her throat. Even as I watch, he licks her there and reaches down to create a V with his fingers, parting her folds to give me unrestricted access to her.

He meets my gaze. "I missed you, too, Nox. So fucking much."

I don't have a response to that that won't break my ribs open and expose my racing heart. So I don't answer with words. Instead, I shift my hand up to join Siobhan's around his shaft and go back to making her come all over my face.

CHAPTER 27

Siobhan

Ever since I fled Lyari and went into hiding, I've fought against being known. Losing the two most important people in my life to violence at the hand of my sister? Even after my scars from the fire faded away to nothingness, the ones from Morrigan's betrayal live on.

I never meant to fall for Bastian, to let him through my walls filled with spikes and traps designed to keep me safe. I certainly never meant to let my friendship with Nox turn into something more.

And yet the joy I feel now, in Nox's bed with their mouth between my thighs, Bastian's naked body pressed to mine ... it's indescribable. I feel like a great, greedy beast, wanting to devour each moment of this pleasure and keep it tucked away inside me forever. I've leaped from a high place, and there may be an inevitable crash in my future, but in the meantime, all I feel is the impulse to go faster, harder.

Nox lifts their head, the bottom half of their face wet with my desire. They look at me and then Bastian, something vulnerable and overwhelming in their gray eyes. "I want to fuck you. Both of you."

I can't quite manage to be cool and collected when they talk like that. "At the same time?"

"Yes."

Bastian's already nodding. "I want that, too." He kisses me, his fingers still moving over my pussy, pressing inside for the briefest moment before retreating again. He's always been a tease when he gets riled. "I want to fuck you while Nox fucks us."

My mind goes blessedly, perfectly blank. There's only one answer, and I can barely get it out in my need. "Yes."

Nox shifts over and takes Bastian's cock into their mouth, sucking him deep. His grip goes tight on my hair. "Fuck, Nox, please. I need—" He cuts himself off as they lift their head and then rise. When Bastian begs, it's a beautiful thing, but he's not quite there yet.

We both sit up to watch Nox pad to their cabinet and dig through the drawers. When they bend over, displaying their pert little ass, I can't help the hungry sound I make. They've tasted me, and as pleasurable as that was, I want to get my mouth on them, to lick my way down their spine, to press their cheeks wide and kiss them there until they squirm and moan, to cover their sex with my mouth and find out exactly what rhythm, what pressure makes their back bow and their fingers dig into my hair.

"Better hurry, Nox." Bastian's voice is ragged. "Otherwise, Siobhan is going to take you right there."

They stand, a contraption hanging from their fingertips and a bottle of lube in their other hand. "Trust me when I say you're not going to want to rush me through this." They return to the bed, some of their customary swagger back in place. I don't know if it's a sign that they're masking their true feelings or if this *is* them relaxing into what we're doing.

The thought bothers me. I clear my throat. "You don't have to pretend with us, Nox."

Instead of retreating, they smile slowly. "I know, love."

Love.

There's no time to let that word wash over me because Bastian has leaned forward, curiosity lighting his beautiful face. "This isn't like any strap I've seen."

"It's custom."

They lightly fondle one of the trio of long, thick lengths attached to the straps. Even as we watch, it appears to squirm to life, growing and rolling with . . . "Water."

"The very same." Nox licks their lips. "Fuck you, fuck myself . . . A lot of fucking in our future."

I see what they mean immediately. The third length isn't positioned outward—it's attached on the inner side, meant to penetrate Nox while they penetrate us. I shiver. "You are a genius, and it terrifies me."

"Remember that next time I come up with a brilliant and questionable plan." They lean down and press a quick kiss to my lips and then grab Bastian's chin. "I want Siobhan on her back, you on top. Get her ready for us, Bastian."

It's as if their words unlock something in him. He pushes me back and slides down my body to press two fingers into me and cover my clit with his mouth. Bastian has always loved foreplay, and he's not fucking around right now, licking me everywhere.

I can barely keep my eyes open as pleasure tightens through me, but watching Nox put on the strap is worth the effort. They move efficiently—except when Bastian sucks hard on my clit as he curls his fingers inside me, surprising a moan from me.

Nox pauses, their gaze so intense that I swear I can feel it on my skin . . . then I realize I *am* feeling it on my skin, air brushing over my nipples, not quite a true touch, but pleasurable enough to make me squirm. At least until I register exactly what they're doing.

I dig my hand into Bastian's hair and tug until he pauses. "Nox." My voice breaks in the middle of their name, and I have to try again. "No magic, Nox. It's not worth the risk to you."

They smile, the expression lighting up their face with warmth. "You don't have to worry about me, at least not with this. It's barely a whisper of power, and even with the concentration to move three separate appendages, it's truly no effort at all." They finish fastening the strap around their narrow hips and close their eyes, humming a little. "Mmm, that feels good."

I open my mouth to continue arguing, but Bastian bites my thigh, opposite where Nox bit me earlier, and says, "Trust them, Siobhan. They're telling the truth, aren't you, Nox?"

Nox opens their eyes, and the two cocks on the front of their strap stir to life. "I could fuck you both for *days* before I start to feel the strain. Tonight won't come close to draining me."

There's a part of me that doesn't quite believe them, but I have to push it down deep inside me. Right now is about trust, and interrogating them might be reassuring, but it will put a damper on what happens next. So I swallow my questions down and nod. "I'm taking you at your word."

"Thank you." Nox turns the bottle and coats each of the cocks in lube. "Bastian."

He doesn't need further clarification. He tugs me to the edge of the bed and presses my thighs wide. For a beat, he stares at my pussy as if he might descend again, but Nox strokes their hands down his chest to grip his cock. They pause. "I'm assuming you've taken precautions to avoid pregnancy."

"I have," I manage.

"Good." Their chin fits neatly on his shoulder as they drag his cock through my folds. He's so tense, I don't think he's breathing. Nox rubs him lightly against my clit. "I like seeing you like this. Both of you." They press him to my entrance and then inside.

My eyes threaten to flutter closed, but I force them open. I don't want to miss a single moment of this. Even as Bastian thrusts slowly into me, he turns his head to kiss Nox. The scene they create is too perfect. They're both so beautiful that, separately, they take my breath away. Together, their tongues dancing as Bastian slides deeper and Nox feathers their thumb against my clit.

It's what I imagine it would be like to be seduced by gods. Terrifying. Exhilarating.

Nox gives him one last kiss. "Down, Bastian."

He obeys instantly, shifting his thighs wide—which spreads me even more—and bending down so his chest presses against my breasts. He cups my face with his hands. "Siobhan—"

"I know," I whisper, cutting him off. Tonight is too perfect. No matter how big the emotions in my chest are, no matter how good all of this feels, I know better than to let my words get away from me. Nox is with us, yes, but I'm still convinced that

it won't take much to scare them off. To end this prematurely—
and I don't mean the sex.

Something cool and wet presses to my ass. I jolt, even
though I expected it. Nox soothes me with a gentle hand on my
leg. "Relax, love. Let me do the work." They must do the same to
Bastian, because he tenses and then relaxes on a ragged exhale.
"There you go," Nox murmurs.

After seeing the size the cocks could swell to, I expect
pain—or at least strain. But it's deceptively gentle and small as
Nox works their cock into me. "Small" being a relative term.
With Bastian buried in me to the hilt, there's just not that much
room. Or at least there doesn't seem to be. While he and I have
used toys in the past, it's never been like *this*.

Even as the certainty that this will change things forever
takes root, the cock in my ass expands slowly, filling me until I
squirm and moan, not sure if I'm trying to get away or closer.

Bastian presses his forehead to mine, his breathing as harsh
as mine. "Fuck, Nox. That feels good."

"Yeah." Their voice has gone husky. "It really does." They
lean over, pushing deeper yet, and drop a kiss on his shoulder
before meeting my gaze. "You doing okay, love?"

Every time they call me that, my whole body goes tense with
want. This time, both Nox and Bastian know it because they're
both inside me. Bastian moans. Nox withdraws a little and
thrusts into us, their eyes fluttering with pleasure.

I reach up and cup their face. "Are you fucking yourself as
careful as you fuck us?"

"Yes." They turn their face and kiss my palm. "Are you ready
for more?"

There's only one answer. "Yes."

Bastian pulls out of me a little, thrusting back onto Nox. "Don't stop. More. Harder."

"Greedy." Nox leans back, the move pushing their cock deeper into me. A bare hesitation and then they're moving . . . except *they* aren't moving. Their cock is. It rolls inside me, almost as if seeking . . .

"Oh, *fuck*." My orgasm hits me without warning. My claws shoot out of my fingers, and it's everything I can do to make sure I don't impale either of them. Bastian writhes between my thighs, thrusting into me and against Nox, driving my orgasm on and on. Just when I think it's about to subside, it crests again.

"There you go, Siobhan," Bastian whispers against my lips. "Let go. We've got you."

Bastian

I'm trying to keep it together, but it's an impossible task. All I can feel is Nox inside me and Siobhan clenching around me as she orgasms over and over again. I can't help trying to get closer to both of them at the same time. "I need . . ."

Nox catches my throat in their hand and uses that hold to force me to straighten. It pushes them deeper yet, pushes *me* deeper yet. "*Fuck*."

"Does that . . . feel good?" From how low Nox's voice has gone, they're close to orgasming, too.

"Yes," I gasp. They hit the spot inside me that makes my thoughts turn to fuzz and words sprout from my lips. "I missed you so fucking much, Nox."

They miss their next stroke. "Bastian . . ."

"I did." I press one hand to Siobhan's lower stomach so I can stroke her clit with my thumb. She's obviously trying to keep her eyes open, but at the first touch, she loses that battle and cries out. "I missed both of you." I know I've said it before, but neither of them can fully understand how deeply I mean it.

Siobhan has been my friend for thirteen years, my partner and lover for ten. We've fought countless times during those years, but this last argument raised the fear that maybe it would be the last. Then, when I was taken captive, I fully expected to be hauled back to Lyari and killed. I would have done my damnedest to not endanger Siobhan and the others; I was all but certain my death would be the end of any hope of fixing what our fight broke.

And Nox? Nox was my first love, the only other person in Threshold who carries a piece of my heart with them, no matter that up until recently, I thought I'd never see them again. It was enough to know that they were out there somewhere, living the life they'd dreamed of, the one I was too cowardly to follow them into.

To spend time with Nox and Siobhan, to sail with them, to have regained enough of their trust to share their bed? It's a gift beyond measure.

Even as swept away as I am, I know better than to speak my feelings aloud. This may feel as right as anything I've ever done, but a few hours ago, Nox was ready to flee. I won't give them reason to run again.

Nox grips my hips. "I'm close," they whisper. "I want you to come, Bastian. Stop being a hero and holding out." They thrust into me, harder than they have previously. The pleasure is almost too much to bear. "Siobhan wants that, too, don't you, love? You want him to make a mess of you?"

Siobhan clenches around me. "Yes!"

"Give the lady what she wants, Bastian." Nox is pure temptation in my ear, their voice as desperate as the feeling burgeoning inside me, one I thought long buried. "Don't make me . . ." They moan, low and long, grinding into me with a frenzy that I can only match.

I thrust hard into Siobhan, keeping up my steady stroking of her clit. Each retreat has me thrusting back onto Nox's cock, still moving inside me with a purpose that has pressure shooting down my spine and gathering in my balls. "I'm going to . . ." And then I'm coming, pounding deep into Siobhan, getting pounded deep by Nox. My orgasm seems to last forever, draining every bit of myself.

I can't even collapse properly at the end of it because of my current position, kneeling between Siobhan and Nox. "Fuck. I—*fuck*."

"Yeah." Siobhan shivers, her eyes still closed.

"Give me a second." Nox is pressed to my back. I feel every single one of their rough inhales and equally ragged exhales. Their cock slowly shrinks and then eases out of me. From the way Siobhan twitches, they've done the same to her. Nox brushes a kiss against my spine and slumps over to the side. "Damn."

Now it's my turn to disentangle myself. My thigh tries to cramp, but I do my best to ignore it as I carefully lie down on Siobhan's other side. She's got a small smile pulling at her lips, and I can't help but kiss it.

I look up and meet Nox's gaze. Pleasure makes their lids heavy, their expression relaxed. Even with all that, there's a growing guardedness on their face. I open my mouth, but they hold up a tired hand before I can speak. "Let's just keep things simple, yeah?"

Simple.

The very idea is laughable. We're three people with an increasingly complicated and tangled relationship, which would be challenge enough if that was all we faced. But it's not.

We're sailing into certain danger—possibly even certain death—as we speak. I refuse to believe that we're going to die, no matter what Siobhan and Nox fear. The horn is the answer, and if we don't know the exact details of how it works, it's enough hope to survive on. We just need a plan and a small, solid team.

I want to tell Nox that we're going to live, damn it. I want to challenge their fear and replace it with hope.

But I know better. For some, hope can be summoned with the right combination of words. Most people *want* to hope, rather than give in to despair. But Nox isn't most people; neither is Siobhan. With the lives of so many people resting on their shoulders, they can only respond to facts and actions, not dreams.

I want to tell them that I'll dream enough for the both of them. I don't. Neither of them will thank me for even saying it.

So I don't challenge Nox's words. I just nod. "Sure. Simple."

They relax instantly, the tension bleeding away from their shoulders. "Thank you." They kiss Siobhan and then slide off the bed to start working on getting the strap off. "That was good. Really, really good."

For a moment, I'm certain they're running again, but then they kick the strap off and climb back into bed to settle down next to Siobhan. She immediately pulls them close and tucks them against her side. It strikes me that it could always be like this . . . that I *want* it to always be like this.

CHAPTER 28

Nox

I SLEEP BETTER THAN I HAVE IN MONTHS—YEARS—AND wake up sandwiched between Bastian and Siobhan as if, even in sleep, they fear I'm going to panic and bolt the first chance I get. I wish they were wrong. I've never felt more conflicted. I convinced myself to stop fighting my attraction and feelings for them under the assumption that we'd be dead long before a broken heart became a real risk.

Except waking up listening to their steady breathing has true fear roiling inside me. I'm not prepared to lose either of them. I wasn't before, but now that I know how Siobhan tastes, have been reminded how sweetly Bastian comes? Now that I've had a night of feeling cared for, I crave it with an intensity that scares me.

I slip from the bed like a thief in the night, easing from under Siobhan's arm and sliding past the leg Bastian tossed over my hip. Neither of them stirs as I dress in hurried, awkward movements. I'm not doing anything *wrong*, but the need to leave the cabin before either of them wakes up is nearly overwhelming. I take a moment to summon my magic to remove the salt from Siobhan's and Bastian's clothing.

I take my first full breath of the morning as I step into the faint sunlight. I should have been out on deck the whole time, ensuring my people were as safe as they can be in this situation. The vote yesterday wasn't only putting their faith in me as captain, but in the mission as a whole. And yet . . . I can't regret a single moment.

Eyal and Poet stand at the helm, expressions serious. I walk over to stand next to them, doing my best to ignore the self-conscious need to shuffle my feet as if I've done something wrong.

"No sign of them," Eyal murmurs. "It won't last."

"It won't," I confirm. "If Morrigan has reported to the Council, then every crimson sail is more of a threat than normal. If they're smart, they'll start a coordinated sweep of this area."

"A tall order." Eyal stares at the horizon as if there are answers there. "Even with Morrigan as the leader, there are plenty of captains who aren't interested in playing nice with a group. There are so many old grudges that they'd need a strategist just to coordinate a plan that doesn't devolve into infighting."

"Hope springs eternal."

"None of that will matter if we flounder." Poet sighs. "Everyone is exhausted. We have perhaps another day or two of operating at full capacity before we need to allow the air-users to rest."

Because magical burnout is a real threat, especially when we've been running so hard with no rest. Or not nearly enough rest. Guilt wraps its claws around my throat. I should have already been taking steps to ensure my crew were protected. "No one has gone down yet."

Despite it being a statement, Poet nods. "Right. Not yet."

Eyal shifts. "If we sail fully east to Drash and then cut south from there, we can hop islands—"

"No." I shake my head. "We can't afford to waste the weeks that route would cost us. Our best chance to be successful means reaching Lyari before Morrigan. If we're favoring stealth at the cost of speed, eventually she'll stop mindlessly pursuing and start wondering where we're headed. If she gets there first, we're all but doomed to fail." Siobhan said something about the ability to make a request when a person summons the Cŵn Annwn. I don't know if it's true, but if it is, the *last* thing we need is Morrigan being the one to get to the horn.

"Nox." Eyal looks away. "Poet and I have been talking. We don't see a route through this where we don't end up dead."

I honestly don't, either, but I'm the captain, and the captain isn't allowed to doubt where others can see. The vote last night meant everything to me, but Eyal has a point now and Poet did then, too. "The *Audacity* isn't going to Lyari." I make the decision as I speak the words. "Get us to Yoth and then take the crew through the portal there. You all should be safe enough until this is over."

Yoth is an island about two days' normal sail from Lyari. It's hot and humid most days, with many rivers despite its small size and a thick jungle that stretches right up to its shores. Over the generations, Lyari has tried to conquer the foliage to create a destination for the rich and bored to vacation at, but developers have been driven back each time. Not violently, but by strange coincidences that lead most people to believe the island is either cursed or blessed, depending on what your goals are.

"Yoth." Poet narrows her eyes. "It's not a bad idea."

"We voted to support you and you're sending us away."

"I'm doing my best to make sure you all *live*." Yoth *is* a good choice. Most of the crew has spent time there over the years. Hedd had a thing with a local for a few years, which brought us south again and again. It gave the crew plenty of time to get familiar with the area. "Or, if you don't take the portal, then spend a couple weeks in the village there. They'll be happy to have our people, and it's as protected as anywhere in Threshold."

Eyal's shoulders drop. "You know I want to support you in this."

"We both do." Poet finally looks at me. "The current system of power doesn't work."

"It's never worked." I clasp her on the shoulder, masking my unhappiness with a bright grin. "But I think a couple weeks on Yoth is more than enough reward for everyone's hard work."

"Easier said than done. We still have to sail there." Poet sighs again. "You're asking for a week more than most of our people have."

A normal ship takes nearly three weeks to reach Lyari from Three Sisters. The *Audacity* isn't a normal ship, and that's never been truer than since I took over and we lost the worthless assholes Hedd kept around. "That's the only option that I can see where we don't all die."

"Let me talk to Orchid and see what we can come up with," Poet says. "If we slow our speed a little, we can offer our air-users more time to recover in between shifts."

I don't want to agree. Obviously more recovery is better, but if we are caught by the *Bone Heart*, it's very likely that the entire crew will be cut down. Making that call is one of the shitty parts of leadership. I'm good at what I do, but I'm just as tired as everyone else. I don't have the answers. "Do it."

She heads off, and I glance at Eyal. "I'll be back."

He waves me away. "I got a solid four hours' sleep. Callen managed not to run us aground during that time, so I think it's safe to say he did a good job."

I make my rounds, chatting briefly with the few crew members up and about. Everyone is exhausted, but they're putting a good face on it. It's only once I've started back to the helm that I realize I've had an audience the whole time. I twist to find Lizzie lurking by the mast. I narrow my eyes. "Eavesdropping isn't looked highly upon."

"Oh, please. Save your false superiority." She waves that away and moves toward me, her long hair swinging with each step. "You're quite the leader. So willing to tuck your crew away in relative safety while you run off to sacrifice yourself."

"The goal is to sacrifice no one," I say mildly.

"And yet that's never the outcome of these kinds of events." She stops just out of reach. "You know, I like you better now that you've mostly set aside the charming-rake bullshit."

"Darling, I *am* a charming rake."

She smiles thinly. "From the scent of Bastian and Siobhan mingled with yours, I believe you." She continues before I can decide how I feel about *that*. "Maeve won't be content to hide with your crew. She's determined to see this through."

I've heard about the feats Maeve accomplished in her time seeking her stolen pelt. I've also heard about how she almost died in the attack that sank the *Crimson Hag.* "This won't be a water battle. She's better off staying in Yoth."

"Undoubtedly," Lizzie agrees easily—too easily. "But Maeve won't listen to reason."

I narrow my eyes. "I would think you'd be invested in keeping her out of combat."

"I am." She shrugs. "But she's not a child to be tucked away while the grown-ups talk. She'll make her own decision about this—and I'll be there to ensure no one lays a single finger on her."

While the selkie's contribution might come into question, no one can argue that Lizzie is dangerous enough for both of them. Her ability to subdue large numbers of people rivals mine. If I were a better person, I'd tell them both to stay behind to keep them safe.

I'm not a better person. I want to live. More than that, I want everyone in Threshold to live a life without fear that a roving crew of Cŵn Annwn will cause havoc in their community. To have even a chance of us accomplishing that, I need Lizzie with us. "I'd be glad to have you."

"I know." This time, when she smiles, she flashes a hint of fang. "And if I'm defending Maeve's life, she can't get grumpy about how I choose to do it."

I give her the look that statement deserves. We both know Maeve would rather incapacitate than kill anyone, even her worst enemy. She's got a big heart, and though she's a fearsome fighter in the water, she will always look for a peaceful resolution. The fact that she ended up with a vampire who enjoys seeing the light leave *her* enemies' eyes will never cease to amuse me.

"Just thinking about it is getting me hungry." Lizzie turns away. "We'll be ready when we reach Yoth."

I watch her walk away. Maybe it was a mistake to change the plan after yesterday's vote, but the growing certainty inside me says otherwise. A small group is more likely to infiltrate Lyari than an entire crew, and most of the people on this ship have specialties and experience that would be difficult to utilize on dry land.

Or maybe it's just that I don't want to lose a single one of them.

It's tempting to return to my cabin—to my bed with a sleeping Bastian and Siobhan in it—but there's work to be done. I climb the stairs to the upper deck and nod to Frost and Derry, both of whom weave slightly on their feet in a way that has nothing to do with the movement of the deck beneath our feet. "I've got it from here. Go get some rest."

They exchange looks. "You were in bad shape yesterday, Captain," Frost says. Ne is a tall half giant with deep purple skin and a mohawk ne likes to wear in rainbow colors. Today, it's pink fading through purple to blue. "We can finish the shift."

"I know you can." The last thing I want to do is undercut my crew's contributions. "But I had a restful night and we've got a long week ahead of us. Rest while you can, because there will be little enough of it in our future."

Frost looks like ne wants to keep arguing, but Derry nudges nem with her shoulder. "You were just complaining about starving. Let's go eat."

Frost mutters a little more, but eventually submits to Derry's nudging and follows her down the stairs to the hatch that leads belowdecks.

I roll my shoulders and tug on the strands of wind surging high above us, guiding them down to fill our sails. Not too much—that way lay ruin—but just enough to increase our pace.

It's draining—more so than normal, due to my reckless magic use in the last week—but not so much that I'm in any danger. Not for hours yet. The next shift change is in two hours. I can hold on until then.

It's a beautiful fucking day. The clouds are low and sparse, giving plenty of space for the sun to shine through. The breeze is playful and more than willing to dance to my whim. It's lovely.

But now, standing here without any crew or quartermaster or navigator to hold my attention, it's all too easy to fall back into the memory of last night.

Siobhan's taste. Bastian's touch. The slick rhythm of three bodies moving in perfect synchronization. It felt like a promise that I'm not sure any of us can uphold. We're sailing into near-certain death, and even if we weren't, playing with tools of the gods is a good way to end up tormented eternally.

Or at least that's what some of our oldest stories say.

I've never put much stock in those stories, but recent events have shown me the error of my ways. Maybe I should have been a historian instead of a captain. It certainly seems more useful.

"Lovely day."

It's a testament to how deep I am in my thoughts that I didn't realize the old woman had climbed the steps, trailing sweet smoke behind her. I give Dia a long look. "You know, smoking will kill you."

"So will everything else in Threshold." She inhales deeply and then offers me a blunt of truly impressive size.

I shrug and take it. With my future numbered in days instead of decades, there's no reason not to take a second inhale. The smoke burns my throat and sinuses, making my head light.

I pass it back. "You know, we're more than happy to drop you at any island on our way south. Any of them would be safer than staying on this ship."

"Undoubtedly." Dia shrugs and exhales a smaller circle into the larger one she just created. Her control is truly inspirational. "But this fight started a very long time ago, even before Siobhan's time. Ezra thought he could change the system from within. He didn't talk much with Bowen about the flaws he saw, which, in hindsight, I realize was a mistake. The boy conducted himself with honor, but he didn't question his orders until Evelyn came along."

Calling Bowen, easily as massive as Frost if not more so, a boy seems a stretch, but who am I to tell an elder how to view someone she raised? "It's impossible to change the system from within. We have to break it."

"I understand that now." She nods slowly. "I'll be little enough help on Lyari itself, but I can assist in ensuring you don't run into weather trouble on the way."

Her divination being specific to weather patterns is invaluable on a ship. "Thank you." I urge a little more air into our sails. We're moving along at a quick clip, but I can't help looking over my shoulder, expecting to see Morrigan lurking on the horizon.

In the hours I was . . . occupied . . . with Siobhan and Bastian, we left Three Sisters far behind. We should be seeing Broax shortly, a strange island where gravity doesn't exist. With the proper precautions, it's possible to explore the space, but the moment your oxygen runs out, you're dead. The island hosts no breathable air on its own.

There are a lot of deadly islands along our planned route. There's a reason the trade route from north to south in Threshold takes a certain path; it follows islands welcoming to humanoid folks, which means villages and towns with ports and supplies. Even with the resupply, we'll be running lean by the time we reach Yoth, but we'll make it without anyone going hungry.

Dia and I smoke in silence for a while before she puts out her blunt and tucks the remainder in her pocket. She pats me on the shoulder. "You'll do fine, Nox. You're a good captain and a good person."

There's no reason for her words to make my chest hurt. I blame the drugs. I smile. "Thanks, Dia. You're welcome on the *Audacity* as long as you'd like to be here."

CHAPTER 29

Siobhan

I WAKE UP IN WAVES. THE WARMTH OF NOX'S BED. THE press of Bastian behind me, one arm thrown over my waist. The scent of sex. My body is loose and lethargic, my eyes heavier than they've ever been. I shift, and Bastian's arm tenses.

"You're awake," I murmur.

"I am." He sighs. "I don't want to be. It feels like last night was a dream that I never want to end."

A dream is a good way to put it. There was the furious and fearful trip from Kanghri, sure every moment that we'd be cut down by my sister. Then coming into this cabin and things changing forever . . . At least I *want* them to have changed forever.

But I'm not the only person in this equation, and my singular desires don't outweigh the needs and desires of Bastian and Nox. Nox, whose absence feels very pointed. There's no reason for that feeling. They're the captain. They can't laze about in their cabin for days on end, no matter how profound last night felt. At least for me.

I sit up slowly and push my hair back from my face. "Nox is going to run again."

Bastian stretches, his muscles flexing beneath his skin and the sheet sliding low on his hips. "Nox was always going to run. They're afraid to want too desperately."

I start to argue, but stop. I may have known Nox a long time, but Bastian *knew* Nox. "Life is too short not to want things desperately."

"I agree." He sits up and presses a light kiss to my lips. "Give them time. They wouldn't have let last night happen if they didn't want this. We just need to stay very still and lull them into a sense of security. Like a wolf and a bunny." His dark eyes twinkle. "Or, more accurately, a hound."

I snort. "Nox is no bunny."

"Of course not," Bastian says gently. "They're a human who can make their own decisions. Just give them time."

Normally, I'm the one who is reasonable and thoughtful, and Bastian leads with his heart. It's uncomfortable for that situation to be reversed ... but also comforting at the same time. At least *someone* is thinking clearly. "I can give them time." What we have of it. Either we die in this mission, or we change the face of Threshold forever.

I'm not foolish enough to think the work stops there, even if we're successful. Nature abhors a power vacuum, and the cesspool in Lyari even more so. We have to hamstring the Cŵn Annwn *and* offer a better way forward.

I hate that the way forward likely means me as leader, or at least part of a new Council, one that is meant to represent all of

Threshold, not just the nobles in Lyari. We should have a representative from each island, voted in from their own people. It's sure to be messy and complicated, but it's still preferable to what we have now.

Bastian gives me one last kiss and slips out of bed. "I'm going to shower and then see what tasks Poet has for us to complete today."

I wait for him to disappear into the bathroom before I stand and stretch, my hands easily reaching the ceiling. I came in here without a single piece of clothing, but I catch sight of the bag I brought from the safe house on the dresser. I hadn't noticed either Bastian or Nox bringing it in here, but Nox obviously used their magic to clean the salt water from the fabric and my boots, because the neatly folded clothes smell faintly of Nox and nothing else.

Putting them on feels like a declaration of something, but it's no more than I already decided on previously. I want Bastian. I want Nox, too. No matter what that looks like.

I dress quickly and head outside, mostly to give my restless energy a place to go. I only make it three steps before I have to pull up short to avoid trampling Dia.

She peers up at me. "We need to speak. Privately."

Curiosity rises. In the short time I've known her, she reminds me a lot of Nox. She's clever and has a wicked sense of humor and doesn't bother to dance around uncomfortable subjects. I have no idea what she's after, but I know better than to brush her off, no matter how much I want to see Nox and reassure myself that we didn't damage something irreparable last night. "My cabin is empty at the moment."

"That will do."

I lead the way belowdecks and to the cabin Bastian and I are sharing. Dia looks around politely and then perches on the edge of Bastian's bed. "I wasn't entirely honest in Kanghri."

I blink. "Excuse me?"

"The information I conveyed. It wasn't complete." Her ancient face is uncharacteristically serious as she contemplates me. "You're Cŵn Annwn, but not the crimson-sailed bastards who have perverted the reputation of the originals. Truly Cŵn Annwn."

I nod slowly. "More or less. There are many generations that separate me and whatever ancestor who held that bloodline. But you knew that already."

"Yes," she says simply. "Just like I've seen how Nox watches you. If I told them what I'm about to tell you, they'd move every realm in existence to change things."

A trail of pure ice drips down my spine. I go still. "What are you going to tell me, Dia?"

She holds my gaze. I can appreciate that, even as her words rip into me with the gentle caress of a too-sharp knife. "The horn will work, but there is a price."

A price.

She continues slowly, but not so slowly that I have a chance to steady the ground beneath my feet. "Do you truly think that horn has just sat there and no one has been foolish enough to attempt it over the years, even if they didn't know the entirety of what it can do? It only works if one of the true descendants of the Cŵn Annwn blows it."

The words make sense, but she's leaving something out. "The price?"

"To summon is to join." She smiles sadly. "The Wild Hunt

never stopped riding, Siobhan. They merely retreated to realms beyond our reach, as is good and right for gods to do after a time. They will answer the call of one of their own, but they will sweep the caller up in the process. Your will becomes theirs, and theirs yours. They will hunt your enemies, but only with you in their midst."

The words worm deep inside me. "That's not what my parents told me. They said we can issue a request, a boon."

"You're not so naive as that." She speaks gently, but the tone matters less than the violence of the words. "There is always a price when it comes to bargains."

I sit down heavily across from her. "So that's it. My life for Threshold." I don't want to believe her, but it feels *correct*. She has no reason to lie to me. Not about something so vital that could save us all.

Or at least save the rest of Threshold.

"I'm sorry." She actually sounds like she means it. "It's not too late to find another way."

All this time, I've been looking for another way—one that wouldn't cost the lives of all the people I've fought so hard to save. "I can't ask the people I want to protect to make a sacrifice I'm too cowardly to make myself."

She smiles slightly, but not like she's happy. "You could. Lots of leaders do."

"But not good ones." I sigh and close my eyes, the weight of the air on my skin too much to bear. "You're sure? This isn't legend and supposition?"

"I'm the last of my family. We've been in Threshold longer than your people, and certainly longer than the colonizers in

Lyari. We aren't the only ones who kept records, I'm sure, but we *did* keep records."

I open my eyes to face her devastating compassion. It would be so much easier to reject her words if she didn't seem to understand exactly what she's telling me and appear to be mourning the loss of a future alongside me. "You're sure."

"I'm sure. The summoner must lead the Hunt."

I force myself to sit with that . . . and then to sit with the possibility of Morrigan summoning them before I can. There's no reason to think she has more information about it than I do . . . but I can't bet our lives and the future of Threshold on it. Dia just said hers isn't the only family who kept histories. We can't afford to assume the Council hasn't kept its own records, incomplete though they may be.

I exhale forcefully. "Okay. Thank you for telling me."

"You're a good girl, Siobhan." She stands and clasps my shoulder. "A good leader. A good person. I'm sorry that the cost of being good is so high." She walks out of the room before I can dredge up a response.

It's just as well. I don't have words. No matter what other options there are, they aren't valid choices. But gods, I didn't expect the cost to be so high.

I drop my head into my hands and laugh hoarsely. That's a lie. I knew there would be a cost and it would be paid in blood. I just didn't expect it to be so . . . eternal.

If the Wild Hunt still rides, just in realms out of reach, then that means I'll run with them until time ends or my life does, whichever comes first. I'm no god, long-lived to the point of being eternal. Maybe the magic of the Hunt will sustain me, but I honestly hope it doesn't.

I suppose it's a good thing I didn't know about this possibility ten years ago. As difficult as it's going to be to leave behind the ones I love, at least I've had a chance to love them. A small comfort, but still a comfort.

"My life was supposed to end in the fire," I finally say to the empty room. "I've been living on borrowed time since then." My throat tries to close, but it feels important to speak this aloud, even if there's no one to witness. *Especially* because there's no one to witness. "This is a way to balance the scales, to do everything I've been fighting so damn hard for."

Will I even miss Bastian? Nox? The friends I've made in my time wandering Threshold? Will I remember what I've lost? Or will my world narrow down to the earth beneath my paws, the taste of blood on my tongue, the flesh of my enemies between my teeth? Will I stop being *Siobhan* and turn into Cŵn Annwn and only Cŵn Annwn?

I hope so. To be trapped in a hunt and *know* I'm trapped sounds like an agony that would drive me mad. Better to lose myself completely.

I can't tell Bastian and Nox. They'll try to stop me, to find a different solution. I'll be tempted to allow them to find another way, even though there *is* no other way. Haven't I played out the alternate scenarios until I'm drowning in the theoretical blood that would be shed? There's a reason the rebellion existed in the shadows for as long as possible. There *is* no viable alternate scenario.

What's one life against thousands?

Because the Cŵn Annwn violence won't stop with those actively rebelling. They'll see the faces of people from so many islands in Threshold and they'll fear that the unrest extends wider than they could imagine. So they'll go on a campaign of terror to break the spirits of everyone under their jurisdiction, to squash any hope of freedom, any semblance of the fallacy that they protect instead of dominate.

I inhale slowly and exhale just as slowly. So be it. I knew my life might be payment for a better future. This bargain is just more explicit than I realized. I'm not even dying, not truly. Yes, *Siobhan* will cease to exist, but my body will go on.

There's no point in worrying about it now. If I dwell on it too forcibly, then I'll panic and try to find another way. There *isn't* another way. There likely never has been.

This means I won't be around to help Threshold get back on its feet, but Bastian is cleverer than he gives himself credit for. He'll step up once he finally stops believing the fiction that he's merely a worthless second son. And Nox will be there, one way or another. They might pretend their allegiance is only to their crew, but if that were true, they never would have joined the rebellion in the first place. They believe in the mission.

More, last night proved that things aren't finished between them and Bastian. They'll take care of him, and he'll take care of them. They don't need me to have a happy life. If Bastian had left Lyari with them fourteen years ago, they would have been together this entire time. The two of them never would have needed me.

That knowledge stings, but it's comforting at the same time. They'll be okay. Nox and Bastian have a community around them that firmly believes in their cause and has the power to back up that belief and make it into reality.

They simply need the threat of the Council and all their followers gone.

I shiver, and not even I can tell if it's in anticipation or fear. No matter how little I've shifted fully previously, I'm a hound down to my very soul. Tearing out the rot in Threshold with my teeth is appealing.

I just have to live long enough to make it happen.

And lie to the two people I care most about in this world in the process.

CHAPTER 30

Bastian

IN SOME WAYS, THE FOLLOWING WEEK IS ONE OF THE HAP-piest of my life. The days are filled with the intense work that comes with keeping a ship like the *Audacity* running, and my nights are filled with Siobhan and Nox. I never would have dared dream the three of us could carve out something that felt as natural as breathing.

And yet . . .

Something is wrong. It's there in the moments after we collapse onto the sheets, our bodies sweaty and our exhales coming hard. It's there in the silences that stretch a little too long when we talk about what happens after Lyari.

At first, I think Nox is the source. They've been cagey from the moment I came aboard, and though they share their body willingly enough, they hold part of themself in reserve. It makes sense. I've hurt them before; they don't trust me not to hurt them again.

But on the morning we'll reach Yoth, I wake up to Nox slipping out of bed the same way they do every morning. They pause to press a kiss to my knuckles before padding to the door and out of the room. I lie there, Siobhan curled around me as if she's afraid she'll lose me in her sleep, and I have to admit that Nox isn't the problem.

There's something wrong with Siobhan.

Her breathing isn't quite steady enough to pass for sleep. I clear my throat. "Are you going to tell me what's going on?"

She freezes. I'm pretty sure her heartbeat even stops for a moment. "I don't know what you're talking about."

She's a noble. She was raised from childhood to hide certain truths about herself, the same as I was. That's why I know her parents taught her to lie from the moment she could talk; it was a matter of survival.

There's no damn reason for her to be so fucking *bad* at it.

"Siobhan." I roll over to face her. She's got her eyes shut, as if she can avoid this conversation simply by pretending it's not happening. That won't work with me. I cup her face. "Talk to me."

"There's nothing to talk about."

"If you want me to believe that, you're going to have to get better at lying."

Her lips twist in something that isn't quite a smile. She finally opens her eyes. "I love you. You know that, yeah?"

"I know that. I love you, too," I say slowly. "But if you're trying to reassure me, you're doing a terrible job of it."

She kisses me then, pressing me back onto the mattress. It would be so easy to let ourselves get carried away, to give in to the body's need for pleasure with one of the two people I care about most in this world.

But Siobhan isn't kissing me because she wants me right now. She's doing it to distract me from questioning her.

I turn my face away, my breath coming hard. "I'm here."

"Bastian." She presses her forehead to mine. "I know. And I appreciate it. Even when we don't agree, I know you have my back."

The fear curling its roots through me flares. I grip her hips. "Of course I always have your back. I love you."

"I love you, too." She slips free as easily as smoke through my fingers. Siobhan's strength has always filled me with awe. There's little we've faced that she can't manage easily. There's no reason to think whatever we find in Lyari will change that. And yet I can't shake the feeling that Siobhan is in the process of a prolonged goodbye.

"Siobhan." I sit up abruptly, following her with my gaze as she pulls on her clothes. "Please talk to me."

She smiles sadly. "Some things are better left unsaid. Keep close to Nox. Between the two of you, you can get out of any mess." She sweeps from the room, her words landing dully behind her.

The two of us. Not three. *Two.*

I don't know what Siobhan believes will happen in Lyari, but she doesn't think she'll be around afterward. Whether that means she expects she'll be dead or taken captive . . . well, it could be anything.

Something happened in the days after we sailed south from Three Sisters. I'm not sure exactly when our lovemaking shifted from pure joy to tinged with grief and desperation. I only know that things *did* change.

I hurry to pull on my clothes and follow. Nox hasn't said

anything about the shift, but they're new to us. I don't know if they would notice it the same way I did, especially when so much of their impressive mind is focused on what comes next and keeping their crew alive.

We've seen crimson sails in the distance a few times, but they haven't seemed to show much interest in what appears to be just another trade ship heading south. It should be cause for relief, but instead it's only caused tension to ride everyone harder.

It feels like a trap.

I need to talk to Nox. They might have a better idea of what's going on, or at least a different point of view. But the moment I step through the door, I know there will be no opportunity for conversation. The entire crew buzzes and rushes about the deck to a purpose I can't begin to guess. I grab Frost's arm as ne moves past me. "What's going on?"

Ne grins, fierce and happy. "Sighted Yoth. We'll be there in a few hours."

The beginning of the end.

I don't know where the thought comes from, or why it brings a dread I can't combat. Yes, this will bring about the end, but that's the goal: the end of the Cŵn Annwn as they function today. This particular ending is an opportunity for new growth and a future without fear.

There's no chance I'll be able to pull Nox aside. They'll have their hands full with getting us to Yoth and making arrangements for the ship and crew. Damn it.

I find a spot on the upper deck where I'm mostly out of the way and watch the island approach. It's small—even smaller than Viedna, the selkie island where Maeve grew up—and so green it looks like a jewel tucked into the rush of waves around it. I've never been here before. The locals aren't fans of visitors, and the currents are even wilder than around First Sister, so most ships aren't interested in fighting their way to an unreceptive populace.

With the help of elemental magic and Nox's keen eye, we easily cut through the currents and into a shallow bay with a sandy beach. No docks to speak of; that would invite the aforementioned visitors.

Nox calls out instructions, and even knowing the plan, it still jars me to watch them intentionally run us aground. The ship shudders as it encounters the sandy beach and then shudders again as both air and water elemental users come together to shove it even farther aground, well away from the greedy tide. It leaves us angled in a way that feels dangerous, the deck canting sharply beneath my feet.

Frost grabs me before I can slide more than a foot. "Careful there, Bastian." Ne grins. "Can't have you falling and breaking something important."

"Thanks," I manage.

Things happen quickly after that. Crew, what little supplies we have left, and gifts for the locals are unloaded. By the time everyone has scaled down the side of the ship to the sand, we have an audience.

The Yothians are a small furred people with dangerously long claws, tufted ears like a hunting cat, and oblong eyes in colors ranging from yellow to a deep green. Their fur is brown with dappled darker patterns, the better to camouflage them in the jungle when they hunt. I'm not entirely certain how they define gender, but the group that meets us wears only small cloths tucked around their hips and nothing else.

Nox moves first, stepping forward and bowing deeply. "Honorable Tia, we come bearing gifts and asking for a boon."

One of the Yothians in the middle, one slightly shorter and rounder than the rest, steps forward on silent paws. "Nox. Captain Nox, I hear. Congratulations on your promotion." They rise. "Ask your boon."

"I would offer the supplies we currently have, as well as a selection of gifts I think your people may enjoy." Nox draws a deep breath. Their tone is perfectly even, but there's tension in their shoulders. "In return, I would ask for a small ship to get us to Lyari. And for you to house my crew for a short period of time. Two weeks, perhaps three. They will abide by your laws and won't cause any trouble."

Tia's ears flick back and forth, but they don't otherwise move. "You know we don't often welcome strangers into our midst."

"I know." Nox doesn't bend in the least. "But I think you have a vested interest in hearing *why* we need this boon from you."

Tia studies Nox for a long moment. "Walk with me."

Nox easily falls into step with Tia, walking down the beach away from us. Both groups eye each other warily but make no move to cause any trouble. A short while later, the leaders have made their way back to us.

Tia steps forward and spreads their short arms. "You're welcome within our community." Their ears flick. "However, if any of you breaks our laws, you will be held accountable by the same laws."

Nox motions the crew forward. "All right, darlings, gather round. Here's the lay of the land." They quickly go through the laws the crew needs to know about. It's pretty standard stuff—don't fuck with the locals, don't damage property, don't make asses of themselves—with a few interesting caveats. All visitors are barred from the center of the island, which is apparently holy ground to the Yothians.

Nox gets agreements all around and then we're off, filing after the Yothians into the deep green foliage. Each island in Threshold reflects a portion of the world in the realm its portal leads to, right down to the climate—in this case, a heat sticky and dense enough to swipe your fingers through. Insects drone in a buzz I swear I can feel in my bones. The trees around us are alive with small animals and movement that suggests much larger predators exist just out of sight.

I shiver and glance to where Bowen walks next to me. "I prefer wide-open spaces to this."

He shrugs, expression carefully locked down the way it so often is. "If something comes at us, I'll stop it."

What must it be like to move through the world so sure of your power and its ability to protect? My glamour is incredibly useful when I dare to use it, but I can't stop acid rain or a giant monster or do anything actually helpful. I've worked hard to ensure I'm not a liability in a fight, but I'll never be as good as Bowen or the other heavy hitters on the crew of the *Audacity*.

We reach the village before too long. At first glance, there *is* no village, but as I stare, the details start to emerge. The buildings are built into the trees in a seamless way that means I can't tell if the inhabitants carved into the trees themselves or did some kind of magic to shift things to make room. The escort

Yothians break off, each leading a small group of crew members in a different direction to where they'll be staying as guests of various households.

Nox waits until they're all gone before bowing deeply to Tia. "Thank you for your hospitality."

"Thank you for your sacrifice." Tia bows just as deeply this time. "Will you share a meal with us before you leave?"

Nox shakes their head slowly. "I wish we could, Tia. Unfortunately, we need to move as quickly as possible. We don't want to bring the Cŵn Annwn down upon you and your community."

"Let them come." Tia smiles, revealing the sharp teeth of a predator. "They have tried before. They will try again. Still, we maintain."

"If we're successful, they will never try again."

Tia waves that away. "Someone will. Someone always does. We still see and honor your plans. You'll find a small ship on the west side of the island." They click their claws together several times in a fast pattern, and two smaller Yothians melt out of the bushes on either side of us. "These are Dao and Cye. They will guide you."

Nox turns to the small group still left. "Let's go." I expected myself and Siobhan, of course, but Bowen and Evelyn remain, as well as Maeve and a put-upon-looking Lizzie. The future of Threshold rests on the shoulders of seven people.

There's nothing more to say.

We file after the youngsters—and they *are* youngsters; that boundless energy of youth is consistent across all peoples—and into an even deeper greenery than we experienced on our way to the village.

Behind me, Lizzie sneezes. Without missing a beat, she snarls, "Not a single word."

"I didn't say anything," Maeve says sweetly.

I can't help looking over my shoulder to see a mask of innocence on Maeve's face that doesn't quite conceal the mischief in her green eyes. She catches me watching and winks. I fight down a shudder and turn back to keep my eyes on the path ahead of me. Lizzie may be useful, but I can hardly comprehend the bravery Maeve must possess to go to bed with the vicious vampire.

It's none of my business. But thinking about bed has me looking up ahead to where Siobhan trudges silently in front of me, her cloak covering her head despite the sticky heat, her shoulders tight in a clear message that she's not interested in talking. Things have been too rushed for Nox to notice something is wrong yet, and there will be little time or privacy after this.

With that in mind, I veer around Siobhan and pick up my pace until I come even with Nox. "We have to talk," I say softly. "Now."

CHAPTER 31

Nox

"BASTIAN, THIS HAS TO WAIT," I SAY SOFTLY. THERE'S nothing resembling privacy here. Not with the Yothians' superior hearing ahead of us and Siobhan's behind us. "We can't stop."

"There's no need to stop." He matches my tone perfectly. Apparently there's no need for secrecy, either, because he starts right in. "Siobhan is hiding something from us."

I glance over my shoulder, but Siobhan has her hood pulled low, concealing her face entirely. It's tempting to use a little wind to push it back to see what her expression is saying, but Bastian takes my arm, distracting me.

"Haven't you noticed?" He pitches his voice lower yet. "She's been saying goodbye."

I don't want to admit that I've been too tangled up in the reckless joy of having them in my bed to register the deeper layers. It's been *so long* since I've let myself fall; I'm simply enjoying the freedom of giving myself over to gravity. When I'm with them in bed, I can almost believe that maybe we *do* have a future. I assumed her ferocity was normal. "What do you mean?"

"I don't know." He curses softly. "She won't talk to me. I just know something is wrong."

I push a branch out of the way and hold it for him to duck under. "Are you sure it's not your own anxiety informing this belief?"

He opens his mouth, pauses, and shoots a guilty look at Siobhan. "No. I'm not sure of that."

"We're out of time, Bastian. If she won't talk to you, she's not going to talk to me, either. We've all agreed the horn is the best choice for a path forward. Turning back now is out of the question." The air is a physical weight against my skin, causing sweat to slide down my spine and pool at the small of my back. I'd rather be soaked in salt water than deal with this discomfort, but there's nothing to do about it except endure. "We have to at least try to see it through."

"I know," he says miserably.

There's nothing more to be said. We might not be in battle yet, but the same rules apply. Once you commit to an action, you better not second-guess yourself or change course. The desire to minimize losses inevitably results in more dead people than there would have been if you remained committed to the original plan. Or maybe that's the insidious glory of hindsight, to think that there was always a better way where less people died. I don't know. Foresight isn't one of my gifts, and for all that it leaves me at the mercy of my own choices, I still prefer things this way. It's better not to know for sure that things would have been better if we took a different route.

There *isn't* a different route available, though. Not in this.

Our only chance is to blow the damn horn and summon the damn Cŵn Annwn and hope they don't kill us on the spot. Maybe they will. Maybe that's what Siobhan believes, and why she's said goodbye in the only way she can stomach. I don't fault her for it. I very much do not want to die, but death comes for us all at one point or another. Might as well make it count.

Cye makes a happy noise that's almost a purr and bounces on their toes. "Almost there."

Within a few minutes, we've left the claustrophobic closeness of the jungle behind and emerged onto a beach with pristine white sand. It's the kind of beach poets wax on about and painters spend days twisting themselves into knots to re-create. It hardly looks real.

Because it isn't.

Dao pounces on what appears to be air, and the entire beach *ripples*. I watch in shock as the image flickers and flickers again, finally fading away to a significantly narrower spot with grainy sand beneath our boots and a trio of ships bobbing gently just past the surf.

I glance at Cye, who purrs again. "We aren't without defenses."

"I see that." I shake my head. The thing Dao jumped on is a large crystal glowing a gentle green. I've never seen anything like it, but Bastian watches it like it's a snake about to strike. I nudge him. "Relax."

"That's a *Boax crystal*. How did you get it?"

Dao's ears flick, and they flash their teeth. "Trade."

As if it's that simple. Boax is inhospitable to the point that it's forbidden to even land there. People still do, of course. The greedy and the desperate are willing to risk their lives to potentially return home with one of the legendary crystals. They're rare enough to be rumor, but it's said they can hold spells for such a duration that it might as well be eternal. To find one *here*, hiding a handful of ships on an island where no one comes ... It's fascinating, to say the least. "Good for you."

Dao points to the ship on the far right. "Take that one."

Cye bounds up with a bag that looks light enough to be empty, but when they pass it over, it nearly topples me. Siobhan comes up and snags it. "Thank you," she says. "For everything. We won't forget it."

The two youngsters exchange a look and bow deeply enough that their tufted ears nearly brush the ground. "Thank *you*, Cŵn Annwn. We wish you luck on your journey and victory in your battles."

Then they're gone, bounding away with the chaotic energy of youth, disappearing into the trees in moments. Lizzie stretches her arms over her head and drapes one around Maeve's shoulders. "Something you want to tell us?"

"No," Siobhan says shortly. She eyes the distance between us and the ship. "We should be able to swim the distance easily enough."

"Go. I'll bring up the rear." The better to help along anyone who struggles with the currents.

Siobhan nods and then she's wading out into the water, the bag looped easily around her shoulders. Bastian and Evelyn follow, Bowen not far behind. Maeve pulls her pelt out and wraps it around her shoulders. In a shimmer of magic, the adorable redhead is gone, replaced by a large leopard seal. She boops Lizzie's shoulder.

"I'm going," Lizzie snaps, but she's moving slower than normal. The vampire fears the water. It's something I noted when she first started sailing with my crew, but she's a proud creature and I like my blood inside my skin, so I only prod her about it periodically.

It's still the height of entertainment to watch her sweet partner herd her into the waves like a wandering duckling. By the time she's made it to deeper water, Maeve swimming circles around her body, the rest of the others have reached the ship.

I follow. There's no need for magic. Honestly, it feels good to swim. For those few minutes it takes me to reach the ship, my mind is clear and there is nothing but the faint strain of my muscles and the steady sound of the waves. There's part of me that wants to exist in this moment forever. We haven't lost anyone yet. Bad things have happened, but we've prevailed. If I never reach the ship . . .

But I do.

Bowen extends a hand to pull me aboard, and he doesn't even need magic to practically toss me onto the deck. I land easily and pull the water from everyone's clothing to send it back where it belongs. "Let's go."

Bastian looks like he wants to argue, but the rest of them quickly move to their respective responsibilities. We won't have a proper navigator for this, but we don't need one unless things go catastrophically wrong—and then we'll have bigger problems to worry about than being lost. All we have to do is sail directly west and we'll come to the east side of Lyari.

I nod at Bowen. "I'll fill the sails. You get us there."

He takes up position at the helm, wrapping his big hands

around the spokes of the wheel with something akin to reverence. Through all his time on the *Audacity*, I've never picked up on even a whiff of ambition, but it's clear he misses being captain. If we survive this, there will be plenty of ships available for use. Maybe even his former one, the *Crimson Hag*.

There's no time to waste. I walk to a good spot at the stern and slowly draw the wind streams to us. Just enough to fill the sails as we turn for open sea. We can't see Lyari yet, but with my magic creating superficial perfect sailing conditions, we'll reach it late tonight.

It's an hour or two later when Siobhan comes to stand next to me. I've worked up a light sweat, but it's a naturally windy day, so I'm using a lot less energy than I would otherwise. I don't have to generate the wind from nothing, just nudge it in the right direction.

She doesn't speak for a long time, and I give her the gift of silence. Maybe I should be like Bastian, demanding answers, but I've sailed with the Cŵn Annwn—and the rebellion, for that matter—long enough to realize that acceptable losses, no matter how much I hate them, are *acceptable* for a reason. There's a decent chance *none* of us survive what comes next. I can't let the fear of losing someone—of losing myself—stop us. Too much hangs in the balance.

Finally, Siobhan says, "Bastian's not wrong."

A shiver goes down my spine. For all my rationalizing, my immediate response takes me by surprise. "You are *not* going to Lyari to die."

Siobhan huffs out a raw laugh. "No, Nox, I'm not going to Lyari to die."

Her words do little to reassure me. I glance at her quickly before turning my attention back to the sails. It takes no effort at all to read into what she isn't saying. "But you don't think you'll be with us afterward."

Her breath hitches, but when she speaks, her voice is perfectly even and contains an edge I've never heard before. A noble's accent, each syllable so crisp I want to sink my teeth into them. "There will be work to do after the rot is purged. I won't be able to travel around with your merry band of sailors and indulge in a life of . . . whatever your plans are. If this is handled poorly, then we'll end up with a worse situation than we have now. We need clear leadership."

This time, I stare. It's foolish to forget where she came from, to ignore the fact that *she* was heir before her sister killed their parents and attempted to kill her, too. Even so, she's never pulled that shit in all the time I've known her. "And you're the leadership we need. Siobhan, the noble Cŵn Annwn, who will lead all of Threshold into a new future."

She lifts her chin. "Who else?"

My old anger surges forth, the still-healing wound of a young person who lost their love to *responsibility* tied to his noble blood. But I'm not that child any longer. I've lived too many years and seen too many things to let a broken heart confuse reality. I narrow my eyes. "Are you telling me that you intend to set yourself up as queen and savior of Threshold?"

"Of course." She's much better at lying than Bastian is, though that's not saying much. They're both terrible at it.

I shake my head. "If you don't want a future with me, Siobhan, all you have to do is say so. No matter my feelings, I won't tie you up in knots and demand you stay if that's not what you want—but don't bullshit me about playing queen when I can see the very idea practically gives you hives."

"Nox." Her breath shudders out and she turns away, wrapping her arms around herself. "You're not making this easy."

"I'm not trying to." I urge a little more wind into our sails, making the deck jerk beneath our feet and Siobhan curse as she bumps into the railing. With a curse of my own, I ease just enough that we're traveling smoothly. "You know, most sailors think it's bad luck to talk about the future before a fight."

She glances over her shoulder. "Oh, yeah?"

No. I'm lying through my teeth. But the thread of hope in her expression is enough to keep the lies spilling. "Yeah. Distracts you, makes you focus on the after instead of the now, which is a good way to get killed. Whatever it is you're grappling with, we'll deal with it after we blow this damn horn and save Threshold."

It's impossible to read Siobhan's expression. There's so much emotion in her honeyed eyes that it threatens to drown me. When she speaks, her voice is hoarse with things unsaid. "I love you."

I hate that the words I've so longed to hear feel like she's saying goodbye.

CHAPTER 32

Siobhan

I<small>T'S BEEN THE BETTER PART OF A DECADE—LONGER,</small>
really—since I've been in Lyari. With the highest concentration of Cŵn Annwn and nobles in the capital city, it's the one
place in Threshold my identity is truly a liability.

Now it doesn't really matter.

We anchor off the coast and swim to shore just as the sun
touches the horizon. Most of the island is settled in residential
areas, with a decreasing amount of space for farming as the
years go on. It forces the population to be dependent on trade
to get food, and somehow that food never quite makes it outside
the city walls—at least not without having the prices marked
up first. It means that folks have started leaving Lyari behind for
smaller communities on different islands.

It's a problem that will need solving if we want the future to
be as hopeful as we've all dreamed. I hate knowing I won't be
here for that outreach, for those changes.

The house we take temporary shelter in has the appearance of being abandoned for years—decades, even. The door hangs half off its hinges, wood swollen by the sea air, and even Bowen has a difficult time wedging it open. Inside, it smells faintly of mildew, mold sprouting in the corners where walls meet ceiling.

"Great," Lizzie mutters. "Now we have to worry about black mold."

No one bothers to respond. Nox pulls the water from our clothes. I dig out some food from the bag the Yothians gave us and pass it around.

"Time to go over the plan," Bastian says. He pulls a rotted wooden table to the center of the room and sets out a handful of rocks that are apparently supposed to represent Lyari. "The Council's building is right here." He points to a triangular rock. "If we time it correctly, we can slip through when they change shifts."

Maeve nibbles on her bottom lip. "We're just going to . . . walk in? Aren't there guards inside?"

"Yes." Bastian sets two smaller rocks next to the triangular one. I'm not sure what these are supposed to represent. Guards? "The Council keeps normal hours. By the time we make it to the city, it will be late—later yet when we reach the library. I'll use my glamour to keep us hidden. Nox and Lizzie will incapacitate the guards as we come across them. Once we reach the library, Evelyn will neutralize the magic on the case around the horn and Bowen will break it. We blow the horn and then this is over."

It does sound too simple to work. A thousand things could go wrong . . .

It's still the best plan we have.

Lizzie looks like she wants to jump out of her skin at the state the house is in, but she's not so distracted that she misses the chance to say, "Why are we doing this alone? Don't you have a network of rebels that stretches the span of Threshold? They could get us up-to-date information and actually, you know, help?"

I'm already shaking my head. "Unfortunately, that's not possible."

She narrows her eyes. "What do you mean, that's not possible?"

"We don't have many people on Lyari." Bastian glances up from his crouched position. "And the ones here are high-risk, so they are roughly three degrees removed from Siobhan and the rest of us. If we go to them for help, they won't know or trust us. It will just waste time we can't afford to lose—and amplifies the risk of being caught."

Guilt and frustration are live things inside me. It wouldn't matter if we had other people to help because I'm the only one who can do what needs to be done. I can't say *that* without explaining what Dia told me. Instead, I focus on Lizzie's suggestion. "The only reason we've been able to work for so long is because the network is just that—a network. I only have direct contact with a handful of people. That wasn't always the case, but it became necessary as the number of people in the rebellion grew. It protects everyone. If one person is caught, they can only draw a connection to one or two of the others."

Lizzie makes a face. "It does make sense when you put it like that. It's still inconvenient."

"Yes." We would have had to change things dramatically to draw people together to fight. I'm not even certain it would work.

Thankfully, that's not something I have to worry about any longer. I just have to get to the horn.

"I won't know if I can neutralize the magic until I see it," Evelyn says quietly. "If you're betting on me, it might be for nothing. This is a serious risk."

Bastian looks at the increasingly chaotic layout of rocks, his brows pulled together. "The current Council is the one who brought the horn out to display instead of keeping it locked in a vault somewhere. Enough of the old members had died off that the younger ones decided to change the way they handle artifacts. The magic will be ritual, and even if the flavor is different than yours, you should be able to find a way around it."

"'Should' is not a guarantee," Evelyn counters.

"It's not. But it's an educated guess and you're an excellent witch. I have faith in your abilities."

Evelyn blushes a little, and though it seems like she still wants to argue, we really have reached the point of no return. I motion to Bastian. "Can you hold the glamour over that many people?" When he hid us on First Sister, they were all on my back, which essentially made us one figure—if a large one.

"As long as everyone is within my eyesight, yes." His jaw is set, his eyes harder than I've ever seen them. He's shown what he's capable of, time and time again. I believe him when he says he can do it.

"Let's go. We're wasting time." I head for the door, moving slowly enough that I'm sure they're all following by the time I press the creaking wood open to the outside. It's significantly cooler here than on Yoth, but we're still well into the summer in this part of Threshold. I tilt my head back and study the stars.

When I'm among the Wild Hunt, will I be able to take moments like this to appreciate the beauty all around me? Or will it be an eternity of constant, churning motion? Of never-ending hunger? I shiver.

"Siobhan?"

I drag my eyes from the sky to Nox. The others have passed us by, following Bastian. I'm proud of him for his initiative here. He's shown plenty of leadership qualities over the years, but he's always been content to hold a second-in-command position. It's a good sign that he's evolving; I won't be around to take a lead from in the future. Someone has to ensure Lyari doesn't set up another Council to replace the first and perpetuate the harm done by past generations. Bastian will do right by the people and the mission. He'll be a good leader.

I wish I could be there to see it.

"Siobhan." Nox slips their hand into mine and pulls me to a stop. "This will work."

Ironic that they're trying to comfort me when I should be doing it for them. "I know." I survey the sky one last time and then let Nox tug me into the trees after the others.

We stick to the trees where we can, and utilize a combination of Bastian's glamour and the dark where we can't. The trip is unremarkable, which is exactly as we'd hoped. The city is too perfectly placed to worry about a large attack from the land side. There's cover for a small group like ours, but not for an army. And who has a standing army in Threshold, realm of the seas? Any attack would be from a navy, and Lyari is well protected against *that*. They have a stranglehold on the bay the city squats in the center of, massive forts on either side of the mouth that ensure only those who are invited successfully enter their waters.

Even slipping into the city itself is easy enough. We scale the short wall in the darkest section we can find. Nox scrunches their nose when we land in an alley filled with refuse and things best left unexamined. "I hate cities."

"We all do," Bowen murmurs.

"Speak for yourself." Lizzie lifts one foot and squints at it. "Though I prefer to hunt in *cleaner* areas." She turns and sweeps Maeve into her arms. "No point in getting your feet dirty. You'll never clean the stench off."

Maeve murmurs something into Lizzie's ear that I do my very best *not* to hear. The dark covers my blush as I weave through our small group to come even with Bastian. "Let's keep moving."

"A moment." He closes his eyes, breathes deep, and exhales on a cough. "Right, that was a mistake. Give me a second to get the glamour in place. It will cover the sounds of our walking as long as no one makes too much noise. You'll be able to see through the glamour, but no one will see you."

"Nifty," Evelyn murmurs. "That's a trick I'd love to learn."

"Sorry, love. He's one of a kind," Nox answers just as quietly. They're smiling, but their gray eyes are serious. "Ready?"

"Ready," Bastian confirms.

Then we're off again, slipping through the dark streets with an ease that sets my teeth on edge. There are guards patrolling here and there, but they never realize how close we are. I know Bastian's magic is formidable, but this feels too damned easy. Right as the horologists are calling one in the morning, we reach the Council's seat of power.

A couple generations ago, it was a normal-sized building. Now it's a monstrosity, bulging oddly and stretching strangely with new additions. Whatever beauty there was in its construction has long since been perverted with the need for *more*. I shudder at the sight, just like I always did as a child being forced to visit this place.

"Is it . . . supposed to look like that?" Evelyn whispers, her eyes wide.

"Apt, don't you think?" Nox answers. They nudge her with their shoulder. "Want to burn it down as we leave?"

"I do like a good fire on occasion." Evelyn flicks a glance to Lizzie, some unspoken history there. I know they used to be in a relationship before Evelyn arrived in Threshold, but there seem to be no hard feelings on either side now. "Just like that time we went gambling in Monte Carlo."

Lizzie rolls her eyes and finally allows Maeve to stand on her own. "It was only a small fire. It hardly counts."

I inhale deeply, sorting through the scents to find what I'm looking for. "Two people patrolling. The last scent trail is old enough that they should be coming . . . *there*."

Nox and Lizzie move in coordinated perfection. As the guards come around the corner, each dressed in the Council's crimson, they crumple, one's eyes rolling back in their head and one with a small trail of blood coming from their nose. Bowen reaches out at the same moment, catching them before they can hit the ground and floating them over to us. Evelyn and Maeve quickly rifle through the guards' coats, the latter coming up with a key and handing it to me.

Nox surveys the building. "No door on this side. Which way?"

Bastian sweats lightly, a small line between his brows as he concentrates. "Left."

We go left. The building may have started as a perfect square, but that was a long time ago. Now its perimeter is as haphazardly designed as its walls. We round four corners before reaching the promised door. The key fits perfectly, and it opens soundlessly, revealing a rectangle of darkness.

"That's not ominous or anything," Evelyn murmurs.

Nox glances at me, prompting another deep inhale, which makes me sneeze. Magic is thick in the air. There are wards on the building, but they've been unlocked with the key, the same way the door has. It's difficult to tell if anyone has come through here—aside from the guards. "I don't know what we're going to find."

"Nothing to do but go in," they finally say.

They start to step forward, but I shake my head. "I'll go first. I see better in the dark than anyone here."

"I see well enough," Lizzie snaps, but it's half-hearted, even for her. "I'll bring up the rear so we don't get ambushed."

No one bothers to argue with the vampire. They file in after me, and Lizzie softly closes the door behind us. It's even darker like this, dark enough that Bastian presses a hand to the middle of my back, and I can hear the others mirroring his motion behind him. It's like a children's game as we file deeper into the building, following the strangely curving hallways.

Nobles usually enter through the public door on the other side of the building. Even so, I finally start to pick up familiar scents after a few turns. *Thank the gods.* It takes several minutes to get my bearings, but I manage to lead us through another series of hallways until we reach a broad archway and the scent of dust. "Up ahead."

"Don't rush," Bastian says. "I'll keep the glamour in place until we're inside."

I go slowly, using every one of my senses to search for evidence of a trap. There *must* be a trap. I'm not one to believe in omens and the like, but this has been too blessedly easy. Yes, the Council is lazy and corrupt and overly confident in their power. The last attempted—failed—attack on Lyari was three hundred years ago. The warriors were cut down in the mouth of the bay; they never had a chance to reach the city, let alone this building. The citizens in the city don't want to draw the attention of the Council, so aside from the random thief who's too desperate to know better, locals avoid this space.

And the attempted thieves? They dangle from the nooses in Hangman's Courtyard until they rot enough to become a hazard. A warning that people heed.

A warning we're ignoring.

We file into the library. I've only been in here a handful of times, and not since I was a teenager, but I could swear little has changed. It's a great dome of a room, with bookshelves running up the walls. Overhead, the curved ceiling has dozens of strange shapes hanging from it. They look like some kind of artifacts, but I can't begin to guess their origins.

The carpet underneath our feet is ancient and faded to the point where I can't figure out what the design originally was. The room curves away on the opposite side from where we entered, fading into deep darkness that not even my eyes can penetrate. That way will have more of what we have here, as well as an office for the person who oversees the collection.

After several long minutes of tension, Bastian drops the glamour. I had barely registered the magical weight of it against my skin, but I can't help stretching the moment it's gone. Everyone is silent as we look around. I very intentionally study the group instead of the large glass square in the center of the room. My fate lies in that case, and even if I have no intention of avoiding it, that doesn't mean I have to stare at it a moment before strictly necessary.

Evelyn looks around with wide eyes. "So many books . . ."

"Don't even think about it," Lizzie and Bowen say at the same time. They exchange irritated looks, but there's a thread of fondness growing between them despite themselves.

Bowen clears his throat. "Some of them will be trapped. It's not worth risking touching anything but what we came for."

"Spoilsport."

"Siobhan, on the door." Nox speaks softly but firmly. "Bastian, sit down and rest until it's time to leave. Evelyn, the case."

"Right. The case." The blonde crosses to the case, Bowen a bare step behind. She glances over her shoulder. "You're lurking. Give me a few moments." Without waiting for an answer, she circles the case. And then does it again, even slower this time, her green eyes narrowed.

Impatience bites at me, but we can't afford to rush. This is the only chance we're going to have to pull this off.

On her third circuit, she stops and nods. "Okay. They tried to be tricky, but whoever put this together didn't expect *me*." She holds out a hand without looking at Bowen. He curses softly under his breath, but doesn't hesitate to offer her a small knife. She pricks the meaty pad of her palm and then presses her bloodied hand to her tattooed chest. A beat where her eyes flare brilliant green, and then she grins. "Oh, yeah, I've got you. Give me five minutes and I'll have it dismantled."

I should be grateful that it won't take long, that it's sur-mountable, but instead my tension rides higher. Too easy. This is too damned easy.

"Almost there." Something sizzles behind me, and Evelyn makes a satisfied noise. "Got it. Bowen, it's safe to dismantle the glass now."

The air in the hallway abruptly shifts, coursing toward us. I take a step back even before my brain catches up with what I'm smelling. "Oh, fuck."

A low laugh emerges from the darkness a moment before my sister steps out. "Hello, Siobhan."

CHAPTER 33

Bastian

WE ALL FREEZE AS MORRIGAN FILLS THE DOORWAY. She's a handsome woman, though where Siobhan has always tried to downplay her strength and blend in, Morrigan seems to embrace it. She wears a sleeveless vest that shows off her powerful arms, and tight pants tucked into knee-high boots. There's no weapon in sight, but why would there be? *She* is the weapon.

"How did you find us?" I don't mean to ask the question, but we took such precautions. She shouldn't have known our destination.

Morrigan shrugs. "Ace is a shark shifter." She grins, revealing too-sharp teeth. "Come now, Bastian. After losing you in the storm—neat trick, by the way—we figured out you were headed to First Sister. Siobhan, you know better than most how I hunt."

Siobhan practically vibrates with tension. "You drew our

attention with Bull's display and sent Ace to place a tracker on our ship."

"I knew you wouldn't come so close to Lyari unless Lyari itself was your destination, and you wouldn't come *here* if you weren't hunting the Council. Now, as much as I like appreciation for my brilliance, we have business to attend to." Morrigan's long fingers shift longer yet and gain a wicked curve of claws. She holds them up and finger-waves at us. "The whole gang's here. Traitorous captains, an equally traitorous selkie, a vampire never properly sworn in to the Cŵn Annwn, a witch who should have been executed the moment she broke her vows, and a noble convicted of using illegal magics."

"I wasn't convicted," I protest weakly.

"The trial was held this week in your absence." She examines her claws. "The trial for your family will quickly follow. We'll discover exactly how much they knew—and how much they're hiding."

Cold unlike I've ever known courses through me. I knew the risk, but I truly thought their legion of connections would keep my family safe. "They know nothing."

"We'll see." Morrigan shrugs before turning her attention to Siobhan. "And *you*. I'm disappointed, Siobhan. I thought you might finally be an opponent worthy of me, but you've been wasting both our time chasing fairy tales." She motions at the horn. "That relic lost whatever magic it had generations ago."

"Maybe." Siobhan shrugs. Her body is coiled, ready to burst into motion. "I suppose we'll see."

"We won't." Morrigan rolls her neck and bounces on her toes a little. "I should thank you. You've handed me the path to leading the Council. All I have to do is kill you, and it kills your cute little movement. They'll beg me to take the position after this." She grins, her teeth too large for her mouth. "Now be a good girl and offer me your throat."

"Fuck you." Siobhan launches herself at Morrigan, who meets her in the air. They're moving so quickly I can barely follow it.

I spin to Bowen, who's taken a step toward them. "The case! We have to blow the horn!"

He turns and slashes his hands through the air. The glass parts, each pane moving independently away from the horn. Without missing a beat, he spins toward the fighting women. "Siobhan!"

She drops to the floor as if they've practiced this move. The panes of glass hit Morrigan in the chest, one after another. By the third, she gets her arms up, her face a mask of fury as she's driven back several feet, her blood splashing the floor and walls.

It's the opening Lizzie needs. The vampire slashes her own arms, her blood surging out as if it's an independent creature, forming into a whiplike weapon that she uses to lash at Morrigan.

Nox skids to a stop in front of the horn and wraps their hands around the smallest bit. Siobhan's eyes go wide and she throws out a hand. "No!"

I'm moving before I have a chance to think it through, responding to the desperation in her voice. I grab Nox around the waist and haul them back before they can press their lips to the horn. "Wait!"

Then there's no more space for anything because Morrigan

has rallied. She tears into Lizzie, easily dodging the vampire's strikes and ignoring the way her blood pours unnaturally quickly from the few wounds she has. It's not enough; they're already closing, healing faster than we can hurt her.

Lizzie goes down from a vicious backhand, but Evelyn throws up a shield before Morrigan can finish the vampire. She pivots easily to attack Bowen, who barely gets a shield of his own up in time to stop her from disemboweling him.

Siobhan hits her sister hard enough to slam them both into the wall and shake the entire building. Dust cascades down from somewhere overhead, and I pull Nox to the floor, half expecting the roof to cave in on our heads. Nox shoves at me. "Let me up, you fool. We have to stop her."

I don't know which *her* Nox means . . . until Lizzie cries out. "Don't you fucking *dare!*"

While everyone was distracted, Maeve has reached the horn. The selkie gives Lizzie a small smile filled with sadness and then blows the horn. Every person in the room freezes, even Morrigan, expecting . . . I don't know. The Wild Hunt, I suppose. Or something so much worse.

Nothing happens.

"No," I whisper. I was *so sure* that this would work. It *has* to work. "It can't be."

Harsh laughter fills the room. Morrigan shoves Siobhan off hard enough to send her rolling across the floor. She laughs. "All for nothing. Just like your little rebellion, sister. I'm going to enjoy crushing every single member, stringing them up on my mast for all to see."

Siobhan struggles to her feet. She's bleeding from half a dozen cuts that I can see, and likely more that I can't. She wipes a river of it from her face. "No, you won't. Not today. Not ever." She staggers a little and looks at Bowen. "Hold her."

Morrigan sneers. She takes a step forward . . . or she tries. Instead, she rams up against an invisible wall. "Cute. Not good enough." Even as we watch, she sinks her claws into the barrier of Bowen's magic and begins to shred it.

He grunts in pain. "Can't . . . hold her . . . long."

"I only need a few seconds." Siobhan staggers to the horn. I try to get there first, but I'm tangled up in Nox and they're attempting the same thing. We topple and hit the ground just as Siobhan reaches the horn. She places her hands gently, reverently, on it and looks at us. "I love you. Both of you."

Did I think the last few days were a goodbye? I'm a fool. *This* is goodbye, and it feels so final I freeze. "Siobhan, wait!"

She blows the horn. I hold my breath, hoping that nothing will happen, that no one will respond to her summons. The horn doesn't make a sound in the traditional sense. Instead, a wave of pure power radiates out from it.

My ears pop and Maeve cries out in pain. It's nothing compared to what Morrigan does. She stops fighting Bowen's barrier, leans her head back, and *howls*. The sound is even worse than the pressure. It's the call of a hunt, the promise of bloodshed and violence. She doubles over and then sinks to the ground.

When Siobhan changed on First Sister, it was with a shimmer of magic both strange and beautiful. That's not what we're witnessing now. Morrigan's skin shreds, revealing bloodstained fur. Her claws grow, swallowing her fingers. I can't be sure, but I think I hear bones cracking over the sound of rushing in my ears.

Oh gods, she's going to kill us all.

Instinct tells me to scramble back against the wall, to put as much distance between me and the monster growling into being a few feet away, but Siobhan is still standing there, her heart in her eyes. Nox wiggles out of my grasp and hauls themself to their feet. "Siobhan, what—"

She begins to change. It's nothing like what's happening to her sister. Siobhan bends in half, shifting to paws instead of hands and feet. Her skin shimmers and then it's silvery white fur, her dark eyes changing to a deep crimson. Her howl joins her sister's, louder and louder. A call to action. A warning.

An invisible band wraps around my waist and hauls me back to the wall. Nox hits the wall a few seconds behind me, quickly followed by the others in our party. Bowen stumbles to his knees in front of us, his hands up as if physically holding something back. I can't see what's going on. I need to *see*, to reach Siobhan. "Stop! We need—"

It's too late.

The first warning is mist coursing from the ceiling, so thick that it quickly obscures the dome. It doesn't stop there, giving the illusion of the walls of the room fading into nonexistence, taking the bookshelves and other obscure magical items with them. I tentatively reach out to where there *should* be wall but find only icy emptiness. "Fuck." I jerk my hand away and shake the feeling back into my fingers.

A tall figure steps out of the mist, dressed in a layered robe of varying greens. They look mostly humanoid, though their features are a little too sharp, the bones protruding too overtly, and horns are curving back from their curly brown hair. Their eyes are perfectly black and set too wide on their face, too large.

They stretch out a clawed hand, so similar to Siobhan's and Morrigan's partially shifted forms. "You've summoned me, little sister. Ask your boon."

Siobhan woofs softly.

They tilt their head to the side, the movement too abrupt and uncanny. "How far our progeny have fallen, to not be able to speak in this form." They casually wave a clawed hand and Siobhan falls to the ground, her soft sound turning pained and agonizing.

I try to stand, but my body is locked in place. I don't think it's Bowen's magic that's responsible. It's this creature's.

Siobhan rises slowly. Her toothy mouth opens and a garbled voice emerges. "Purge the rot from Threshold. Eliminate those who use your name and pervert your true purpose, but leave those who have been forced into a life they never would have chosen for themselves."

The creature smiles, and I truly wish they hadn't. They have too many teeth, and they're shaped entirely *wrong* for a humanoid mouth. "Do you think I have the power to know mortal souls?"

"Are you not Cŵn Annwn?"

Their smile widens, seeming in danger of splitting their face in half. "I am the leader of the Wild Hunt, little sister. I am more than Cŵn Annwn. Much more." They straighten. "It has been a long time since my Hunt has ridden in Threshold. Very well. I'll grant your boon."

My breath leaves in a rush. It's happening. We did it. The Wild Hunt will ride and . . .

"Come along, little sister. It's time to join your people."

No.

Their gaze goes over Siobhan's head to where Morrigan cowers against where the wall used to be. "And you. Come as well. You'll do well with a few centuries of proper training." They turn away.

"Wait!"

"Stop!"

Nox and I shout over each other, but it's too late. The creature walks into the mist, Siobhan and Morrigan trotting on either side of them. She never even looks back. She's just . . . gone.

"What the *fuck*?" Evelyn whispers. "That wasn't the Welsh god of their Otherworld. I'd stake my life on it."

"Arawn only leads the Wild Hunt in some myths," Lizzie says absently. She crouches next to Maeve and takes the selkie's chin in her hand. "Don't you *ever* try some shit like that again, do you hear me? You could have died."

"I didn't." Maeve seems untouched by the vampire's anger. She covers Lizzie's hand with hers. "I'm okay. We're all okay."

"Not all of us," I say dully. Outside, howls have started, so many that they weave in and out, creating a haunting melody that makes my skin crawl. Then the hoofbeats come. An army's worth. Laughter and calls in a language I don't understand and yet it's familiar in a way I can't put into words.

The Wild Hunt rides.

And it took Siobhan with it.

CHAPTER 34

Nox

I HAVE ENCOUNTERED—AND FOUGHT—MONSTERS BE-yond knowing. There is no terror like wading into a pack of feral mermaids or knowing a water horse is on your trail. This is worse. I've never felt so small in my life, never felt so much like *prey*. There's nothing I want more than to press Bastian into a small space and hide with him until this is over.

But they took Siobhan.

"Stay here." I climb shakily to my feet. The strange mist that obscured the ceiling and walls is fading; I can see the door now.

"Nox!" Bowen has his arms around Evelyn. "It's too dangerous."

"They took Siobhan."

"She went willingly," Lizzie says.

I shake my head. "No, she fucking didn't." I exchange a look with Bastian. He was right when he said she was saying good-bye. *This* was the outcome Siobhan knew would happen, and this is why she didn't want Maeve to blow the horn. I've listened to Evelyn talk about the myths surrounding the Wild Hunt. Some folks they sweep up are deposited elsewhere. Some ride with them forever.

I have a feeling I know which fate awaits Siobhan.

He rises as well. "I'm coming with you."

I want to argue, but there's no time. We stagger our way through the door, the air so cold that my breath ghosts the space before my lips. The voices of the Cŵn Annwn are fading, a great sound rising in its place. It takes my exhausted mind a few steps to place it.

Screaming.

Bastian picks up his pace, and I match him without hesitation. We burst past two spatters of blood on the walls, but don't see a single soul until we shove through the doors and out onto the street. There's no point in subterfuge now; no one is paying us the least bit of attention.

Lyari is a relatively flat island, and the city itself is nestled in between two small hills on either side. I catch sight of riotous clouds overhead, but I can't *see* anything. "We need to get higher."

"We need to *save her.*"

"We can't do that if we don't know where she is." I don't wait for Bastian to argue further. I grab two fistfuls of air and shove it down, propelling myself up onto the roof. I put too much power behind it and nearly topple off before I find my footing.

When I see what the Wild Hunt is doing to the city, I almost wish I had fallen. It's . . . massive. Beyond comprehension. The only hunting parties I've seen are among ships, but I thought I had an idea of what a hunt on land might be. I was wrong. This is no gathering of dozens of warriors, eldritch or otherwise; this is a *horde*.

It sweeps through the streets of Lyari like a tsunami, mist and hounds and warriors on horses. Some of them look similar to the creature that answered Siobhan's call. Some of them are more humanoid . . . and some significantly less. As they ride away from us, I catch sight of a hunter that seems to be made entirely of tentacles and wet laughter.

"Do you see her?" Bastian calls from the ground.

I shake my head slowly. "There are hounds, but I don't know which one is Siobhan." Or Morrigan, for that matter. The giant beasts dance around and under the hooves of equally giant horses with glowing eyes, whose every exhale seems to add to the mist following the group.

"We need to go after them!"

How? Even if we could find her, how could we possibly fight *this?*

Despair rises in me, so strong that I choke on it. I've barely come to terms with the reality of *wanting*—of *loving*. It wasn't supposed to be like this. If we were on a suicide mission, then we would go out together, martyrs to the greater good. She wasn't supposed to sacrifice everything and leave us to pick up the pieces.

I love Bastian—I don't think I ever truly stopped, for all that it turned to hate for a time—but I love Siobhan, too. One is not a replacement for the other. The relationships are similar, but not identical. How am I supposed to go on when half of my heart now rides with the Wild Hunt?

"*Nox.*"

"Coming." The descent is just as chaotic and rushed as the ascent. I hit the ground too hard and my knees buckle, but Bastian is there to grab my arm, already rushing us in the wake of the Hunt.

There's no way we should be able to close the distance, but magic is a strange thing and sometimes the rules of reality bend around it. That's the only explanation for our reaching the docks seconds behind the Hunt. Bastian almost keeps going, but I grab a fistful of his shirt and yank him to a stop before he can enter the mist churning around the Cŵn Annwn—the *true* Cŵn Annwn. "You'll join them."

"You don't know that!"

Yes, I do. I don't know how, but I just *know*. I take a step back, even though it's pure agony to put more distance between us. The Hunt surges from one ship to the next, sending up screams and cries with each pause. I can't tell if they're killing their victims or sweeping them into the Hunt itself. Possibly a combination of both.

It takes seconds for them to clear every ship docked and start out across the water of the harbor, racing across the surface of the water as if it's solid dirt. "We can't catch them."

Bastian takes one step farther and then hits his knees. "*Siobhan!*" he roars.

In the distance, one of the massive white hounds misses a step and slows. I rush forward and grab his shoulder. "Again! I see her!"

He draws in a full breath and, when he calls her name again, he puts the full force of his glamour magic behind it. I use my wind magic to increase the range, desperation pushing me hard. The result is amplifying the sound until each syllable rings like a bell out across the water. "*Siobhan, come back to us!*"

For a moment, I think it might work. She hesitates, going so far as to turn around and look at us. But then the Cŵn Annwn call and a horn sounds and she's gone, sweeping after the Hunt as they leave the harbor and descend upon Threshold.

Bastian's shoulders shake against my palms. "What have we done? Did it even work or was it all for nothing?"

"I don't know," I whisper. "Come on." I make myself release his shoulders and head slowly toward the closest ship with crimson sails. It's nestled between two mundane trading ships, both of which seem to have their entire crews on their respective decks.

A burly person leans over the railing and shouts down to me. "What the fuck was that?"

There's no reason to lie. For better or worse, today is the stuff legends are made of. "The Wild Hunt."

They frown. "I don't know what the fuck that is, sailor."

I don't expect them to. "Have you suffered losses?"

"No." They shrug. "Swept through that one." They nod at the Cŵn Annwn ship. "But left us alone."

That, at least, is a good sign. I don't know what metric the Wild Hunt might use to define "rot," but at least they're confining it to the Cŵn Annwn and not all of Threshold.

Walking aboard the crimson-sailed ship makes my skin break out in goose bumps. I almost tell Bastian to stay on the docks, but he won't listen and I'm not keen to face whatever I'll find alone. "Hello?"

There's a sound belowdecks, and it takes me several long beats to realize it's the sound of someone weeping. I glance at Bastian. "Stay behind me."

"Let's go."

It's not an agreement, but it's the best I'm going to get under our current circumstances. I head to the hatch and carefully raise it. Down below, there's no pocket dimension to speak of, just a rank and filthy room with gently swinging hammocks. I inhale carefully and wince at the coppery scent that lingers. Blood.

We follow the sound of weeping to find a trio of people huddled in the corner. One is barely more than a child, clothed in the same robes Orchid and the people of Drash favor, their head bowed and their thin body shaking. The other two are older, but not by much. From the wideness of their eyes, they're in danger of going into shock.

I crouch down, trusting Bastian to watch my back without a second thought. "You're safe."

"They came," whispers the one on the right, a woman with deep purple skin and too-large eyes. "They took them all, but I think they killed the captain and the quartermaster." She shudders. "Good. They deserved it."

I want nothing more than to find a proper ship and sail after the Hunt to call Siobhan home to us, but . . . I can't. If this trio, obviously traumatized by more than just the Hunt, are any indication, we're going to have a significant number of refugees to either see settled or guide back to their home realms. I can't just drop that task into someone else's hands.

Siobhan wouldn't want me to.

"Fuck," I breathe.

Bastian finally gathers himself enough to speak, directing his question to the man who looks slightly steadier than the other two. "We need to search for anyone else aboard. Can you show me the way?"

The man reluctantly nods. I busy myself herding the woman and child up onto the deck. By the time we reach the dock, the rest of our party has arrived. Bowen takes in the situation with a single glance. "Maeve, start with the Cŵn Annwn ships on the far side of the docks. Lizzie, let Maeve lead." He ignores the vampire's hiss. "Evelyn and I will start on the other side. We'll bring all the survivors here. Once they're gathered and safe, we'll come up with a plan for what to do next."

The sheer enormity of the task sets me back on my heels. It's not just docked ships that will be affected. If the path of the Hunt is any indication, they'll hit every ship with crimson sails. There will be some crews left more intact than others, but the latter are in active danger. Most of the ships are too large to be sailed by a handful of even the most knowledgeable people, and I doubt any of the survivors will fall into that category.

"Fuck," I say again.

Bastian leads another dozen people down to the dock. He speaks softly, reassuringly. "We'll get you sorted shortly. Please just sit here and rest in the meantime." He crosses to take me by my arm and speaks in a low voice. "I questioned them briefly. Every single one of them is a conscript who didn't want to die. Half of them want to return home. The others just want a new start."

I close my eyes and try to *think*. Being captain of a single ship was one thing. What we're looking at is a widespread catastrophe. "We need to move, and fast. But we have a scattered network, no central communication, and—"

"Nox." This time, it's Bastian who takes my shoulders. His expression is absolutely haggard with grief. "We can make it work. The Cŵn Annwn ships have the ability to contact the

Council, so we just need to find that room and set up someone to gather information and locations. You and I can both get word out to our respective contacts. It will take time, but we'll make it work. Even if Siobhan is . . . gone." He sucks in a pained breath. "But we have to deal with Lyari first. If we sail off, we're going to leave this space wide open for some aspiring noble to undo the potential for so much change."

It's both amazing and horrific to understand exactly what's needed—and the sacrifice demanded. "You have to do it, Bastian," I say softly. "You're the only one who can."

He flinches. "What? No. I can't. They won't follow me. I'm only a second son and—"

"You won't be alone." The pieces snap together, faster and faster. "Lizzie has participated in more court politics than most of the current nobles combined. She can stay and guide you. Or at least watch your back. Maeve was one of our best informants for a reason. She will help." The reality of the situation spins out, faster and faster, pieces clicking into place in my head. "Once we have the locations of the ships most in danger, Bowen and Evelyn can take one of the ships left here and a crew of volunteers on rescue missions. I'll head back to the *Audacity*. From there, we'll coordinate and condense, gathering up folks left stranded. Once we've managed that, *then* we can work on getting everyone home."

He looks at me, the shattered heart I can see in his dark eyes a perfect mirror to mine. "But . . . Siobhan."

"I know," I whisper. "But she's not in active danger. The people at the mercy of the sea are. We have to do this, and we have to do it now, Bastian. Otherwise, she sacrificed herself for nothing."

He pulls me into his arms and holds me tight—as tightly as I hold him. "We're going to get her back, Nox. I swear it. No matter how long it takes."

"But first—"

"But first we'll ensure her sacrifice is honored." He releases me slowly and presses a gentle kiss to my forehead. "Let's get to work."

CHAPTER 35

One Year Later
Bastian

I THOUGHT IT WAS EXHAUSTING HELPING TO RUN A REBEL-
lion. That was nothing compared to what it's taken to keep
Threshold from ending up in an all-out war after the Wild Hunt
rode. I am . . . so damned tired. More tired than I knew I could
be. Every day is filled with bickering nobles and more and more
representatives showing up from the various islands in the
realm. We will be setting up a new Council tomorrow, a truly
representative one. Each inhabited island is sending two people
who have been voted on by their people. The fact that it took *a
year* to get to this point just speaks to how effectively the last
Council—and the many before that—have misused power and
policy for their own gain.

No longer.

I've seen Nox only a handful of times in the last twelve
months, short intervals where we spent as much time as we
could manage wrapped up in each other. It's not enough, never

enough, but with so much at stake, we can't prioritize our relationship over the good of the realm. We speak regularly with the new desk they installed in the *Audacity*. They're personally escorting the representatives from Three Sisters, so they should have arrived in Lyari hours ago.

I meant to go meet them on the docks. Truly, I did. But the sun started to set before I could, and *this* is not something I skip for anything. Even Nox.

As the sun sinks to the horizon behind me, I climb up onto the roof of the old Council building. It's the tallest spot in Lyari. I don't know if the height actually helps, but it can't hurt.

I kick off my boots and step into the permanent amplification circle Evelyn created for me on her and Bowen's most recent stop in Threshold. I have to draw out the pattern each time I use it, but she burned the template into the boards so it's easy enough. I kneel in the center and carefully draw a few drops of blood. I hadn't thought I was any good at ritual magic, but apparently all I needed was the motivation to *become* good.

As soon as the power stabilizes, I take a deep breath and exhale just as slowly. It hurts to do this. Not the power expenditure, but the hope that I should have killed long months ago. Instead, here I am, a year later, trying to call her home.

Another deep breath and I'm ready. I send my magic out, farther and farther and farther, to the very edges of my ability. The amplification circle drains my magic twice as fast as normal, so I can only hold it for about fifteen minutes.

I close my eyes. "*Siobhan. Siobhan, come home. Your hunt is finished. You've saved us all. Come home to us.*" Again and again and again, the words carrying a lilt of melody that helps the magic cling to them.

At the end of fifteen minutes, I reluctantly release the magic. Beneath me, the chalk amplification circle has blurred to the point of being unrecognizable, its use fulfilled. I sit back on my heels and let loose a shaky breath.

"That's beautiful."

I look up to find Nox standing before me. They're dressed in black, which somehow suits them even more than crimson, their duster flowing dramatically in the light wind, their clothing beneath fitted to their body. I use my forearm to wipe the sweat from my brow. "I'm glad you made it in time."

"Me, too." They carefully step into the circle, avoiding the sigils and offering me their hand. "Tomorrow, the next step starts."

"Yes." I let them pull me to my feet and then hug them close. "Fuck, I missed you."

Nox holds me just as tightly. "I missed you, too."

Tomorrow, the newly formed Council votes on how to proceed with returning the refugees to their home realms—and settling the ones who have no interest in returning in communities with room to spare. People will get a choice; I'm determined to ensure it's so. We're starting the new Threshold on the right foot, on the promise of being better.

Even though I know I shouldn't, I can't help but ask. "Have you seen her?"

"I don't think so," Nox says slowly. "We caught the edge of the Hunt a month ago. I don't know if they were coming or going, but we heard them and saw the mist. No hounds or riders, though."

We had thought the Wild Hunt would disappear the same way it's been gone for time unknowing. Instead, wherever they ride, they seem to use Threshold the same way normal people do—as access to other realms. There are regular sightings, but they don't bother any of the people left after the purge of the Cŵn Annwn.

If they had disappeared, maybe I would have been able to give up hope that Siobhan would return to us someday. As it is, I can't help doing everything in my power to summon her home.

Nox loops their arm through mine and turns us toward the door to the stairs. "You know, you're getting quite the reputation. The young eligible nobles wax poetic about the Lyarian Banshee, calling his lost love home. It's considered quite the coup if they can seduce you out of your sadness."

I wince. There have been plenty of attempts in the last year. "You know I'm not interested in any of them."

"I know." They press a kiss to my cheek. We share a bed when they're in town, and we've spent no little amount of time losing ourselves in pleasure, but there's no escaping the grief of Siobhan's absence. I keep thinking it will fade, will lose some of its jagged teeth, but it endures. Instead, it's as if it's compounded when Nox and I are together, two-thirds of a whole that might never be whole again.

"What if she never returns?" I hate to give voice to the fear I can't escape, but if I can trust anyone to hold space for it, it's Nox.

We walk in silence through the building and out onto the street. "I'd like to join you tomorrow night. Give a little warm wind to carry your call farther."

I glance at them. "Do you think it will help?"

"It can't hurt."

It's not until we're back in my bed, sweat cooling on my skin and Nox sleeping beside me, that I realize they never really answered my question.

Siobhan

Blood in my mouth. Flesh between my teeth. The ground falling away beneath my paws. Always the next surge, the next prey, the next call from the Hunter to change direction. There is nothing else.

Except . . .

Siobhan.

I miss a step and nearly fumble into my siblings around me. One of them snaps at me, but it's half-hearted at best. We're picking up speed again, intent on our next destination.

Siobhan.

I shake my head roughly, trying to clear it. I know that voice, though it's strange in the cadence. I've heard its owner say that name a thousand times, a million, until it's as familiar as my own heartbeat. I've heard him speak . . . my name?

Siobhan, come home.

I slow, letting my siblings rush on without me. A warm wind comes from the south, ruffling my fur. I close my eyes, my body straining toward something I have no name for. The wind brings more than those soft, singing words, more than the name I didn't realize I'd forgotten. It brings scents as well, each so vivid that it feels like a blow to my body. Cedar and spice. Salt and blood.

Yearning rises within me, a longing for something just out of reach. I inhale deeply, and then again. I . . . know these scents, these . . . *people.*

Your hunt is finished.

No. Impossible. The Hunt is everlasting. A singular purpose with no end. There is no shortage of prey across all the realms in existence. There never will be. The Hunter blows their horn in the distance, directing us to the next portal.

You've saved us all.

Saved . . . I slow further. What have I saved? Even as I think the question, the answer echoes deep within my mind. *Threshold. The realm we now ride through on our way to the next.* I don't understand and yet my paws plant and my body freezes. Every bit of me is crying out to surge forward and follow the Hunt, but I can't stop my ears from straining backward, trying to find more words sung in that lovely voice.

Come home to us.

Us.

Bastian.

Nox.

Thinking the names is like a spell breaking over me. Me, *Siobhan.* Not *little sister* but a person who is also a hound. A person with two lovers waiting for me. How long has it been? I don't know. I can't know.

But it doesn't have to be longer.

I turn away from the Hunt, from my people, and start running south.

Nox

Three days after arriving in Lyari, I'm sitting in on yet another endless meeting for the new Council in a large room that I'm nearly certain used to be a ballroom for events. I maintain no position—and want none—but Bastian found me a spot near the wall to observe history in the making. All observing has done is prove that the closest I want to get to true authority is captaining the *Audacity*.

There are already factions and alliances and petty politics, but there's no escaping those things. We *have*, however, ensured that all the people of Threshold are represented in making the policies that will affect them. No one island or people holds the power over any others. And these policies are only for the realm politics—the laws of each individual island will be reverted to their respective peoples.

I catch Tia's eye as she and an unfamiliar Yothian pass by. There will be no further sanctioned attempts to turn Yoth into a vacation destination for Lyarians. Good.

I don't think anyone quite reckoned on this process taking days, especially when today clearly won't be the end of it. As the hours stretch on, I start craving the sea air against my skin with a desire that has me fighting not to fidget. Right when I'm nearly at my breaking point, Bastian calls a recess until tomorrow.

He's good at this.

No matter what doubts he held, he manages the occasionally heated conversations with ease. He holds no voting position; instead, he's taken up as the moderator for the discussions and votes. Not everyone was happy with that choice, but no one had a better solution so it stuck. Thankfully.

By the time the last person files from the room, the light has changed as night approaches. Without a word, Bastian and I make our way to the roof, and I watch as he painstakingly traces out the amplification circle. We step into it and repeat the same ritual we have the last three evenings.

Calling Siobhan home.

In my dark moments, I suspect we might be calling Siobhan home for the rest of our lives, might go to the grave with her name and longing on our lips. I'll never voice that suspicion, though. It feels unspeakably cruel to do so.

As the last bit of the circle dissolves and Bastian allows his glamour to fade, he slumps against me. "I don't know how much longer I can do this. It hurts too much."

"I know," I say softly.

"What if—" He straightens abruptly. "Nox, do you see that?"

It takes a beat to understand what he means. And even then, I don't know what I'm looking at. Something small and quick racing through the gap in the harbor and heading for the docks, moving faster than I've seen any ship. "What *is* that?"

"Come on!" He takes my hand and then we're running, down the stairs and out the building and through the streets. My breath saws in my lungs, but I don't tell him to slow down, don't pop the bubble of hope that's risen in both of us. Surely it's not her. It can't possibly . . .

But it is.

We reach the docks at the same time the hound does. I was sure I hadn't forgotten her size, but I'm still staggered by it as Siobhan—because it *must* be Siobhan—stumbles off the surface of the water and onto the dock. Between one step and the next, she shifts, a shimmering veil lowering and rising, revealing a naked woman.

Bastian gets to her first, pulling her into his arms. I'm there a moment later, needing to touch her, to ensure that she's truly here. She's thinner than she was a year ago, but not dangerously so. She's *here*.

Siobhan blinks down at us as if waking up from a dream. "Bastian? Nox?" Her voice is rough and gravelly, nearly identical to how it had been when she spoke in hound form after the creature did . . . whatever they did to her.

"You're here." Bastian kisses her and then she's kissing me and, *gods*, I missed her so much I think I might die from it. "You're safe."

"Safe," she repeats slowly. "It feels like a dream. How long?"

"A year," I whisper.

"So long." Siobhan frowns and shakes her head as if trying to clear it. "You called me home."

"Bastian did." Tears streak his face, or maybe it's me who's crying. I don't know. I truly thought she was gone forever and now she's *here* in our arms and I don't know how to process it. I don't think any of us do. "Let's go home."

"Home." Siobhan smiles, some of the strangeness fading from her expression. In that moment, she looks less like an uncanny creature accidentally wandering into civilization and more like the woman we both fell in love with. She looks at Lyari and then back at us. "Tell me everything."

Bastian pulls off his tunic and tucks her into it. She's taller than him, so it barely covers her nudity, but it's better than walking through the streets without. This city has seen some shit, but Siobhan is a force of nature, even looking slightly bewildered at the rapid change of events.

We fill her in on the new Council, on the effort to save those stranded by the Wild Hunt, on all the changes we've fought for, as we make our slow way to the harbor house Bastian keeps. He intentionally picked a place where he's accessible to people, rather than being tucked behind the gated communities the nobles occupy—or what's left of the nobles. Their purge wasn't as thorough as that of the Cŵn Annwn, but it was enough to ensure they haven't done more than grumble about the new government.

She showers and dresses in clean clothes, and while we feed her, exchanging wild looks because neither of us can believe this is happening, we tell her about the programs we're getting set into motion—courtesy of the wealth the old Council had spent generations hoarding.

"It really worked." She reaches out and takes each of our hands, pulling us down into the chairs on either side of her. "You've both worked so hard." A single tear slips free. "Things are working. And you still called me home."

"Siobhan." I wait for her to look at me to squeeze her hand. "Of course we did—well, Bastian has done most of the work, but the point remains. We love you." Even after a year, it feels so strange to say aloud. "We were never going to stop trying to bring you home."

Another tear slips free. She looks at me and then Bastian. "I love you both, too. So much. I don't think anyone else's voice could have reached me, could have given me pause."

"You know I love you. I never stopped. I never *will* stop. None of this would have been possible without you," Bastian says softly. "The revolution, yes, but all that came before. You put a decade's worth of work into making Threshold a better place. We've just been continuing the work you started."

"And doing a damn good job of it." She smiles slowly. "I

know it's selfish, but I'm grateful I don't have to be the face of the new future. It sounds like you have it well in hand."

"There's nothing stopping you from—"

"*I'm* stopping me." But she's smiling as she says it. "There's still so much work to be done, and I'm happy to be there, working hard alongside you—both of you."

Fuck, now I'm going to cry. "I want that. More than anything."

"Me, too."

I'm not sure who moves first, but we end up on our feet, our arms wrapped around one another. Siobhan hiccups. "I'm so glad to be home. To be with you both."

Now, with Siobhan back, it truly *will* be a home.

CHAPTER 1

Evelyn

M**Y GRANDMOTHER TAUGHT ME EVERYTHING I KNOW.**
She was a withered old crone when my mother died,
leaving me alone at the ripe old age of six. Bunny, as she insisted
I call her, pulled up in an ancient car, took one look at me, and
tsked. "Look just like her, don't you? Get in, little bird. No point
in standing around with your thumb up your ass."

She didn't have much respect for laws—human or otherwise—
but Bunny had an endless list of rules that were nearly impossible to keep track of. Don't do spell work during an eclipse. If
you're going to lie, make it a good one. It doesn't matter what
path you tread in life as long as it's the right one for you.

And stay the fuck away from vampires.

Bunny is probably rolling in her grave right now. Or she
would be if I'd buried her when she died, the day after I turned
eighteen. Our kind don't like graves—another thing she taught
me. We prefer to be scattered with the elements, our ashes little
bits of stardust going back to the earth and sea and air and fire.

She held on to this life until she was no longer needed, and then she moved on to walk paths I can't follow.

It's just as well she's not around anymore to see what I've become.

Case in point: the gorgeous vampire leaning against the bar at my side. Lizzie isn't my girlfriend. She doesn't do labels, and I'm too much Bunny's child to *date* a vampire.

Sleeping with one, though?

I've always liked to play things too close to the edge. Hopefully this time won't kick me in the ass. My track record says otherwise, but hey, I'm a slow learner when there's fun to be had. It's not like I spend much time with Lizzie. We met six months ago, and after spending a glorious two weeks in bed that I wasn't sure I'd survive, we've been asteroids pinging into each other before flying away to commit destruction elsewhere.

I didn't even know she was back in town until I got a text two hours ago with a time and place. Imagine my surprise when I show up to a hole-in-the-wall bar filled with an equal mix of humans and paranormal folk. Most of the time us magical people avoid regular humans. They don't know we exist, and we prefer to keep it that way. But there are places that are exceptions to that rule, and this bar is one of them.

It doesn't seem like Lizzie's speed, but what do I know? It's not like we spend our time together *talking*.

"What about that one?"

I follow Lizzie's chin jerk to the pretty, petite woman sitting by herself at the end of the bar. It's considered rude to scan other paranormals, so I don't risk it, but she gives off a human vibe.

Which means Lizzie wants to play. We've done it a few times, picked up a human at a bar and taken her to the nearest hotel to have a night of sex and, occasionally, magic. As a bloodline vampire, Lizzie's bite is orgasmic, which paves the way for a whole lot of fun.

I'm not in the mood tonight. I shouldn't have answered Lizzie's text at all, or at least I should have begged off. It's the twenty-third of April, which means I turned twenty-five yesterday.

It also means Bunny's been dead for seven years as of today. A lucky number, but it doesn't feel lucky right now. Grief is a strange thing. Most days, I get by on the warmth of doing spells Bunny taught me, or cleaning with the particular concoction of kitchen-witch magic shit that she swore warded away negative emotions.

On the bad days, I go through a whole systematic process of remembering her. Cleaning and spell work and baking her favorite cookies, culminating in a tearful trip through the box of photos I keep tucked away in my closet. She'd whack me upside the back of my head if she saw me on those days, would remind me that the dead aren't gone for good and there's no point in wasting my living years mourning someone who's stepped through a door to the next part of this grand journey we call existence.

On the good days, I believe her. On the bad days? Not so much. And the anniversary of her death is always a bad day.

"Evelyn." Lizzie's voice is cold, but that's nothing new. She might be downright sizzling when we're in bed, but she doesn't fuck around with the warmer emotions outside of it.

I sigh and try to focus. Giving her any less than one hundred percent of my attention is dangerous, which is exactly why I shouldn't have come out tonight. I look at the human woman again. She's rubbing her straw against her bottom lip in a really enticing way as she watches us . . . watches Lizzie. "She's pretty."

"Do you have another choice?"

I glance half-heartedly around the room. Nearly everyone is watching Lizzie, though most of them aren't doing it overtly. I can't blame them. She's a sight to behold, a lean white woman with a tight ponytail of dark hair and a penchant for athleisure. Her leggings and fitted long-sleeved shirt *should* make her look like a soccer mom who wandered into this dingy bar on accident.

Like prey.

Lizzie, being a bloodline vampire from the family that possesses the magic to control the blood in a person's body, money beyond comprehension, and an orgasmic bite, has never been prey in her life.

The other predators in the room know it, too. I catch sight of a female werewolf hauling her partner out the front door, and there's a demon with a wickedly skillful glamour in the corner who's motioning for his tab.

Clearing the way for Lizzie to hunt.

Too bad I'm not in the mood tonight. I knock back my third—fourth? fifth?—tequila shot and set the glass on the bar, trying to ignore the stickiness of the counter. "Whatever you want. She's fine." Any other night, I'd be sidling up to the woman at the end of the bar and giving her my best charming smile as

I buy her a drink and lead her back to Lizzie. Tonight, it feels like too much work.

"Getting jealous, Evelyn?"

Even if I was—and I'm not—I know better than to say as much. Lizzie might like fucking me, but I'm not foolish enough to think she'd ever let orgasms get in the way of murdering me if the mood strikes.

Really, Bunny was right. I'm a damned fool. It's the only explanation for the way I jump into bed with Lizzie over and over again, part of me thrilled to be dancing right up to the edge of ruin.

It's that desire that has me leaning into Lizzie. I can have fun tonight. I'll *make* myself have fun tonight, even if it kills me. I don't have a death wish, normally, but nothing's normal on April twenty-third. Not anymore.

"Maybe I'll take her home instead of roping her in for you." I grin up at Lizzie. "Want to make it a wager?"

She studies me with her eerie dark eyes. "Are you drunk?"

"No. Probably not. Okay, maybe a little." I'm just being sentimental and letting it get the best of me. Not that Lizzie would know that yesterday was my birthday or that today marks Bunny being gone seven years. That's not the kind of relationship we have. What we have can't even be called a relationship. It's a . . . What do my mortal peers call it? A situationship.

"If you're not drunk, then what's wrong with you? You never act like this."

If I were a different person, if *we* were different people, this would be the turning point for us. I would confess why I'm so down, and she'd do something to comfort me. That's the stuff of romantic movies, though. Not real life. "I don't want to talk about it."

"Evelyn."

"It's fine. *I'm* fine." I lift my hand to flag down the bartender for another shot, but Lizzie catches my wrist. "Don't bother. We're leaving."

I blink. "Excuse me?"

"I'm not in the habit of repeating myself." She drops a wad of money on the bar and drags me toward the door. She's moving fast enough that I can barely keep my feet. I catch sight of the woman at the end of the bar and her disappointed look, and then we're at the door. No one moves to help me, though I'm not exactly in danger.

At least, I don't think I am?

"Lizzie?" I almost knock my hip into one of the tables, but somehow Lizzie senses it and jerks me to the side at the last moment. I hiss out a breath. "Where's the fire?"

"You're walking wounded right now. Every predator in that building was about to come sniffing."

I blink, but my response is lost as she hauls me through the door and the cold nighttime air slaps me in the face. It *should* sober me right up, but somehow it makes me realize exactly how drunk I am. I weave on my feet and jerk my arm out of Lizzie's grasp. Or I try. All I get for my trouble is what will probably be an outstanding bruise tomorrow. "Let go."

She ignores me. "If I put you in a cab, are you going to go home and sleep this off?"

Ten minutes ago, that's all I wanted to do. Now, I dig in my heels, buoyed on by the promise tequila whispers through my blood of a good night that couldn't possibly end in ruin. "It's early."

"Evelyn."

"Lizzie." I mimic her tone. "You wanted the pretty lady. Let's go get her."

"I'm not in the mood to babysit a melancholy drunk."

"That's rude. I'm not melancholy. Melancholy is for poets and people writing the Next Great American Novel. I'm *happy*. Fun. A riotous good time."

"Mmm." We reach the curb and she lifts her hand, I'm assuming to flag down a cab. But the car that pulls up is dark and without a single identifying thing on it. I'm not even sure of the make and model.

I peer at it. "Is this one of those expensive black-car experiences? Because I might pay my bills just fine, but I do that by not wasting money on shit like this. It's ostentatious, Lizzie. Honestly, just wasteful."

She looks at me, and I could almost swear I see her considering whether or not to rip my throat out and just be done with this mess. She finally shakes her head. "Get in the car, Evelyn, or I will make you get in the car."

"If you—"

Apparently we've reached the end of Lizzie's patience. She pulls a move that I might be impressed with if I weren't so damn irritated, jerking me forward with one hand and grabbing me by the back of the neck at the same time that she opens the door. I barely have the opportunity to curse when she's shoving me into the back seat.

"Stop treating me like I'm a threat!"

"You're not a threat. You're a liability." She slides in behind me and slams the door. I reach for the handle of the other door, but the car pulls away from the curb fast enough to throw me back against the seat.

She just . . . She honestly just . . . I spin around and look at the driver. A quick scan—it's rude, but I don't care—tells me they're a vampire. *Damn it.* I lean forward and knock on the back of the driver's seat. "Excuse me, I'm being kidnapped."

Lizzie rolls her eyes. "You're not being kidnapped. I'm saving you from yourself. You're welcome."

"No, I'm definitely being kidnapped. Stop the car."

The driver doesn't answer, but I honestly didn't expect them to. They're one of Lizzie's minions, a bitten vampire who serves a bloodline vampire. Funny how vampire culture mimics capitalism so thoroughly, but she's never appreciated it when I point it out. Bunny was really onto something with her rule about staying away from vampires.

"I'm not a liability," I mutter. "And I don't need saving."

"Sure." She snorts. "Whatever you say, Evelyn."

I slump back against the seat, my brain sloshing about inside my skull. "I think I hate you."

"No, you don't."

No, I don't. I slide over and lay my head on her shoulder. "Fine. I don't hate you."

"I know."

I poke her arm. Just when I'm sure Lizzie has no sense of humor to speak of, she lets little glimpses of it out. I'm nearly certain she's making fun of me right now, but when I look up at her gorgeous face, there's only a small smile curving her lips. In the darkness of the back seat, I can almost convince myself that her eyes have warmed a little, too. "I guess I should thank you for saving me from myself. Will orgasms work in payment?"

"Evelyn." There's fond exasperation in her tone. "Close your eyes and rest."

I don't know if it's vampire magic or alcohol, but my eyes slide shut despite my best efforts to keep them open. Sleep flickers and flirts, finally sweeping me away into its dark embrace. It's almost enough to convince myself I feel Lizzie's fingers stroking soothingly through my hair.

CHAPTER 2

Evelyn

W AKE UP, EVELYN."

I lift my head from the pillow and blink at Lizzie. My head pounds in time with my heartbeat and my mouth tastes . . . well, best not to think too hard about how bad my mouth tastes. "I need a toothbrush." I look around, recognition rolling over me in waves. I've been here only a few times; I recognize the large bed with its absurdly high-thread-count sheets and nice down comforter. I'm still not even sure if vampires sleep, but Lizzie does nothing halfway. The bedroom is a luxurious dark oasis. Too luxurious for my tastes. Too dark. But I can appreciate it in small doses.

"Why am I in your bed?" I sit up and have to press my lips together to keep from being sick. "Why did you bring me here? You should have just sent me home." I have a vague memory of her carrying me into the house and tucking me in with her usual capable briskness. It might warm my heart if I didn't feel so nauseous.

Of course, then she promptly ruins it. "So you could choke on your own vomit and die alone? I don't think so." She waves a hand. "It doesn't matter now. There's no time. You need to go." Her expression is cold and her voice remote, not even a hint of the warmth I've gotten used to. There's definitely none of the softness she showed me last night.

Silly to miss something I'm half-sure I imagined in the first place. I shove my hair out of my face and try to focus past the hangover making me want to burrow back into the bed and not move for another few hours. "Why? What's going on?"

"This thing between us ends. Right now." She looks away, her skin so pale it's almost translucent in the moonlight streaming in from the open window. "I just received word that my mother is on her way. She'll be here soon."

Suddenly, I'm not worried about my hangover. Lizzie might have a soft spot for me, but her mother has an even more fearsome reputation than she does. If she finds out her daughter has been sleeping with a lowly witch, she's liable to yank every drop of blood from my body.

Damn it, Bunny was right. I never should have messed with vampires.

I happen to like my blood right where it is, so I jump up. My stomach sloshes in a worrying way, but I don't have time to be sick right now. I start throwing my clothes on. "How long do I have?"

"Not long." She sounds almost bored. Like I've been a fun toy she's amused herself with, and now it's time for that toy to be discarded.

No reason for that to sting. I knew what this was when I let her seduce me in that club all those months ago. Silly me for getting sentimental. But last night felt . . . different. Or maybe that was the tequila making me silly and sentimental. Lizzie brought me back here because I was making a fool of myself—not because she actually cares.

If she cared, she wouldn't be standing idly by while my death approaches.

Gods, but I'm a fool. I actually started to fall for her. I yank on my boots and tie them quickly. "If you had just let me go home, this wouldn't be an issue."

"Just another mistake in a long line of them."

Well, fuck, that *definitely* stings. I drag in a breath, trying to think past all the emotions swirling with leftover tequila in my system. I can focus on my bruised heart later. If I don't get away, Lizzie's mother might rip it right out of my chest. "You have to get me out." Lizzie has the same powers as her mother—as the rest of her family. She can protect me long enough for me to run for my life.

"I don't have time. I have to meet her when she arrives." She drags off her clothes from last night—from earlier tonight?—and sets about dressing in a clean outfit. Fool that I am, I can't stop myself from mourning each inch of skin covered by her plain button-up dress. I've never had a lover quite as physically perfect as Lizzie, and what she can do with blood heightens every sexual encounter we've had.

And she . . . took care of me last night? Even though I know better, I can't help thinking about that soft moment in the car. I didn't imagine it. I swear I didn't. I hesitate, my heart pounding. Maybe I was wrong about this being nothing. Maybe . . . "Come with me," I blurt.

Lizzie lifts a brow. "Evelyn."

I know better than to fight a losing battle, but my foolish heart has run away with my mouth. "Please, Lizzie. You're more than the weapon they use you for. You could be so much more." I don't want to change her. Never that. But what could she be if she was actually free of her family's shackles? I never would have dared ask if I wasn't scared for my life.

She crosses to me and catches my chin lightly. Her dark eyes are fathomless. "I honestly can't tell if you're trying to manipulate me or if you actually believe that." She shakes her head slowly. "Either way, it won't work. I have no need to be more than a weapon. I *enjoy* being a weapon." Her grip goes tight and for several beats I think she might do something truly shocking, like kiss me. Even though I know better, I go a little soft in response.

Then she pushes me away. "Get out."

I don't have a heart left to break. Life is cruel and merciless at the best of times, and people even more so. I know that. Of course I know that. It doesn't change the fact that it *hurts* to have the woman I've spent six months sleeping with basically admit that she doesn't care if I live or die.

On the heels of the emotional turmoil from last night, there's a part of me that wants to curl up and just let what will happen happen.

The impulse doesn't last long, but it shames me nonetheless.

I watch Lizzie walk out of the room, her stride long and predatory. She's not even going to stick around to ensure I make it to an exit before her mother comes calling. *That's all I'm worth to her. Less than nothing.*

The thought is at least a little bit a lie, but somehow that just makes it hurt worse. She *does* care about me, but not enough to stand between me and her family. Not enough to save my life. "You are such a *bitch* sometimes, Lizzie."

I'm not going down like this.

I go to my knees and reach under the bed to pull out the pack I stashed there the second time Lizzie brought me to her house. As Bunny used to say, always have an exit route or six planned. It pays to be prepared for any eventuality in normal life, and sleeping with a vampire makes that doubly true. You never know when you'll run into your not-girlfriend's murderous mother.

I sling the backpack on and turn to the window. We're on the second floor facing the front of the house, so that exit is out of the question. No reason to present a target. There's a staircase used by the human servants near the back of the house; a door there will get me out. It means hiking through the forest that surrounds the estate, but it's a small price to pay.

I start for the door, but pause in front of the dresser with the big antique mirror attached to it. Lizzie doesn't wear jewelry as a general rule, but there's a bowl of it just sitting there for the taking. Bracelets, necklaces, rings, and brooches, all studded with jewels. Many of the pieces look like they're hundreds of years old. This kind of haul could set me up for years . . . or at least a few months of lavish living.

I don't make a habit of stealing from friends or lovers, but Lizzie's just proven that she's neither. That makes this jewelry fair game. I cast one furious look at the door and then shrug out of my backpack to dump the jewelry into it. The satisfaction I feel at the thought of her rage when she finds it gone . . .

I'm being petty and I don't give a fuck.

The hallway is blessedly empty and I don't bother to be quiet as I sprint toward the stairs. It's not like I can effectively hide from a vampire of Lizzie's family. Their magic is even more blood-based than normal bloodline vampires. In addition to a whole host of tricks, they can sense any creature with blood in their bodies within a certain range.

Makes for a quick game of hide-and-seek, I imagine.

I take the staircase down, moving so fast I almost trip. I'd love to say all the sex with Lizzie has improved my cardio, but the truth is that I only run when jobs go bad, and my jobs rarely go bad. *If you have to run, you're already fucked.*

Each breath feels like a knife in my lungs, but I can't afford to slow down. Not a single person appears as I burst out of the doorway at the bottom of the stairs. Where's the door? I clocked it when I explored the house, but adrenaline and my hangover make my head buzz and muddy my memory. There are dozens of doors dotting this hallway. Servants' quarters? Was the exit four doors down or five?

A shiver shoots down my spine as my sensing ward around the house pings the presence of . . . Five. Ten. Twenty-five. Oh fuck, that's a lot of vampires. What is this, a family reunion?

I yank open the fourth door and rush through. Right into a dusty sitting room. I stop short. "What the fuck?" I was sure this was the way out. A moth-eaten couch squats against one wall, directly across from two equally decaying chairs. There's a dresser that appears one sneeze away from collapsing and a large swivel mirror on a stand that seems completely out of place.

Hushed voices sound in the hallway, accompanied by the

sound of quick footsteps. I scan them without thinking. Humans, but that doesn't mean I want to get caught. I pull the door shut softly behind me and hold my breath as I wait for them to move past.

Except they don't.

They stop a few feet away from my door and continue speaking in soft, harried tones. I could wait them out, but I have mere minutes before the vampires reach the house.

The window it is.

I head for the window, scrunching my nose as each step sends up clouds of dust. Why don't the maids clean this room? Every other part of this house I've explored has been pristine. I shove the curtains aside and instantly regret it when a sneeze threatens. It doesn't matter. I just have to get the window open . . .

It's painted shut.

"You have *got* to be kidding me." I don't have time to cut the damn thing open. Surely there's another exit somewhere. I take a few steps toward the door but pause when the mirror in the room flickers oddly. Even knowing I don't have time to explore, curiosity takes hold. It will take only a moment to investigate. I move to it and send a flicker of my magic at it. What I find makes me grin.

"Lizzie, you've been keeping secrets." She's got a *portal* in her house. No wonder this room is forbidden to the staff. Having them fall through a portal when they try to clean the mirror would be a nightmare to deal with.

Where does it go, though?

I glance at the door and bite my lip. Trying to find the exit is still a good plan, but I can't move as fast as the vampires outside, and if Lizzie figures out I stole from her, she'll come after me. And not in a fun way.

But the portal? I can go through it and ensure no one can follow. It won't stop her from hunting me, but I've spent my entire life learning to lose myself. I can stay ahead of her long enough for her mother to send her off to do some murderous shit or for Lizzie to find some other poor soul to torment.

Easy peasy.

The words feel like a lie, so I ignore them.

It takes two precious minutes to cut my thumb and carve a quick spell onto the mirror frame. Once I trigger it, it will explode in thirty seconds, closing the portal behind me. A risk, but giving Lizzie a direct way to follow me is riskier.

I hope.

There's no time to hesitate. I pull my shirt open a bit more to reveal the network of tattoos on my chest. Each is a prepped spell, just waiting for a bit of blood to activate it. I press my bleeding finger to the one in the center of my chest, drawing a shield around me. It will only hold as long as my concentration and power do, but I don't know what I'm walking into.

The door flies open as I take one step into the portal. Lizzie rushes into the room. "What the fuck are you doing?"

"Escaping." I just have to trigger the spell to destroy the mirror after I step through. Damn it, I'm going to have to time this right.

My backpack clinks as I shift farther into the mirror. She narrows her eyes. "You didn't."

"Don't know what you're talking about." My heart is beating so fast, she has to be able to sense the lie. I need to go, and I need to go now.

I thought all warmth was gone from Lizzie. Turns out I was wrong. The last bit of softness disappears and she bares her fangs at me. "Drop the bag right now, Evelyn."

It's the smart thing to do, but I haven't been doing the smart thing for a long time. No reason to start now. "Nope." One last deep breath and I trigger the spell on the mirror frame.

Lizzie lunges for me, but it's too late. The last thing I see is her furious face as she screams. "I'm going to fucking *kill* you!" Then the mirror explodes, cutting us off from each other.

I realize my mistake the moment it does. This isn't a direct portal at all. Of course it's not. I should have known Lizzie wouldn't keep an open door to somewhere else in her house.

Darkness presses close, thick and syrupy. I can't see a single thing, can't breathe, can't think. Oh gods, please tell me I didn't flee from Lizzie only to die in this space of nothingness.

Damn it, *no*. Instinct gets me moving, despite the difficulty it is to take one step and then another. The only other option is holding still and suffocating, and I'm not going out like that. Panic flutters in my chest, screaming through my mind. I've heard drowning is a peaceful way to die, but there's no peace in this. Just terror.

Keep going. Keep moving. One foot in front of the other. You still have strength, and you're going to fucking use it.

Step after step after step. It feels like the abyss is swallowing me whole, but I'm walking on *something*, even if I can't see it. There has to be a way out. There *has* to be. I just need to find it.

But nothing has changed by the time my lungs start screaming for air. In desperation, I pick up my pace. I don't have much time left. Hard to say if black dots are dancing across my vision when I can't see anything at all. The very non-air seeming to fight against me, trying to hold me still and slow me down.

Fuck you.

I'm running now, pumping my arms as fast as I can while my lungs shriek. I clamp my lips together to keep from gasping, but I'm seconds away from my body taking over.

I'm moving so fast, I don't realize the ground beneath my feet is gone until I'm falling.

Between one blink and the next, the darkness is replaced by pale dawn light. I drag in one glorious salty breath . . . and then hit something hard enough that everything goes black.

Photo by Bethany Chamberlin

KATEE ROBERT (she/they) is a *New York Times* and *USA Today* bestselling author of spicy romance. *Entertainment Weekly* calls their writing "unspeakably hot." Their books have sold over two million copies. They live in the Pacific Northwest with their husband, children, a cat who thinks he's a dog, and two Great Danes who think they're lapdogs.

VISIT KATEE ROBERT ONLINE

KateeRobert.com
Katee_Robert
AuthorKateeRobert

Ready to find
your next great read?

Let us help.

Visit prh.com/nextread

Penguin
Random
House